Seduced by the Sliver Cat

Emilia Abraham

The Cryptid Chronicles #2

i

Dedication

iii

For anyone who needs a little more cryptids in their life.

And hopes they're all fuckable.

And for Krysten-who makes sure all those pesky typos I missed
get cleaned up. You're the best.

Author's Note:

Seduced by the Sliver Cat is a paranormal shifter romance.

The content warnings are as follows:
Adult Language
Explicit Scenes
Light BDSM activities
Depression
Anxiety

While I don't believe that depression warrants a content warning, I also want readers to be aware it does play a part in this book. Kira has struggled with it for awhile. She also doesn't recognize it for some time. She does her best to ignore the symptoms until she's numb to them. Along with the depression, comes some anxiety. It doesn't play as large of a part, but it does make an appearance.

I want to make it clear-falling in love does not "cure" her. There's not enough in the book to show this. However, it probably will be brought up in subsequent books in passing. . Love doesn't magically make her not depressed. For Kira, her healing starts with choosing herself. Chase merely gives her the space to do so.

I hope, if you struggle as so many of us do, with either depression or anxiety, you can resonate and felt seen while reading Kira's story.

Table of Contents

Chapter 1: Fuck the Moon
Chase

Let the moon guide you.

Fuck the moon. Honestly, if I hear "let the moon guide you" one more time, I might just disappear into the woods and live among the trees. Gemma has been telling me the adage for the past three weeks. Jake told me to just fucking pick a place. Because apparently, the option to find a shifter community to help me through my transition was not actually an option. More like a demand.

I don't blame them. My best friend is annoyed at my whining and his woman feels hopeless. Yet neither one of them knows what I'm going through. It's not like it's normal to go from being a completely regular human being to being a cougar shifter over the span of a week at the ripe old age of twenty-nine. And I'm not taking it well.

My phone rings, and I groan as Jake's name flashes across the screen. I roll up the window of my truck, though I can't do anything about the rumble emitting from the engine.

"What do you want, Jake?" I growl, heat flashing through me when he chuckles. "Just wondering how close you are to Moon Cove."

I grit my teeth, reminding myself he's not the problem. "You mean Gemma wants to know and asked you to call since she thought I'd bite her head off. Which I wouldn't, by the way."

"Sure. We'll go with that. Also, her mom won't stop calling her. So spare me from hearing her worry about it and tell me how close you are," he hisses.

"About twenty minutes. Where am I going again?"

Gemma wrote it all down, but her directions are tucked away behind my seat.

"Uh, the general store? Apparently, it doesn't look like ours does. Kind of like if you took the pop-up store Paul sets up every year for Samhain and merge it with the general store, then add a shit ton of knickknacks in the shapes of supernatural creatures. Gemma said you'll know when you see it." He sighs, then clears his throat. "You know you can come home anytime you want, right?"

I huff, keeping my eyes on the desolate road in front of me. "I need to do this, Jake. Gemma can't help me, and you don't have time. I need to figure out who I am now. Think of this like a journey to find myself. If I don't learn how to be a shifter, I'll end up getting shot by some random hunter and then you'll have to bury my naked body deep in the woods."

Gemma groans in the background and he chuckles. "Nobody needs to see that."

"Hey," I cry mockingly. "Some lady might enjoy gazing at my virile form."

"Shit. Do not say virile. And no one wants to see an ass with fur all over it."

"It went away. I never should have told you about that shit," I grumble. "Listen, I'll call you when I get settled. Need to figure out where the hell I'm going."

"Alright. Remember what I said." He hangs up before I can protest. Because that's exactly what I'd do.

If I didn't have to go to Moon Cove, I wouldn't. I was content to spend all of winter and most of spring holed up in my house on the lake right outside Whispering Pines. I have everything I need there and could order in whatever I didn't. Staying there would have been fine if it weren't for Jake and Gemma getting on my ass to figure out who I was now.

I spend the next fifteen minutes grumbling to myself, determined to shed my bad attitude by the time I get there. I may not have wanted to go, but Gemma's family is going out of their way to help me. They didn't have to offer up their house or their time to teach me about being a shifter.

At least I'll have some connection to home through them. Nerves dance along my skin, electrifying the air around me. I roll down my window, hoping it's not another shifter thing I know nothing about.

Moon Cove comes into view and my jaw drops. Gemma tried to warn me about what it is like. Her explanations didn't come close to what it truly is. The main street is set up much like Whispering Pines, with shops lining each side. Small businesses boasting everything a person could need living so far north.

Beyond the typical town, though, it's like stepping into another world. One I've seen on television. Massive log cabins surround a large parking lot, advertising the latest cryptid sightings and next town celebration. A long banner stretches across the biggest store, welcoming some show I've never heard of. It's at least three stories tall and made up of logs taller than me. And at six foot two, that's saying something. There isn't a lot of commotion this early, thankfully. Then again, I could get lost in the crowd if there was one. Now, I'll stick out and probably labeled a tourist by the townsfolk.

I park in front of the general store, though it's labeled Moon Cove's Country Market. Pushing from my truck, I try to take it all in. My door almost clips my elbow, I'm gawking so much. If whoever's watching wondered if I was a newcomer before, I've solidified their opinion of me. Which is not what I want. I'm going to be here for a bit. At least until I've learned what I can to help settle into my new life. Then I can retreat to my cabin and live out my days pretending I'm merely human and nothing else.

An older woman with grey streaked through her brown hair steps out onto the porch, a broad smile gracing her face. She wipes her hands on her apron as I climb the stairs. Gemma made some comments about her mother—loving, always smiling, super friendly, and passive-aggressive to a fault, but only with her children. Apparently, I'd know I was accepted when she got onto me about cutting my hair or washing my truck. When I told Gemma I was due for a trip to the barber, she didn't laugh.

"You must be Chase. Are you hungry? Oh, what a question. Of course you're hungry. Was the drive good? Come on, dear." She waves me forward, then pulls me into a crushing hug. "We'll get you fixed up."

"Thank you, ma'am," I mumble, unable to keep a grin from my face.

"Oh, you." She smacks my arm with the back of her hand. "None of that ma'am stuff. You can call me Gladys. Bennie should be in soon. He's just checking the traps."

I follow her inside, trying to focus on her prattling on about people I don't know. Nothing could have prepared me for the inside. It's massive, filled with all sorts of things, from stuffed animals to road trip snacks. It's like I stepped into a truck stop smashed together with a souvenir shop. I tip my head back, taking in the beams soaring above me. I thought there were multiple levels to this place, but it's just open. My feet slow as I attempt to take it all in. I can't imagine what the rest of the shops look like. This place seems like the main hub, though it's empty right now.

"How was the drive? I know it probably took a few days. When Slade took Gemma to college, it took them forever." There's a slight tightening to her voice when she says college, but I ignore it.

"It was fine," I murmur as she leads me into a labyrinth of items.

"You know, Gemma said she might come visit while you're here. It'd be so nice to see her. Does she have everything she needs out there? I know he's your friend, but I don't know much about this Jake fellow. She said they're fated mates. I'm not saying she doesn't know. That would be ridiculous. As a mother, though..." Gladys continues, and I'm starting to see what Gemma was talking about.

I follow her around a massive counter lining the back wall. There's a hallway leading into what I assume is storage. Instead of taking me back there, she slips out the back door marked *Emergency Only*. I wince, waiting for an alarm, then hurry after her when there is none. We take a path covered with an archway. Flowers mask the outside world and I pull in a deep breath. They're still blooming even though autumn is right around the corner.

"Sorry. This will be a bit of a trek. I was afraid of sending you to the house, especially since I knew I'd be at the shop. Don't worry. We won't put you to work while you're here. Although you seem like the type to get restless, so you're welcome to jump in whenever."

She smiles at me over her shoulder, deftly hopping over a vine snaking across the path. I wonder if her reflexes are due to her shifter nature or because she's walked this way a thousand times. It's a tossup and I'm not about to ask. I may be here to learn more, but we haven't really established how it'll happen. I also don't have it in me to tell her I'm pretty lazy in the winter. Jake's summer camp is the only reason I've been active since my parents died.

"You're putting me up, ma'am. I'm more than happy to help wherever I can," I say, smiling.

She spins as we reach the end of the path and plants her fists on her hips. "Now, what did I say about calling me ma'am? Before long, you'll be calling me Mom, I suspect."

She sends me a sneaky grin I don't understand, then nods. She turns again and I shake my head. I'm sure she's like that with everyone who's associated with her family in some way. I imagine she was the type of mom who had an open door and cookies ready for her children's friends. My heart clenches, wondering what that must have been like. I shove the ache down to its usual place. No use reopening old wounds. It won't magically fix my childhood.

"Would you like me to move my truck back here? Or is there another place I can stash it while I'm here?" I ask as she climbs the stairs to yet another log cabin.

It's smaller than the shop, as she called it, with what looks like only two stories. The porch wraps around the whole thing and overlooks a small lake half the size of the one back home. Relief floods me when I see the forest stretching toward the horizon on the other shore. I'm not surprised since most of the countryside on the way here was woods, but the fact it's so close makes me feel better. I haven't been able to control my shifts like Gemma and Jake can.

"You can leave it at the shop for now. We'll deal with it later. I'm sure we'll find where you'll fit," she murmurs.

She sweeps through the front door and slips off her shoes. I follow suit, slipping off my boots and flexing my toes. Weaving through the house, I barely catch the den to my right. With so many kids, I'm sure these spaces were used often when they were all home. The space opens up, revealing a huge kitchen opening up to a dining area and living room. It's the massive fireplace leading upward to the vaulted ceilings and flanked by windows on each side that gives me pause.

"The stairs lead up to the loft and most of the bedrooms. The master is down the hall, though," she says, gesturing down another hallway.

"You have a beautiful home, ma—Gladys."

She gives me a satisfied smile. "We don't need as much space nowadays, but it's nice when there's festivals. Lots of things to store and people to house during those times. It'd be nice if my children would come to visit more, but I understand they have their own lives."

"Mom, the Peterson's kids got into my garden again. If you can't get them to stop, I'm spraying them with a hose," a woman yells from the back of the house.

Gladys winces, then wrinkles her nose. "My daughter, Kira. I promise she's not always so...abrasive."

I struggle to keep my face neutral. Gemma didn't want to tell me much about her family beyond her parents, but Jake filled me in as best he could. Kira, just a year older than Gemma, is the second oldest daughter. And apparently those two do not get along. I was told to steer clear of her if I liked my balls attached to my body. My hand twitches in an effort to not protect them.

When she steps into view, though, I tense. Before me stands the most beautiful woman I've ever seen. It's almost too much to keep my jaw from dropping.

Her long hair spun with what looks like pure gold sweeps over her shoulder. I swallow hard, trying to get my shit together before she notices me. I can't get caught gawking at her. Then her amber eyes find mine and I'm a goner.

Before I can even utter a word, she scowls, planting her hands on her hips and turns to her mother. "What the hell is *he* doing here?"

Chapter 2: You've Got to be Kitten Me

Kira

I swear if he doesn't stop looking at me like I've hung the fucking moon, I'm going to lose it. I told my mother I wanted nothing to do with Gemma's new friend. Mom didn't put much stock in my words. She never does. And now he's staring at me with his ridiculously blue eyes and running his long fingers through his already messy blond hair. When he glances away, it's as if I can breathe properly again.

My question hangs in the air as my mother shoots me a disapproving glare. I don't care if I'm being rude to a guest. He doesn't belong here, even if he is a shifter now. We don't have time to take in every stray the Goddess deems worthy enough to be changed. Plus, if he's here, there's a chance Gemma will come back, which would be terrible for everyone involved.

"Kira," my mother snaps. "Be nice."

I plaster on a fake smile. "Lovely to meet you. Hope your drive was particularly wonderful. Perhaps you'd like to make it again? Now?"

His eyes widen, blinking at me like the spell is finally broken. Thank the Goddess. Hopefully, he'll take my advice and run straight back to wherever the hell Gemma is living now. As long as I don't have to deal with him tracking my movements and following after me like a little puppy, life will be perfect. The town's already in an uproar about the Samhain festival even though it's just under two months away. We don't need someone seeing the inner workings when the production company rolls into Moon Cove.

He clears his throat and tucks his hands in his pocket. When he rocks back on his heels and gives me what I'm sure is supposed to be a devastating smile, I groan. It was supposed to be internal, but the sound echoes through the large space. Mom shushes me, fire blazing in her eyes.

"Pleasure to meet you, Kira," he says, his voice rumbling through my body, and I suppress a shiver.

"It's Ms. Livia to you," I sneer.

The wooden spoon comes out of nowhere and smacks me in the arm. It clatters to the floor, and I whip my head toward my mother, rubbing the mark left behind.

"Don't test me, Kira. Now, Chase will be staying in Moon Cove and you will be nice to him," she hisses, and I nod, then tuck my chin to my chest. It's been a while since she's scolded me, and I feel like I'm fifteen again.

I peek at Chase, and he grins. "It's okay, Gladys. I'd rather be in Whispering Pines as well."

I close my eyes, sucking in a deep breath. "How long are you going to be here?"

"No idea." He shrugs and I swear his grin grows. Does he ever fucking stop? If he's going to be here for a while, I might make it my mission to piss him off.

"Great. Fantastic. I'm going home. Mom, talk to the Petersons and get them to control their crotch goblins," I say as calmly as possible, and her lips press together. "Please."

I pivot, not bothering to address Chase. Mom clears her throat, and I spin back. Her eyes dart to Chase, then back to me. Whatever she's planning, it can't be good. Least of all for me. I cross my arms, more to stop the trembling in my hands than anything else. I'm sure she'll see it as a sign of defiance, but that can't be helped.

"Chase, I don't know what Gemma told you, but we have a big festival coming up. We've run out of space and had to use the empty bedrooms upstairs. Obviously, we're not going to put you up in the lodge or the hotel. We wouldn't do that to you, would we, Kira?" She sends a sharp look my way, and I shake my head. "Therefore, you're going to need a place to stay."

"Oh. Yeah, of course. I can always stay in the next town over," Chase says, his grin falling from his face.

"It's two hours," I say, narrowing my eyes at my mother.

"Well then. I'll figure it out, ma'am. I don't want to put you out." Emotion flashes in his eyes, too quick for me to name.

"Nonsense," Mom cries. "Kira has room. She'll be happy to have you."

It takes a minute for me to process her words. My head snaps to her. "What?"

Her glare tells me all I need to know. There's no way in hell I'm getting out of this. I wonder how long she's been planning this. Was it a flash of genius for her? Or did the idea sprout when Gemma called her up? Fucking Gemma. All of this leads back to her. She just had to meddle in affairs back home. I told her to stay away and while she may have listened, she obviously can't keep her nose completely clean.

"Honestly, ma'am. It's fine. As someone who values my own space, I wouldn't want to invade Kira's place." He smiles again, but this time it's forced.

My mother sighs, then starts her campaign. It's nothing I haven't heard before. Guilt mixed with passive-aggressive comments are her go-to tactics. Chase doesn't stand a fucking chance. I'm sure she's talking to me too, but I tune her out as I study him. He doesn't look very threatening. Looks can be deceiving, though. I know that firsthand. Before long, he'll show his true colors and I'll understand why my gut tightened when I first spotted him. It'll make sense why there's an ache in my chest and a low ringing in my ears.

"It's fine. I have a spare room," I murmur, and both of them stop talking.

I don't know who appears more surprised—Chase or my mother. Until I know what he's truly here for, I'd rather keep him close. Like hell am I going to allow him to charm my family just to turn around and hurt them. Gemma may say he's a good guy, but she's been hoodwinked before. And she hasn't known him very long. She's not the best judge of character, which is exactly why Mom is still making comments about the shifter Gemma's fated to.

"Are you—" Chase starts, but Mom shushes him.

I don't know why she's so insistent on this. It wouldn't be hard to move things around or find him a room somewhere else. She'd never put him up in a hotel, though. One doesn't foist a guest off on someone else. Unless that someone is me.

I spin and glide down the hallway, keeping measured and quiet steps. My skin itches the farther I walk, the urge to turn back chasing me as I close the door behind me. It follows me all the way to my front door and I slough it off as I step over the threshold.

My cabin may not be as large as my parents, but it's home. Slade called it cozy, though I suspect he was mocking me. I gaze around the space, wondering what Chase will think. I huff, shoving the thought away. I don't give a flying fuck what he thinks. His opinion means little to nothing to me.

Then again, I'll hear it from my mother if he complains. He doesn't seem the type to bitch needlessly about things, but I'm not willing to risk it. Muttering under my breath, I rush around my cabin, grabbing random clothes and piling them into my arms. I toss them into my bedroom and slam the door. I'm halfway through gathering all the random cups scattered around when the air around me rumbles. I close my eyes, shoulders sagging. Fuck my life.

A minute later silence descends, and I hold my breath until there's a knock at my door. It's possibly the politest knock I've ever heard, which only pisses me off more. I don't want to share my safe space with Mr. Goody Two-shoes. I curse my mother one more time before pulling the heavy door open.

Chase turns, the late summer sun hitting his blond hair and creating a halo around his head. I blame the Goddess for his good looks. He was probably a troll before she got ahold of him. None of the other turned shifters I've met have magically transformed, but I cling to the idea to make myself feel better.

I step back and present the way to him. He throws his bag over his shoulder and slips past me. His arm brushes mine as he passes and a shock rolls to my fingertips. Flexing my hand, I kick the door closed. He's already scanning the space, and I shove my anxiety away, reminding myself I don't care what he thinks.

"Rules," I say, trying to keep my voice steady. "No going through the window if you spontaneously shift. No visitors. Don't leave your shit out. And no matter what, do not tell my parents what I do. If I catch you spying on me, your ass will be catapulted through the window."

He turns, a smirk firmly in place. "Thought you said no going out the window?"

I scowl, then stomp past him to the stairs. Halfway up, I glance over my shoulder. "You coming?"

He hurries after me as I start climbing again. When I reach the top, the heat from his body seeps into my back. It distracts me enough that my toe catches on the runner covering the floorboards. His fingers brush my side and I snarl. My wolf whines in my head, though whether it's him or my falling, I don't know. He doesn't heed the warning as he wraps his arm around my waist.

"Whoa there," he murmurs, his breath coasting across the shell of my ear.

My heart pounds in my chest as I shove him off, then spin. "I don't need your help."

The words come out harsher than need be. Except I would have been perfectly fine without him. His gaze dips to my hands, and I suck in a sharp breath. I will the claws away, then tuck my hands under my armpits. They didn't pop out because of him. He doesn't need to know that, though. Then again, I shouldn't scare him. I might not want him here, especially *here*, but he shouldn't be afraid of me. I have enough people who actively avoid me.

"They were just to catch my fall. It's a defense mechanism," I mutter and glance away.

"No harm, no foul. I shouldn't have grabbed you."

I narrow my gaze as I study him. He smiles, but there's a heaviness resting in the blue depths. Chase may present as a happy-go-lucky guy, but there's something else there. Something he doesn't show anyone. I shake my head, reminding myself it's none of my fucking business.

"This is your room." I swing open the door and he shuffles inside.

It's not big and I'm worried he won't fit on the mattress. He'll deal. He spins around slowly, taking in the small closet, bed, and nightstand. There's not much room for anything else. When he peers out the window, I feel like I'm intruding. The longing on his face is something I'm not used to seeing except in my reflection.

"You're really close to the lake," he murmurs as he presses his palm against the glass.

"Yup. I like the water. The window opens so you can hear the small waves lapping at the shore." I wince, wondering why the hell I said that. He doesn't need to know anything about me. I'm usually better at keeping my mouth shut. There's something about this man who sets me on edge. That's all it is.

He angles his head, gazing at me. "Got the same thing back home. Though my lake is bigger."

"It's not a competition," I mutter as I shuffle away from the door.

"Where's your room?" he asks, and my head snaps up. "In case there's an emergency."

"I'm capable of handling any emergency without your help."

He nods as he fights a smile. "What if I need something? You want me to walk around screaming your name? Neighbors might hear."

My mouth drops open and I snap it shut. He raises an eyebrow, his smirk back. Bastard. Now all I can think about is what it would sound like if he was underneath me screaming…I cut off the thought. Nope. No reason to go there. No matter how hot he is or how my skin heats the closer he gets.

"I'm across the hall. Don't ask me for anything."

"Is that another rule?"

"Yes. You stay out of my way, and I'll stay out of yours. Before you know it, you'll be back home and this'll be a distant memory."

I pivot and make my way downstairs. As I reach the bottom, he clears his throat behind me and I swallow down a groan. I spin and cross my arms.

"Little problem with your plan there, sunshine."

I sniff at the nickname yet choose to ignore it. "What's that?"

"Gladys told me to stick with you today. Said you'd give me a tour. Maybe you'll find out I'm not as bad as you seem to think I am." He chuckles as if there's anything funny about this situation. "And no, you weren't hiding it very well."

I smirk right back at him. "I wasn't trying to hide a goddamn thing. Perhaps I should have been less subtle."

I scowl, wishing I could wipe the smug look off his face. My wolf strains against my chest and I hold her back. No reason to destroy my cabin because he pissed me off with his little grin. I march out the door and slam it behind me. Bastard can figure shit out by himself. I refuse to allow him to put me under his spell. I'm perfectly fine right where I am.

Chapter 3: Too Many Beds
Chase

A shudder runs through me as the door slams behind Kira. The urge to chase after her settles in my bones and I roll my head, stretching my neck. It doesn't help, but I doubt anything will. Gazing at my hands, I inspect them for anything unusual. My fingertips tingle, yet no claws come out, no fur sprouts along the backs of my hands. The tension in my muscles ease, and I sigh.

I retreat into my temporary room to unpack. Kira didn't tell me where the bathroom was. Or where anything was, actually. I doubt the bed is long enough. It probably won't matter since half the time I end up curled in the fetal position at the foot. Hopefully, Kira's rule of staying out of bedrooms applies to her as well. The last thing I need is her finding me like that. In fact, this might be the worst idea ever.

It's probably nothing she hasn't seen before.

She's lived in Moon Cove her whole life. It's strange to imagine growing up in a community where everyone understands what's happening to them. Being a shifter of any kind is probably the most normal thing in the world to them. Gladys told me not to worry about the townsfolk with a gentle pat on my arm. Her touch didn't elicit any physical reaction like Kira's did. I could chalk it up to Kira's beauty, but it seems like there's more to it than that.

I don't have the energy to figure it out. This day has already dragged on too long, and it isn't even noon. I open the window, letting the breeze from the lake filter in. Shouts of laughter float up, and I glance outside. Three children, who look like triplets, chase each other through Kira's backyard. They must be the Peterson kids. Their giggles are contagious, but I assume all four-year-olds' giggles are. We don't get a lot of kids that young at Jake's summer camp, but every one of them acts exactly like these kids do. I don't know why Kira seems to have such a problem with them.

As soon as the thought crosses my mind, the little rascals head straight for what is clearly Kira's garden. They each grab a large tomato from the plants and chomp down on them. I jerk back and smack my head on the sash when they transform into fawns, the tomato still in their mouths. They gallop away, although I don't know if deer gallop. Someone shrieks and I wince.

Kira bounds around the corner, dragging a hose behind her. She sprays it at the kids, but they've already disappeared. I lean on the sill, my head hanging out the window, and watch her. She huffs, mumbling under her breath, then blows a piece of golden hair from her face. I grin when she glances up and spots me.

"I think you almost got them," I call, and she scowls. I have a feeling I'll be seeing that look a lot.

She flips me the bird before stomping back around the house. Shaking my head, I pull back inside. Maybe being here won't be so bad. Messing with Kira might be the highlight of my stay. My phone vibrates and I snatch it off the bed. A text message from Gemma greets me and I scroll through the massive list she sent me. It's a guide to all things Moon Cove, containing everything from residents and their shifter forms to the best place to eat while here. There's also a hefty paragraph on Kira, though I skip most of it.

"She warning you away from me?" Kira asks from the hallway, and I jolt.

"What? No. More like go here for the best fried chicken." I tuck my phone in my pocket.

From the look on her face, I haven't convinced her at all. "Sure. Come downstairs. We clearly need to talk."

She walks away and I follow, practically tripping over her heels down the stairs as she leads me into the living room. I stop short, flabbergasted at the scene in front of me. She plops down on a couch situated in front of a fireplace and glances over her shoulder.

"Why the hell are there so many beds?"

She rolls her eyes, then turns back. "Surprised you didn't notice before. Because my siblings think they can stuff all their junk in my house instead of getting rid of it or keeping it at our parent's house. I plan on having a bonfire later."

"There's at least five in here. How the hell did you even get them through the door?" I lean back and peer down the hall. "Are there more in the kitchen? What about the bathroom?"

"Would you sit down? You're freaking me out, hovering behind me." She huffs and crosses her arms when I don't move. "Fine. There's like nine. Two in the room in the back down here. One in my room and one in yours. And five in here. So there's only eight. Wait...nine. But you're not going to be fighting a bed to cook eggs. Now sit the fuck down."

I slip between the couch and the foot of one of the beds and settle next to her. Her nose wrinkles and she moves to lean against the arm, tucking her leg underneath her. I mirror her, my heart pounding as I wait for her to start.

"I don't like you," she says, and I fight a smirk.

"You don't know me. How can you hate me already?"

She grits her teeth. "I didn't say I hate you. I said I don't like you. Which might seem like the same thing, but it's not. I don't like anyone. I don't want you here."

I sigh and tuck my chin to my chest. I don't want to get Kira in trouble with her mother. But I won't put Kira out either. This was a bad idea from the start. Gladys was able to convince me she'd come around. An hour isn't enough time to get used to each other. I'm not going to make her uncomfortable.

"Okay. So, how do we get me somewhere else without your mother coming down on you?"

Her spine straightens, shock flitting across her face. "What?"

"You don't want me here. Fine. But if I leave without an excuse, Gladys seems the type to blame you for it instead of me. So, how do we convince her you didn't run me off?"

"That's it?"

"Was there something else you needed to discuss?" I raise an eyebrow when she just stares at me.

"Where would you even go?"

I shrug, glancing around the room to escape her eyes. "I'll figure it out. More important part is fending off your mom."

I don't want to sleep in my truck, but I will if I have to. It might be the only option other than going back home. The thought sends numbness spreading from my gut, immobilizing me. Leaving shouldn't be a dreaded thing. I shake my head and my vision blurs. I can see Kira's mouth moving, but no words come out. Or maybe I just can't hear her. I dig my nails into my palms, the small bit of pain turning the world back on. Kira says my name, something close to concern in her tone.

"Sorry, what was that?" I ask, tilting my head.

"Are you—never mind. I was saying you can stay. It would be more trouble than it's worth. But I'm watching you. You're hiding something, and I'll eventually figure out what it is." She narrows her eyes, daring me to refute her.

"I mean, we don't know each other. So, there's probably a lot of things you think I'm hiding. Which I'm not, by the way." My spine straightens as a realization comes over me. "You're a werewolf, aren't you? I mean, a wolf shifter."

She nods slowly, and her tongue darts out to lick her bottom lip. My gaze dips down at the motion, and I will my cock to not react. Of course it doesn't work. She does it again, and I wonder if she's doing it on purpose.

"What kind did the Goddess decide to make you?" she whispers as if she already knows the answer.

I clear my throat and pull my gaze away from her lips. "Cougar. Which probably explains that feeling in your gut."

She groans, tipping her head back. Her body slithers down until she's sprawled across the couch, her foot inches from my leg. I have the irrational urge to grab her bare ankle and do...something I probably shouldn't. Like rub the arch of her foot or trail my fingers along her inner thigh. Her shorts leave me with a lot of skin to work with. I shift, burrowing into the cushions more.

I clear my throat again. "Maybe it's not the shifter thing, though."

Her lids snap open, and she glares at me. "What else is there? Are you planning on murdering my family? Or exposing us to the world? Perhaps you'd like to sabotage the festival?"

"What?" I laugh, the tension breaking around us, and her lips twitch. I might make it my mission to make her genuinely smile. Seems like a good way to pass the time while we're stuck together.

"You said it might not be because of our shifter forms, so what else is there?"

I wiggle my eyebrows at her. Confusion swirls on her face until finally she gets my meaning and scowls. I laugh again as she huffs, then throws a pillow at my head. I bat it away, still grinning. This really could be fun.

She crosses her arms and stares at the ceiling. "Do *not* say shit like that around my parents. They'll get ideas you won't be able to escape."

"Gladys did say I could call her mom," I murmur.

"The hell she did. For fuck's sake. This is going to be a fucking disaster." She pops off the couch, her toes brushing my leg, and I desperately wish I wasn't wearing jeans. "Get some proper clothes on and we'll get this over with. The sooner you learn your shit, the sooner you can leave. And I'll have my home and my life back."

She stomps up the stairs, and a minute later, a door closes. I glance down at my black t-shirt and jeans and wonder what the hell constitutes proper clothing. I launch over the back of the couch and bound upstairs. Hopefully shorts will be good enough for Ms. Grumpy Pants. Giddiness overwhelms my system, and

I end up tipping over onto the bed as I push down my pants. Once I kick them off, I spin around in a circle, forgetting what I was doing.

I freeze when there's a knock at my door. At least I remembered to close it behind me. I search for my bag and spot it on the other side of the bed. My knee clips the footboard and I howl, pain shooting up my thigh. Crashing onto the bed, I clutch my leg, hoping she doesn't come in. The door swings open and I groan.

"What the hell is going on in here?" she snarls. She plants her fists on her hips and the move pulls her shirt tight across her breasts. I groan, slamming my eyes shut.

"Nothing. I'm fine," I gasp. It doesn't even hurt anymore, but with her hovering over me in those shorts and her low-cut shirt, golden hair swirling around her face, I can't fucking take it.

She spins and stalks out of the room, muttering, "Thought cats were supposed to land on their feet."

"I'd get on my knees for you, sunshine," I call after her.

She shouts something back, but I'm too busy laughing to listen. She'll end up punching me before long. And I'll welcome it. At this point, I'll take whatever she'll give me. Clearly, there's something more between us, whether she wants to admit it or not. I'm not too concerned about the ramifications anymore. A little harmless flirting never hurt anyone. Unless she's spoken for, in which case I'll have to back off. From the way she's reacted, though, I doubt it.

I tug on my shorts and swing around the door frame, ready to leave my doubts behind and engage in something much more exciting.

Chapter 4: Fix Your Face

Kira

"Over there is the school," I say, pointing at a single-story brick building. I'm desperately trying to ignore Chase's presence, which isn't working very well. Especially since he keeps brushing against me.

"Who goes there?" He leans close, his chest pressing into my arm.

"Kids. Don't you have schools in…" I lose my train of thought when his fingers skim across my palm.

He chuckles under his breath. "Whispering Pines. And yes, we do. Well, in the next town over. Is it a shifter school, though?"

I nod, forcing myself to move away. This man is going to drive me to the brink and I'll either end up running into the woods or cuddled up next to him. Neither one is acceptable. I'm not leaving him in my cabin by himself. Who knows what he'd end up doing to it. Am I being unfair? Probably. Knowing he's a cougar shifter along with everything else just makes this all the more precarious. This can't end well.

"It *is* a shifter community, after all," I say, and continue down the path. Thankfully Moon Cove is small enough we can walk most places. And if Chase can't handle it, so be it. I did my duty of showing him around and my mother can't bitch.

He hurries after me, his arm brushing me again, and I grit my teeth.

"Are there fights?"

"At the school?"

"Yeah. With so many different types of shifters, you'd think they'd clash every once in a while. Plus, Gemma said—"

I stop, holding up my hand. "Whatever Gemma told you isn't relevant. She's not here. So, I suggest you just ask your questions so we can get this done with and I don't have to hear about her."

It takes him a few seconds to catch up to me when I start walking again. "Why do you hate her?"

"I don't," I say through gritted teeth. The last thing I want to do is talk about Gemma with him. He'll clearly be on her side, even if there aren't any sides.

"Seems like you do. And if you're trying to act like you don't, well, I hate to break it to you, sunshine—"

"Stop calling me sunshine. I am the furthest thing from sunny. And a little word to the wise, when a woman makes a statement, maybe you should believe them the first time," I snap.

He skips in front of me, and I stutter to a stop.

"I do believe you. But when your words don't match your attitude, what exactly am I supposed to do? Let it slide?"

"First of all, we're not friends. Unless you're my friend, you don't have a right to question shit. Second of all, you can't say you believe me and then turn around and say something that questions that belief." I poke him in the chest, then do it again for good measure. Certainly not because his muscles have muscles and I'm trying to find out how deep they go.

He glances down and I poke him once more. He steps back and tucks his hands in his pockets. When he studies my face, tilting his head, I brace myself for the gaslighting. Or the arguments. Or the doubling down. It's usually one of those three.

"Okay. You say you don't like Gemma, but you don't hate her. And we're not friends. Got it." He drops his head, the gazes at me from beneath his long lashes. I wonder how many women have swooned from that one move.

"You know when you do shit like that, it kind of negates your words," I snap, and his brows pull low.

"What shit?"

I roll my eyes and step around him. Of course he didn't even notice what he's doing. It's probably second nature to him to flirt. With his grinning and his witty comebacks, I'm sure he's popular with whoever he turns those baby blues on. They probably fall at his feet. I won't be one of them.

"Wait." His fingers graze my arm. "Kira, please."

I pivot and poke him one more time. He holds his hands up in surrender.

"What could you possibly want?"

"I'm sorry. I forgot you don't like me. Why don't we get this tour done and I'll get out of your hair?" He presses his lips together.

"Spit it out."

I swear he blushes as he fights a grin. "I don't think you'd appreciate it. Should we continue?"

I continue with him falling into step next to me. Silence stretches between us, and I find myself peeking at him more often than not. I didn't think he noticed until his arm whips out, stopping me in my tracks. A car filled with teenagers drives past, and I realize I almost walked into the road. What the fuck is wrong with me?

He maneuvers me to the inside of the sidewalk. "Do I need to hold your hand?" Chase asks, laughter in his voice.

"The sun," I mutter. "It blinded me."

"Alrighty then. We should eat."

My head whips up and I glance around. "We're not going on a date."

He chuckles, latching on to my elbow and steering me toward Harriet's Cafe. The bell overhead jingles as he pushes open the door, and I wince. Hopefully Harriet isn't here. She's probably the nicest lady in the town, but everyone comes to her for the town gossip.

I'm already pushing the limit by showing him around. Excuses could be made for that, though. Eating with him? Nope. Rumors will fly, and I don't need to deal with any of them.

Chase leans down and whispers, "Doesn't have to be a date, but I'm more than willing to take you out if you'll let me."

He grabs my hand and drags me toward a table in the back before I can cuss him out. At least we're in the corner. I snatch a menu from behind the ketchup bottle and prop it in front of my face. Chase sticks out like a sore thumb, gazing around and smiling at people. A finger appears at the top of my menu and pulls it down.

"Are you hiding?" he murmurs, raising an eyebrow.

"No. I'm perusing the menu. Seeing what the selections are. As you should be," I snap.

I already know everything, though. Harriet's mother owned this place before her. And her mother before that. Her family was one of the first ones to settle in the town after my ancestors started it. At least that's what Harriet boasts. At this point, I'm not even sure if the history I've been taught is based in reality.

Chase clears his throat. "Question. Who exactly is going to be teaching me? I doubt I'll fit in the desks at the school."

"They don't teach that stuff at school. There's afternoon school classes, but they're wrapped up in the puberty talk." I drop the menu and smirk. "Didn't think you'd want to go through that again."

"Definitely not. Gem—your mother didn't say what would be happening, though. I suspect she's got a lot on her plate with Samhain coming up." He flashes a smile at Dotty, one of the servers, who blushes. As soon as she sees my face, though, she disappears into the kitchen.

"I think Dad, Ben to you, will probably tell you a lot of the lore. Depends on what your issue is," I mutter. I don't want to get into this here, but he seems like a glutton for punishment. "Do you like gossip?"

He sucks in his cheeks and rocks his head back and forth. My lip twitches before I can stop it and I glance away.

"If it's handed to me, I won't plug my ears. Depends on what type of gossip it is. If I'm in the middle of it, well, depends. Why?" He scans the menu, then looks up.

"Because if you don't start controlling your face, you're going to be in the center of town gossip for-fucking-ever. And you're going to drag me into it as well. So, knock it off."

I duck my head so I don't have to see his reaction. I've been in the middle of rumors before. Most of them I was dragged into kicking and screaming. When I was a teenager, I loved it. If they were talking about me, then it meant I wasn't invisible. As I got older, I realized how toxic that was. Most of my friends who weren't really friends either moved away or found their mates. I got sucked into the family business and made it a point to stay as far away from being the center of attention as possible.

Chase clears his throat, pulling me from my thoughts. "I'll try to control my face. What's good here?"

"Everything. Though the chicken fried steak is—"

"What's wrong with my chicken fried steak, Kira Livia," Harriet demands from across the dining room, and I wince.

"Nothing, Miss Harriet. It's perfect if you like chicken fried steak." I try to smile, but she huffs anyway.

Chase's shoulders shake, and a low rumble erupts from me. Harriet stomps up to the table, her dark hair cascading down her back. She may be in her sixties, but she still looks like she isn't a day over thirty. I wonder what it's like not to worry about wrinkles or stretch marks. She's rail thin and ethereal. I've never plucked up the nerve to ask if she has Lorelie blood in her. When I was younger, I thought she was a dryad. Slade, my older brother, just shook his head after I asked him.

Harriet narrows her eyes at me, and I shrink down in my seat. She's a force to be reckoned with, and I don't want to tangle with her today. I wish Chase would have dragged me into the cafe down the street. At least we could walk and eat at the same time. Her gaze looks Chase up and down and then she smiles.

"You new here?" she asks, her voice sugary sweet.

"Yes, ma'am," he says, returning her smile. Something twists in my gut, and I fix my eyes on the menu.

"What's your name?"

"Chase Holbrook, Miss Harriet. I hear you have the best chicken fried steak."

She smirks and I roll my eyes, though I'm mindful enough to turn my face away. They chitchat while I try to ignore them. As they talk, I find myself watching his lips. The bottom one is plump. I swear they're the color of cherry blossoms in full bloom. It takes longer than I'd like to pull myself away. I move on to studying his cheekbones and wondering if one would consider them apple cheeks when Chase's finger taps the back of my hand. I jolt, an electric shock wrapping my wrist.

"What do you want to eat, Kira?" Harriet asks as if it isn't the first time.

"Oh, uh, nothing. I'm not hungry," I murmur, wondering what the hell is wrong with me.

Chase points at something on the menu and Harriet nods. She gives me a funny look before gliding off to the kitchen. Chase laces his fingers together, and my attention is drawn to them. Instead of waxing poetic about them, I think about chestnuts. Because anything is better than swooning over him.

"What are you thinking about?" Chase asks softly.

"Chestnuts." I grimace and he raises an eyebrow.

"Are you craving chestnuts or..."

"It's spelled wrong. There's a random letter in the middle no one pronounces. And why the hell are we roasting them? It doesn't make any sense. Why not roast walnuts? Also, they're covered in fur." I cross my arms and glance around the diner. More people are coming in and it sets me on edge.

He sighs and we fall into an uncomfortable silence. The urge to fill the empty space builds the longer it stretches. I fold my hands in my lap, biting my tongue. It's not my job to make him comfortable. It's not my job to be agreeable. Except I don't have to be a bitch. It's not his fault Mom foisted him off on me. I don't know how to hold him at bay yet not take it out on him. I'll just keep my mouth shut and hope we can get this over with quickly. Life will go back to normal soon. The thought doesn't make me feel any better.

Chapter 5: Paw-sessive

Chase

Kira's shoulders keep climbing the longer we sit. I've figured out pretty quickly I shouldn't have brought her here. Now I'm wishing I would have paid more attention. Kira doesn't seem like the type to go along with someone else's plans.

I lean over the table and whisper, "We can leave if you'd like. Or you could slip out and I'll bring the food to your place." A million other options pile up, but I keep them to myself.

"If I leave now, there will be even more talk. Especially with lunch rush. I wouldn't be surprised if one of my family members sweeps through the door by the time your food comes. It's fine." She huffs and stares at the table. "What questions do you have?"

I straighten, wondering where to start. "I don't really know. Hard to have questions when you only have snippets."

She huffs again, then focuses on me. "What did Gemma tell you?"

"Thought you didn't want to hear about Gemma?"

Her eyes narrow and I brace myself. Then her face smooths out and her gaze fixes on my shoulder. At least I think it's my shoulder. I glance behind me, but there's nothing but the end of the counter and the wall. There aren't even any posters or pictures there. When I face her, she's relaxed the slightest bit.

"Gemma's and my relationship is complicated and none of your business. But I need to know where you're at so I can decide who can help you. Why don't you tell me how you got like this?" She waves her hand at me, and I wonder if I should be offended.

"Maybe now isn't a good time for that. I'd rather my story not be fodder for the masses," I mumble.

Harriet makes her appearance, setting my plate of breakfast food in front of me gently. She drops a salad in front of Kira and spins. Kira's nose wrinkles and annoyance bubbles in my gut.

"Harriet," I call, and she turns.

Her head tilts and she scans my plate. "Something wrong, dear?"

I tug Kira's plate closer to me. "This isn't what I ordered. I'm happy to eat this too...and pay for it, of course. But could you bring the other dish as well, please?"

Her lips press together and she nods sharply. I may have made an enemy, but I don't give a shit. Whatever is going on between them isn't my business. Doesn't give her a right to be a bitch to Kira. I push my own plate of eggs, sausage, and hash browns toward her, then drizzle the dressing over the salad. At least it looks good and isn't a small one with only a couple leaves in a bowl.

"I'm not eating your food," she hisses.

"Why not? I know not everyone likes over easy eggs, but they're cooked well. Or are you a vegetarian? Wait, is that a thing with wolf shifters?" I shove a forkful in my mouth as I ponder what it would be like to be a wolf who didn't eat meat.

"Fine. But I'm only doing this so you don't make a scene."

She cuts around the egg whites, leaving the yokes behind. My salad is fine, but I'm definitely going to be hungry by the time I'm done. These days I'm eating twice the amount of calories.

"Is it a shifter thing to eat more?" I ask softly.

Her fork stops halfway to her mouth. "Uh, maybe? I mean, I eat more. But I burn a lot of calories during a shift and being like...this."

"What does that mean?"

She ducks her head and shoves her food in her mouth. "Some of my friends in high school were smaller shifters. They didn't eat as much, I suppose. I don't know how to describe it."

"Jake said shifters can turn into everything. But he's a bigfoot shifter so, I don't know how much he knows and he's pretty vague."

Her head snaps up, eyes wide. "Bigfoot? Have you...has he...what the fuck."

I fight a grin. "Yup. Full on bigfoot. Don't call him a yeti, though. Gets a bit pissy."

"I doubt I'll ever meet him, so that won't be a problem. You know they're really rare, right? I don't know anyone who's met one of them. They're almost as uncommon as Lorelie. Does he have a temper?" Concern flits across her face.

"Nope. He's a loner. Took me four fucking years to befriend him. Grumpy, but definitely doesn't have a temper. Unless you fuck with Gemma. Practically threw Rick out the window when he was a dick to her."

"Did he know she was his mate then?"

Shoving the last of the greenery in my mouth, I try to remember. I was dealing with a lot of my own shit what with all the changes I was going through. I should have been there more for Jake. Instead, I focused on my own shit and left him to navigate everything.

"I don't think so. He almost ripped my arm off when I touched Gemma once. That's normal, right?"

She nods, her gaze darting over my shoulder, then back to her plate. Harriet appears with a club sandwich and a plate of fries. Her eyes narrow at the empty bowl, but she takes it away without a word.

"It's normal. Mates get possessive, even before they know it." She grabs a fry and munches on it. I don't think she even realizes she's taken my food. I nudge the plate closer and pick up one of the sandwiches.

"How do they not know it?"

She tips her head from side to side. "Lots of reasons. Usually, people's own issues get in the way. Sometimes the goddess just makes them wait. There's some who don't believe in fated mates, so until it snaps into place, they're just real confused. Mates are drawn to each other. They want to spend time with each other. Gemma probably had a great time pulling Jake out of his shell."

"Not exactly. She spent most of her time keeping secrets and calling him out on his bullshit."

Grooves appear between her eyes, and I wonder how long it's been since she's talked to her sister. It's not my job to fix their relationship. Being a conduit would be on-brand for me, but I have enough to deal with.

"What happened when you first shifted?" she asks, and I struggle to keep my face from falling.

"Don't remember at first. After that, it was weird. Happened when Gemma came around. Jake had to shift and run me off. I don't remember a lot of it. When I came to, I was home on my porch." I don't have memories of what happened other than flashes of images I don't like to recall.

"First, what were you doing on the porch?" She grabs one of the sandwiches and props her elbows on the table.

"Nothing?" Actually, I was sunning myself. I'm not about to admit that. If I keep shit from her, though, I may not get the answers I need. "I was lying down in the sun."

She nods and licks her finger, drawing my eyes to her lips. My nostrils flare and her scent washes over me. An ache blooms in my chest, and I shake my head. If she keeps it up, I'm going to end up bending her over the table and...I cut off the thought and shuffle in my seat. I'd just gotten my shit under control and she's derailed it just by eating.

"So you were acting like a cat. Makes sense. What about before?"

"Told you I don't remember," I mutter.

She waves away my words, another fry in her hand. "I mean, before you shifted."

"Uh, I was sick. Thought I was sick. And I started blacking out. At first, it wasn't that bad. I'd wake up at the end of my bed or out on the couch. Then

I ended up coming to three miles away from home covered in blood. I wasn't injured, so I assume I killed something." The thought turns my stomach. I'm more aware now when I'm shifted, but it's still just a mess of images instead of an actual memory.

"You realize that's normal, right? I don't know a lot of made shifters, but they've all said something similar. It'll even out. Is that why you're here?" she asks skeptically. "Because nothing about your experience seems out of the ordinary."

"How long?" I raise my eyebrow. "How long do I have to wait for everything to even out? Because I'm still waiting to not black out."

She paws at my plate, seeking out another fry, but they're all gone. I didn't even eat any of them. Not that I'm complaining. As long as she's full, I'll be fine. That's what they invented snacks for. I might have to ask where the grocery store is, though. Maybe I can get Kira to come with me.

"Let's go," she says, reaching for her money. I beat her to it, dropping some cash on the table.

She scowls and slides from the booth. She's halfway across the diner by the time I've gotten up. Huffing, she stomps back to me and grabs my hand. I can't keep the smile from my face as I allow her to drag me out the door. She doesn't seem to notice the others watching us. Nor does she notice when I lace our fingers together.

A low hum of energy thrums through me and I wonder if she can feel it, too. She doesn't give any indication she does and eventually it fades away. Or maybe I just get used to it. It's calming in a way I've never experienced before. I've been on edge for months now.

"Where are we going?" I ask as she pulls me down another street. We've left Main Street behind, the spaces between the houses growing with each block.

"I don't know many goddess-made shifters, but there's one who might be able to answer your question. Dad might know. I figured it'd be better to go straight to the source. Vincent traveled around a lot after he became a shifter. Then he settled here."

Jealousy hits me hard, and I resist the urge to whisk her away. I'm not one to attempt to control who someone hangs out with. Especially Kira. We literally just met. I keep hold of her hand, anyway. I can't seem to make myself let go. Telling myself there's no reason to be envious doesn't help.

Vincent's house isn't big, but it's tidy with bushes planted around the porch. She tugs me up the stairs and knocks. As soon as the door swings open, she drops my hand. Vincent doesn't look much older than me. His light brown hair is cropped close to his head. He wraps his arms around Kira, pressing his sharp cheekbones into her temple.

"Such a lovely surprise," Vincent says. His smooth voice rolls over me and sets me on edge. "What brings you around?"

He leans back, his hands settling on her shoulders. There's nothing sexual about the act. Doesn't stop me from wanting to shove him away from her. My fingers curl into fists and my nails dig into my palms. I can't pull my gaze away from them as they chat. It's innocent and easy, their conversation, and it tears at me. I close my eyes and pull in a deep breath.

"Chase," Kira says sharply, as if this isn't the first time she's tried to get my attention.

I open my eyes slowly. "Yes?"

"This is Vincent. He's like you."

"How lovely," I murmur and hold out my hand to him. He grips mine briefly, then drops it.

"Come on in." Vincent spins and walks inside.

Kira glares at me and hisses, "What the hell is wrong with you?"

"Nothing. Let's go. Clearly, Vincent has a lot to share." I gesture her to go in and she scoffs before following him.

I don't know what the hell is wrong with me. The new moon isn't for another two weeks, though that doesn't seem to matter for me. There's a lot of fucking things that don't seem to matter for me. The rules don't apply to me and it's driving me to the brink. This is my last chance, my last attempt to do something to stop myself from running off into the woods so no one else has to deal with me.

I barely notice our surroundings as I plop onto the couch. I'm too focused on Vincent asking Kira if she'd like anything to drink. She sits next to me and there's a swooping in my stomach. I expected to feel better since she chose the couch, but it only adds to the tension.

This entire day has been a rollercoaster of emotions. Being so close to a wolf shifter has set me on edge. I didn't think being surrounded by other shifters would affect me so much. I should have asked Gemma about it, but she grew up here. She wouldn't know what it was like to be shoved into a situation like this.

Vincent settles in his chair and crosses his ankle over his knee. "So, what exactly can I do for you?"

I glance at Kira, silently urging her to speak up. We're only here because of her. Vincent is my best bet at figuring out what's typical for made shifters. If she doesn't start talking, I'll end up filling the quiet just to get this over with. Not that I actually want to do this right now. I thought I'd have time to adjust to being in Moon Cove before diving in.

"Chase," Kira mumbles.

"What kind of shifter are you?" I bite out.

"Fox. You?" Vincent raises an eyebrow, the corner of his lip twitching.

"Cougar." I don't elaborate as I struggle not to glare at him.

Vincent clears his throat, fighting a smirk and losing. "Perhaps we should take a walk, Chase."

"Great idea." I shove from the couch and follow Vincent down a hallway and out the back door.

We end up on the porch, and he turns to me. "Feel a bit better?"

"Excuse me?" I don't know what the fuck he's talking about. Now that he's mentioned it, though, the tension in my muscles has eased and my stomach has settled somewhat.

"Ah, I see." He nods knowingly. "Fresh air helps sometimes. You looked like you were about to shift right in my living room. Wouldn't have been terrible, but it might have triggered Kira, and I didn't want a fight breaking out. How long?"

He doesn't have to elaborate. And the sooner we get this over with, the sooner we can leave. "I shifted the first time last year right before Samhain. I don't remember a lot when I'm shifted even now."

"And the first time you chose to shift?"

"Chose? It's not a choice. It happens, I wake up, I figure out where the hell I am, and I go home." I cross my arms, more to protect myself from his judgement than anything. I knew I was fucking this thing up.

He sighs, leaning on the railing as he gazes around his yard. "You're blacking out because you haven't accepted your shifter side. It's hard, but your cougar is a part of you. If you keep pushing it away, you'll never find peace. Start by trying to shift voluntarily. Might find out a lot about your life once you accept who you are now."

He leaves me on the back porch and I scrub my hands over my face. As much as I want to reject his words, I can't. I don't want to accept shit. I want things to go back to the way they were. My life was fine. I was content. And I'm afraid I'll never find that peace again.

Chapter 6: Chasing Chase

Kira

"Maybe I should go…" I mutter, my eyes fixed on the hallway as if I can see through walls. Vincent came back at least fifteen minutes ago, yet Chase hasn't reappeared.

"You'll stay in your seat and let him work through his shit." He sighs, running his hands through his hair. "This isn't going to be easy, Kira. He needs someone who will work through it with him. Is that something you're up for?"

"I don't have an option." My throat swells, cutting off the excuse I was going to throw at him. It's the truth, though there might be something more I can't figure out. I shove the feelings aside. I'll deal with it later—or not at all.

He snorts, shaking his head. "This should be interesting."

Chase stalks down the hall, then stutters to a stop. He grins, but it seems forced. Whatever Vincent said to him clearly didn't help. Or maybe it did, and he's just not ready to deal with everything. I'll need to talk to Dad before long. I'm not equipped to deal with this. I don't *want* to deal with him. He's a stranger who waltzed into my life and will waltz right back out again before long. No reason to get attached.

"Ready? Unless you need to stay. I can make my way back alone." He's already across the room, practically shouting over his shoulder. I don't know why he's running away.

I push to my feet and wave at Vincent, who chuckles as I rush after Chase. The front door shuts and I'm reaching for the handle by the time it hits me. My hand drops and my vision blurs. Why the hell am I chasing after him?

"Something funny?" Vincent asks from behind me, and I groan internally.

I didn't realize I'd snorted out loud. "Chasing Chase. Just sounded funny."

"You going after him?" he asks, peeking out of the front window.

"Why would I do that? We're not together. We're not even friends. He wants to leave, so be it." I take a step back, then another. Going out the back will get me closer to the forest. Magic buzzes under my skin and I'm about to lose it.

I make my way through his house in a daze and I'm almost out the back door when he calls, "Can't run from the truth forever, Kira. Remember that."

I shake my head and push outside. Running between the houses, I keep my breathing even. If I let the magic overwhelm me, I'll end up shifting in the middle of the neighborhood. The town is probably already ablaze with rumors and gossip and all sorts of talk about Chase. And I'm in there too. My mind races, remembering our entire time at the diner.

"I held his fucking hand," I cry.

As I reach the edge of the forest, I gather the magic thrumming within me and shift. I'm sure if someone is watching, they caught the flash of light, but my paws are hitting the ground. Weaving through the trees, I take the familiar paths toward the spot I've been going since childhood. I usually don't go during the daytime. The outcropping is exposed, hanging over the lake. Hopefully, a random wolf won't draw attention.

I rest my head on my paws as the sun beats down on me. I've been putting off shifting, too wrapped up in the humdrum of everyday life. A peace settles over me and I close my eyes. I don't know how long I doze with birdsong lulling me. My mind keeps wandering back to Chase, preventing me from falling asleep completely. This is exactly what I didn't want when he came here.

A twig snaps behind me, and I whip my head around. Another wolf appears, loping through the trees. I huff and turn back to the scene in front of me. My brother is the only one who ever found me here. Or maybe he's the only one who bothered to look for me. Magic ripples through the air, and I thank the goddess for the foresight to allow our clothes to stay with us when we shift.

He drops down next to me and nudges my head. I growl but shift regardless. I settle next to him, dangling my feet over the edge. Hopefully I don't lose my shoes. No way am I going into the water after them.

"What are you doing here, Slade? Thought you were off on another adventure?" I ask.

"Well, I went by your house and some random guy was there. Took me a minute to figure out he's Jake's friend. Then I went to Mom and Dad's and neither of them had seen you since this morning. Figured you were hiding here." He leans back on his hands.

"Just needed a run. Been a while. Why are you in Moon Cove? You said you weren't going to be back for Samhain."

He tips his head back, basking in the afternoon sun. "And I'm not. I'll be gone in a couple days. Got a call from Holden. They got a bit of a cryptid problem. Wants me to check it out."

I sniff, biting my tongue to keep my retort in check. "I don't know who Holden is. How the hell do you know all these random people?"

"Helps I can sense other shifters. Comes in handy when I'm traveling. Met Holden about five years ago when I was down south. His car had broken down, and I helped him get back on the road. Ended up crossing paths a couple more times and shit just stuck. You know how it is."

He says it so nonchalantly I don't have it in me to burst his bubble. Slade always had a way of making friends with anyone. He's got that air about him. He just has the kind of personality that makes people feel comfortable. High school was a playground for him. Slade would flit from group to group, engaging everyone. I didn't have the same experience. He thought because I was popular, we had the same results. We didn't. Not by a long shot. Slade was liked while I was feared.

"I haven't left Moon Cove in ten years, Slade. So I have no idea what you're talking about. Plus, I'm a bitch. People don't flock to me like they do you." So much for keeping my mouth shut. I sound whiny and bitchy, which isn't the reason I came out here.

"You're not a bitch, Kira. You're just...rough around the edges. And you don't let people in." He sighs, then grabs my hand in his. "What's Chase like?"

"He smiles too much," I mutter. "And he talks a lot."

"You need someone to fill the silences when you refuse to speak."

I roll my eyes and tug my hand away. "It's not that. He just seems to be...overly communicative."

"Is that a thing?"

"Apparently. I called him out when he tried to analyze Gemma's and my relationship. He turned around and apologized."

Slade gasps dramatically, pressing his palm to his chest. "He. Did. Not."

"I'm not going to talk to you if you're going to be like this."

He smacks my leg. "You need to lighten up."

"And you need to not interrupt." I crack my neck, trying to figure out how to explain what Chase is like. "It wasn't just him saying sorry. He detailed where he went wrong and how he was going to do better. I felt like I was being gentle parented by him. But I couldn't even be mad about that because he wasn't condescending."

"So he apologized, validated your feelings, and lined out how he was going to change. Sounds fucking terrible. Do you think you maybe just haven't been around any guys who are decent people other than your amazingly awesome brothers?" He flashes me a grin and I roll my eyes.

"Mom's making him stay at my house. I'm going to be stuck for goddess knows how long with a man who constantly smiles, overcommunicates, and keeps trying to find a way to leave." I huff, realizing how ridiculous it sounds.

"Why is he trying to leave? Jake said Chase needs this. Something about not dealing with his transition well."

I pick at the skin on my knee, thinking back to Vincent's words. "I've known the man less than a day, Slade. Not like he's opened up and told me all his troubles. He keeps trying to leave because I'm being a bitch, but you know Mom will never let that happen. He's trying to find a way around her."

"Fat chance at that," he snorts. "You're not usually sucked into other people's shit so easily. Could you have a little—"

I slap my hand over his mouth as his eyes dance in glee. "Less than a day. Nothing is going on. Nothing is happening. I'm pissed because I don't like people in my space. That's all this is. And so help me, if you start spouting to Mom and Dad I have a crush on *anyone*, I will bury you so deep in the woods they'll never find your body."

I remove my hand slowly, daring him to keep going. His lips twitch like he'll pop off once more, but he stays quiet for once in his life. I huff, staring out at the scene in front of me. None of my moroseness has anything to do with Chase. It has nothing to do with him staying at my place. Or him insisting we have lunch together. Or his disappearing act at Vincent's. I'm just tired. Exhausted from my life.

"You ever wonder what it would be like to be human? Fully human?" I whisper, my voice barely carrying over the breeze rustling the trees behind us.

"Nope. But I'm also pretty sure I figured out who I was a long time ago. You didn't get the chance."

"What's that supposed to mean?"

I've done well for myself. Sure, I didn't go off to college like Gemma did. I'm not like Slade, who disappears for weeks at a time for another adventure. Throw in all my other siblings and I don't exactly stand out. But I have my cabin and my job and my garden. Though my job is working for my parents. And my dad was the one who built me my cabin. The garden was all me. That's my claim to fame.

"Have you ever thought of...leaving?" Slade asks, wincing.

"Like Gemma did? Or Alister and Sloane? Or maybe like Alissa did. I could go off into the woods and completely cut off society. You know Eli talked about bouncing after winter? He wants to go to the desert. As if he wouldn't die from the heat." I sigh, shoving to my feet. "Everyone else got to make their own decisions. They didn't think twice about what they were leaving behind. You know she cries? When Mom thinks no one else is around, she whispers to the goddess, begging her for reassurance she made the right decisions for us."

"I knew. But she's not crying because we left, Kira. She's crying because most of us haven't found our mates. She wants us to have what her and Dad have."

I shake my head, refusing to believe him. "You think you're so damn smart, Slade. Gemma was the catalyst. She went off and found her mate. Then one by one the others slinked off into the shadows. Hell, Alissa left in the middle of the goddamn night. Within a year Mom lost us all. Except for me. Like hell am I going to break her heart completely. I'm content where I am. Stop trying to change who I am to fit whatever picture you have in your head."

Stomping toward the trees, I pull on the magic within, calling up my wolf. She's already close to the surface, ready to protect me from my own emotions. Slade calls my name and I glance over my shoulder.

"Don't close your heart off because you're afraid of change, Kira."

I don't bother to answer before I shift. It's harder to hold on the reins instead of letting my wolf take over. I'd end up halfway to Canada before I came to. While the run might be nice, I'd have to turn around and come back. As much as I don't want it, I have a responsibility to Chase. He'd tell my mother if I disappeared for too long. No reason to worry anyone.

I thought my talk with Slade would make me feel better, but all it's done is mess me up more. I just need to keep my head on straight while Chase is around. Plans form in my mind as I trot back toward town. First order of business is getting him set up with Dad. Chase can spend his days learning shifter history, and I won't have to think about him.

By the time I hit the edge of town, I'm calm and determined. Just a couple months and I'll be able to wash my hands of him. If I'm lucky, I can cut that down to weeks. It'll be fine. Everything will be just fine.

45

Chapter 7: Awkward Family Dinner
Chase

I shouldn't have walked out on Kira. She seems perfectly content with Vincent, though. She probably didn't even notice I left. It's not like me to leave, regardless of what the hell is going on with me. This town is doing something to me—something I don't entirely like. Might just be my inability to be a shifter.

Shoving the few things scattered about the room into my bag, I ignore the ache building in my chest. My phone rings and I snatch it up before answering without checking.

"Yeah?" I snap, grabbing my pants to empty out the pockets.

"Chase?" Gemma's voice rings down the line, and I freeze.

"Hey, Gemma. What's up?"

"I just wanted to see how things were going. Slade called, said I should reach out to Kira. Thought I'd call you instead."

I don't know what to say. Kira and I spent a couple hours together. That's all. I'm not about to butt into their relationship. It's not my job to repair whatever is between them. If Gemma wants to avoid Kira, so be it.

"Everything's fine. It's real busy here, though. Thought I might come home and help with the festival back there. Then I can try again next year." Even I can hear the lie in my voice. There's no fucking way I'm coming back. I'll end up back in Whispering Pines and I'll never leave.

Silence stretches down the line, and I pull the phone away to glance at the screen. The numbers flash, counting the seconds. Maybe I can fake a dropped call. It happens all the time at Jake's place. I could blame it on the mountains.

"You remember the first summer camp session at the beginning of the season?" she asks softly.

"Yeah. It rained the first day and everyone complained about not having a bonfire. Why?"

"Do you remember what happened at the end of the week?"

I close my eyes, trying to remember three months ago. I've been through a lot of sessions at the summer camp Jake owns. The kids blended together in the beginning until they started coming back year after year. My memories are much the same with each one melding into the next unless something significant happened. Like the time a Jacob at the ripe old age of ten set his tent on fire.

"No? It was a long summer, Gemma."

She hums, though I doubt she agrees. "You don't remember because you disappeared. You ran off into the woods and didn't come back for a week. When you did, your clothes were in tatters and you were covered in blood. You spent another week holed up in your house, hacking up small bones and hairballs."

"Any other time and that'd be funny," I mumble, trying to lighten the mood.

"Maybe. Listen, I know you don't want to be in Moon Cove. I get it. Believe me, I do. But we can't help you here. We both know you won't go back if you come home now. If you give it a chance, I'm sure you'll find what you need. Don't throw it away because of her."

My spine straightens as indignation washes away the idea of leaving. "Let's get one thing clear—none of this has anything to do with Kira. I have no idea what the hell went on with you two and it's none of my damn business. But I'm not going to continue this conversation if you're going to mindlessly blame her when you have no idea what's going on."

"That's not...I wasn't trying to..."

"Yes, you were. You were assuming she was the problem. She's not. In fact, she's been nothing but kind to me. If anything, I'm the problem. If you need someone to blame, then blame me." I pull in a deep breath as something uncoils within me. "Anything else?"

"No," Gemma whispers, and I hang up.

I toss my phone on the bed and grip the back of my neck. Closing my eyes, I try to control the emotions rattling around in my chest. I'll have to call her back and apologize. Just not yet. First, I have to get my shit together before I explode in the middle of Kira's spare bedroom. Breaking a rule on the first day won't be a good look.

"You didn't have to say all that," Kira mumbles from behind me, and I spin around. "You left the door open."

"Didn't say it for your benefit."

She raises an eyebrow, calling me out on my lie. Except I wasn't doing it for her. Not completely. I'm tired of everyone telling me what I should do. Gemma wanted me here. Jake wants me to go back to normal. Hell, even Gladys seems to have an ulterior motive I know nothing about. Kira's the only one who doesn't seem to have an agenda for me. She just wants me to stay out of her way.

She glances away. "I've gotta go into work. Mom wants you to come around for dinner tonight. Slade might be there. Just a heads up."

She turns and my hand shoots out, then drops to my side. "Who else is here? Of your siblings?"

Sadness flashes in her eyes, too quickly for me to find how deep it goes. "No one. Everyone's gone. Dinner's at eight up at the house. Come or don't. Up to you."

She disappears down the stairs, leaving me to wonder how the hell I got in so deep in so little time. I spend the rest of the afternoon unpacking and repacking ten minutes later. I'm not usually this indecisive. Once I've made up my mind, I don't turn tail and run, but this town sets me on edge.

It took a long time to come to terms with the idea of magic and even more to understand it was now within me—fucking with my life, changing who I was, and forcing me to do things I didn't choose to do. As soon as I showed up in Moon Cove, it's like the magic is bubbling up, demanding I pay attention. I'd rather ignore it like usual.

I roll up my sleeves as I make my way to Gladys and Ben's cabin. I didn't expect Kira to come pick me up, but I wish she would have. Walking into the wolf's den sets my nerves on edge. It takes everything in me not to hightail it back to Kira's place. We both knew she was lying when she said I didn't have to show up. So I shove the anxiety aside and knock.

An older man with a shock of white hair opens the door. He nods at me, a stoic look firmly planted on his face. I hold out my hand and he takes it in his own. I'm not ridiculously tall, but Ben towers over me. He reminds me a bit of Jake with his broad chest and thick arms.

"Chase Holbrook, sir. Thank you for inviting me for dinner." I smile, attempting to hide my nerves.

"Well, I didn't invite you. Still glad you came. Come on in. Hope Kira hasn't yelled at you more."

He leads me inside, thankfully not searching for an answer. He doesn't seem to be a man of many words, which is just fine with me. I wonder if their family dinners are the same as mine were. Usually, one of my parents was rushing out to take a phone call. The rest of the time, it was silent. Somehow I doubt it. Gladys might be carrying the conversation, but it's definitely not a quiet affair.

"You a vegetarian?" Ben asks. "Won't be a problem, but there's some meat on the table already."

"No, sir. Hard to be a vegetarian with the kind of shifter I am."

"Ah well. No harm in asking."

Ben shuffles into the kitchen. I'm not entirely sure I'm supposed to follow him. I glance into the dining room and spot Kira with her head buried in a book. My body sways, torn between greeting Gladys and finding out what Kira's reading. Ben's rumbling voice and Gladys's subsequent giggle decides it for me, and I slip around the table.

I ease into the seat next to her, waiting for her to greet me, but she stays quiet as if I'm not even here. When I peer over her shoulder, she angles the book away and I grin. My arm settles on the back of her chair as I gaze at the cover.

"Do you mind?" she murmurs.

"Not at all. What are you reading?"

"None of your business."

"Could I borrow it when you're done?" I grin as she glares at me.

Huffing, she tucks what looks to be a leaf between the pages and closes the book. "You want to read about vampires fu—"

"Kira Livia. Watch your mouth at the dinner table," Gladys snaps from the kitchen.

"You're not even in here," Kira calls. I press my lips together, trying not to laugh as she rounds on me. "Don't even think about it. She's got the hearing of a...a..." Her eyes dip down to my lips, and I realize how close we are.

"A wolf?"

She shakes her head. "Obviously. Why are you here?"

"You invited me," I say, leaning forward to grab a baby tomato. They probably have a name, but I don't know what it is. I pop it in my mouth and Kira scowls.

"You're not supposed to eat before everyone is at the table. Why do you think I haven't busted into the bread yet?"

I barely hear her words, too busy savoring the small piece of fruit. I grab another one. "Is a tomato a fruit or a vegetable? And does it matter if it's a baby one?"

"Those aren't baby tomatoes. They're cherry tomatoes. And they're both."

I grab another to examine it, my mouth already watering. "How can they be both? I thought it was one or the other. Also, how the hell are these so damn good? I've had them before and they've never tasted like this."

Her cheeks redden and she glances away. "They come from a flower and contain seeds. So, they're fruit. But most people use tomatoes as a vegetable in cooking. And they're homegrown. Probably why they taste different."

Gladys sweeps into the room and sets dishes on the massive table, though we're seated in the middle. Ben follows with even more food, and I wonder who else is coming.

"They come from Kira's garden. That's why they taste so good. Actually, all the vegetables come from her garden," Gladys says, smiling at her daughter.

"Well in that case, we're going to have to deal with those crotch goblins who keep stealing them, huh?" I wiggle my eyebrows at Kira. Not that she's paying attention to me. She's too busy actively avoiding everyone's gaze.

Somehow, the hours pass and night falls outside. It definitely isn't anything like what I grew up with. The longer we sit, the more Kira opens up. By the time Ben brings out dessert, she's laughing along with a story her mother is telling. I'm having a hard time keeping my eyes off her. At one point, she giggled, and I swear my heart skipped a beat.

If I'm not careful, I'll end up sleeping with her. And that definitely can't happen. She might not even be attracted to me, though from the way she was staring at my lips earlier, I doubt that's the case. Either way, I'm not staying in Moon Cove. I wouldn't want one of us to get attached, only to break it off in the end.

"Chase, tell us about your childhood. We've regaled you with tales from Moon Cove. Did you grow up in Whispering Pines?" Gladys says, pulling my attention away from Kira.

"Uh, no." I clear my throat, dropping my arm from Kira's chair and straightening. "I grew up in the city, actually. Not a lot to talk about. Had a normal childhood."

Gladys opens her mouth, and Ben shushes her. "Don't push the boy, sweetie. He'll open up when he's ready."

I shake my head, plastering a smile on my face. "Nothing to get ready for. Had a mom and dad. They passed a while back. No other siblings or relatives. Moved to Whispering Pines and that's about all."

Ben nods, though I can tell he doesn't believe me. I wouldn't either if I was on the receiving end. Kira stands abruptly, practically knocking over her chair.

"I'm out. I'm opening tomorrow. Mom. Dad, maybe now would be the time." She whisks out of the room without a backward glance. I wonder if this is how she felt when I left her at Vincent's—like a hole had opened in her chest. I dismiss the thought, chalking it up to this whole fucking day.

Ben examines me over his steepled fingers. "When would you like to get started on shifter lessons, Chase? I'm free tomorrow."

Shit. There's no way I'm going to say no to this man. Especially with the way he's looking at me. Since I don't have an excuse, I smile.

"Sounds good to me."

Chapter 8: Blame the Magic

Kira

After almost a week, Chase and I have settled into some semblance of a routine. I go to work, he tags along to talk to Dad, we eat dinner at my parents' who have decided this is totally normal. Then we go home and dance around each other until we retreat to our respective bedrooms. It's smothering, to be honest.

Tonight is no different, except I didn't skip out at the end of the meal and leave Chase to fend for himself. Not that he seems to mind. He has a better relationship with my parents after a week than I've had in the last thirty-odd years. Maybe it's because there's no baggage between them. Or because there are no expectations when it comes to him.

"Why are you running, Kira?" Chase calls after me.

"I'm not. I'm walking. Like a normal person." I slow anyway so he can catch up.

He sighs, gazing around as we make our way through the neighborhood. Stars pop out in the darkening sky, and I consider whether I should shift tonight. The new moon is coming up soon, though I don't really have to worry about it. I shift enough not to be forced into it unless we have a festival and I'm on shifting duty.

"Why aren't there any streets around here?" he asks, his fingers brushing mine.

I shiver and my mouth goes dry. "Way back when they founded Moon Cove, there weren't any cars. It's always been a shifter community, so it wasn't an issue. Everyone would just shift or walk. When the world changed, so did the town. They built the tourist part of town and separated the main street for the actual residents."

"Except I never see the tourists on main street even though there's a road. And no one seems to go to the residential part." Grooves form between his eyes and I have the urge to smooth it away.

"Oh, that's the magic."

"Why the hell does everyone just blame magic? There has to be a *reason* behind it. And what the hell is up with the moon?"

"Some things you can't explain, Chase. It's not like math with a right and wrong answer. Sometimes you just have to have a little faith." I'm sure learning about all this is disconcerting, but he's not going to find the secrets of life here. "I'm guessing you're getting frustrated with the moon?"

"Let the moon guide you is bullshit. Everyone keeps saying it as if it's this grand revelation, yet no one can explain it."

I chuckle, wondering what Dad's been telling him. Benjamin Livia never was a man of many words, but he knows more about the history of shifters and the lore behind the town than anyone else. It's why he teaches most of the after-school shifter classes. Mom tried once, but she got off track talking about periods and they didn't ask her back. It was traumatizing for Gemma and me, though we never talked about it. Now I wish we would have. By that point, we weren't on speaking terms.

"The moon dictates when you shift. As it goes through its cycle, so does your inner animal. It's like...being reborn. We're both human and animal. Rejecting one of them is as pointless as denying the phases of the moon." I don't know how else to describe it and I search for a way to explain. "Just because you can't see the moon doesn't mean it ceases to exist. Just like your shifter side. When the new moon comes around, your shifter side comes out to remind you."

"And the guiding part?" he asks gruffly.

"It's mostly a metaphor, obviously. But usually when you're struggling with a decision, you need to rely on both sides of you—the human and the shifter. It's a reminder not to forget who you are and realize just because you don't know where you're going, doesn't mean the answer isn't there. At least, that's how I always understood it. Some people think the goddess sends us signs through the moon, but I don't believe that."

"Like the feather thing," he murmurs as we reach my cabin, and I stop him with a hand on his arm.

"What feather thing?"

"You know, the white feather. Before I fully transitioned, there was a flash in the middle of the lake. Jake said it was a feather to indicate a new shifter was in the world or some shit like that. He said the same thing happened the first night Gemma was at his house. Don't know if that was because of me or her, though. Probably a fated mates thing." He tilts his head, a serious look on his face. "That's not typical, is it?"

I bite my lip, searching the multitude of lore I've hoarded in my mind. "I don't know. I've never seen it, at least that I can remember."

Chase grins, his blue eyes sparkling in the dark. "Maybe I'm just special."

I roll my eyes and drop my hand. I shouldn't have been touching him, yet I didn't even notice. I'm too preoccupied by this mysterious feather. That's the only reason.

He clears his throat. "You're special too, sunshine. Promise."

"I don't want to be special. I'm perfectly fine just the way I am." I take a step back as I make up my mind.

"You can be perfectly fine and still be special," he whispers.

"I need to go." This feather thing will bother me until I get answers. Dad would know, but he's probably sleeping.

Chase reaches for me, and I take another step back. "Are you okay?"

My head snaps up. "Yeah. I just need to go. I'll be back."

I don't know why it sets me on edge. It's just one more thing that doesn't make sense in the grand scheme of things. I slip my phone from my pocket, contemplating whether I should try Dad or not. Instead, I put it back in my pocket and take off around the cabin. Chase calls my name and I run faster. This time, I don't wait for the trees to close around me before shifting.

Weaving around the trunks, my paws thud against the rough ground. I let my wolf take over, allowing my mind to sift through the lore I've learned over the years. Feathers and flashes of light are on par with the goddess. Either it's never happened in Moon Cove or I've just been kept in the dark about it. Why, though? There's no reason to keep the knowledge from me.

If Chase is right, it's an omen—a premonition straight from the goddess. She hasn't interfered with shifters directly in hundreds of years. I don't know when she started making shifters instead of letting us die out. There may be one person who does.

It takes me at least two hours of bounding through the forest before a cabin comes into view. No one else knows it's out here. At least as far as I know. My parents never mentioned it. They've taken the stance of never talking about my sister, the pain too fresh.

I shift on the edge of the small yard and approach the front door cautiously. After being shifted so long, my clothes are wrinkly, and I smooth my dress down. It doesn't do much, but at least I'm not naked. My hand trembles as I lift it to knock on the wood. Seconds later, it swings open, and I struggle not to react.

"Hey, Alissa," I say softly.

She sighs, swinging the door wide and gesturing me inside. It's smaller than I expected, consisting of one large room with stairs leading to a loft area. It's sparsely furnished, and I wonder how she got what little she has up here. There's no roads leading to here. Hell, she probably doesn't even have plumbing.

"What brings you by my humble abode?" she snaps as she hops onto the counter in her tiny kitchen.

"How are you surviving up here?" I glance around, taking in the small fridge and countertop stove. She never was a baker, so I'm not surprised she doesn't have an oven.

"Is that why you stopped by? Thought I was dead?"

"You're my baby sister. Can't I be concerned about your welfare?" I cross my eyes and she raises an eyebrow. "Okay, fine. What do you know about feathers being an omen or warning of shit to come?"

Her nose scrunches up and I'm thrown into the past. Maybe she hasn't changed as much as I thought. Her clothes may be more rugged than the cute dresses she used to wear. And her hair is shorter. A lot shorter, actually. She must have chopped off at least a foot.

"You're going to have to be more specific. What kind of feather? When does it show up? And can you actually handle the feather, or does it disappear?" she asks, and I avert my gaze before she realizes I was staring.

"White feather. Appears when change comes around, it seems. Disappears in a flash of light." I bite my lip as the gears turn in her head. "Wait. Is there more than one thing dealing with feathers?"

She hops down and makes her way to the fridge. "Yeah. There's a couple old stories about feathers being a sign of the goddess's visits. An ancient shifter whose line long since died out had a tale about a feather leading him to his mate or something. Doubt that's related. I'm banking on the first one. She hasn't been seen in centuries, but when she would appear, she'd leave a feather behind. Based on the color, you'd be able to tell if you were in her favor or not. Why?"

"You ever heard of it happening when a shifter is made instead of born?"

She spins, a bottle of water in both hands. She gives me one, and I drain it before she responds. I was so focused on making it here, I didn't stop to rest along the way.

"There's been an uptick of shifters being made. Numbers are dwindling at a faster rate. Would make sense she's leaving clues to point to them. Especially if there are other shifters around. It wouldn't be an omen. More of an alert system.

Like, *look here and take care of them.*" She leans against the counter, completely at ease. I don't think I've ever seen her so at peace.

"You look...happy," I murmur.

She shrugs, glancing away. "I'm better than I was. I don't know if I'd go with happy, though."

"Aren't you lonely?"

She smirks, shaking her head. "After spending most of my life trying to force the spotlight on me, I can confidently say I am glad to be alone. Sure, I talk to myself more often now, but it's a tradeoff I'm willing to make."

"I should have come sooner."

"Nah. I would have kicked you out. I wasn't ready. Still not, really." She gives me a pointed look. "But I will offer to let you stay here if you're hiding from our parents."

I smile, probably the first full-fledged grin I've had in months. Mostly I've been forcing myself to go through the motions at dinner, at the store, at home. I've been close when Chase makes an off-hand comment or joke, but letting him in would be ridiculous. He'll be long gone and I'll be alone again. Maybe I'll move to the woods like Alissa. She seems to be doing amazing.

Alissa clears her throat and I focus on her face. "Are you okay?"

I shake my head and smile again, though it's forced this time. "I'm fine. The store is getting busy again, so I've been working a lot more."

"And the guy?"

I scowl, glancing away. "Guy? Gonna have to be more specific. There's a lot of guys in Moon Cove."

"Oh, is that the way we're going with this? Seriously?"

Crossing my arms, I roll my eyes. "Fine. His name is Chase and Mom passed him off on me. He's a made shifter and Dad's been giving him history lessons."

"Bet Dad's loving that," she mumbles.

"Oh, he is." I need to get out of here before she pushes any more. "Well, I'm going to get going."

"Is he hot? Is that what it is?" She presses her lips together, not hiding her grin one bit.

"Is that what *what* is?"

She pushes from the counter and grabs another bottle of water, then hands it to me. "Not ready. Okay. Slade may have mentioned your new friend was in town and staying with you. You should come visit later—tell me how things are."

"There won't be anything to tell. Nothing happens in Moon Cove you haven't seen before."

"Well, I wouldn't mind meeting him. Especially if he's sticking around for a while and getting under your skin."

"He's not getting under my skin." I roll my eyes. "He might end up in the woods while he gets a hold on shifting voluntarily."

"You still didn't answer whether he's hot or not," she murmurs slyly.

"I'll tell Mom and Dad you say hi. And maybe think about coming to Samhain," I say, ignoring her comment. "They miss you."

She smiles sadly but ducks her head quickly. We say our goodbyes, but it's awkward. I shift when I reach the edge of the forest. I don't bother to look back. She's already inside, not waiting for me to disappear. Alissa isn't a worrier—never has been.

Having so many siblings isn't easy. We all have different personalities and were stuffed in one house for years, trying to deal with all the hormones and changes that come with being a shifter.

I'm not surprised Slade came out to visit Alissa. He likes to be in the know and he'll spread it to the other siblings whenever he deems it necessary. He thinks he always knows best, at least with us younger kids. For once, I wish he'd butt out of my life. Telling Alissa about Chase is exactly something he'd do. Now Alissa probably thinks there's something going on between us. Thank the goddess she's sequestered in the woods and can't play matchmaker.

If there was a future between us, which there definitely isn't, Chase is exactly the type of man I'd look for. He's kind and present and compassionate. Despite the hand he's been dealt by the goddess, he hasn't crumbled or lashed out. I wouldn't blame him if he did. It's what I do.

I've learned to push people away before they walk away. I'm not easy to be around, which is why I didn't want him to stay with me. That and I knew he'd be harder to resist.

I've spent the last week ignoring my attraction to him. Every time he walks around without a shirt on, every time he smiles, every time his hand brushes my lower back, I'm reminded of his allure. There's a magnetism swirling around him that draws me in. I've been fighting it, but the more time we spend together, the harder it is.

Unless I stop resisting and give into the desire. I paw at the ground while my wolf whines in my head. I have no idea whether she's okay with my latest train of thought. Chase probably won't make a move, anyway. With the way I've treated him, I'd be surprised if he did. If he does, though...

Clouds gather overhead, cutting off what little moonlight is left. I slow as I weave through the trees and jump over fallen logs, the sound of my pants overshadowing creatures scurrying through the forest. A low rumble from my left has me pausing and I glance toward the source. There's a grunt, followed by a twig snapping and I take off.

It could be nothing more than another animal foraging for food, but I'm not about to take that chance. I race through the trees as fast as my four legs will take me. My shoulder brushes against the bark of a tree and I overcompensate by veering away. My hip slams into another trunk and pain radiates from the injury. When my back leg buckles, I crash to the ground. A yelp leaves me and echoes through the night. I sit for a minute, hoping nothing sneaks up on me while I'm lying here.

The pain recedes gradually, and I resign myself to limping my way back home. Here's hoping there's no lasting effects and I can keep my shit together long enough to make it. Because I have no idea what Chase will do if he finds out I'm hurt.

63

Chapter 9: I Can Be a Good Girl

Chase

I should have gone to bed hours ago. Kira's a grown-ass woman who's completely capable of taking care of herself. There's no reason I should be pacing through the living room, weaving my way around the ridiculous number of beds.

I check the clock for what feels like the hundredth time. She's been gone for at least four hours and it's almost midnight. If she doesn't come home soon, I'm going out to find her.

My ears perk up at the straining wood on the porch. I sink onto one of the beds facing the front door. The knob turns slowly and the wood swings open. I probably shouldn't be sitting in the dark like a half-dressed creeper, but I can't force myself to move. She ran out of here, didn't tell me where she was going, and definitely has some explaining to do.

Kira tiptoes inside, wincing when the door creaks as she closes it. When she slips off her shoes, she rests her forehead on the wall. Her hand goes to her hip, and she sucks in a sharp breath. I narrow my gaze, gritting my teeth.

"What the hell did you do?" I growl, and she jolts upright.

"Nothing. I'm fine. What are you doing sitting in the dark?" she snaps. She tries to hide her limp as she walks past me, and I grab her wrist.

"Want to try that again?"

She can't even meet my eyes. We both know she's lying.

She tugs her hand away. "I'll be fine."

"Which means you're hurt right now." I shove to my feet. "Out with it. What did you do to your hip?"

She turns to glare at me. "I ran into a tree. It's not a big deal. We're shifters, Chase. I'll heal before the night is over."

I gesture behind her. "Okay. Let's go, then."

She huffs as she spins, then stomps up the stairs. Halfway up, she slows and a whimper leaves her. I take one more step, ready to catch her if she falls. I don't know if I believe her about the tree. If someone hurt her...rage swirls in my chest and I shove it down. There's no reason to think she's not being truthful about that, too.

"I'm fine," she gasps as we reach the landing.

My hand lands on her lower back, sending a shockwave through my arm. "Sure you are."

I guide her into her room, intent on getting her into bed. I don't know what I expected when I stepped inside, but it wasn't the splashes of color on every surface. There's the soft blue of her comforter next to a bright green nightstand. Paintings cover every wall, depicting the night sky complete with constellations. The walls themselves are a pale pink. She must have sanded down the logs to get the color right. It's like walking into a whole other world compared to the rest of the place. There's nothing downstairs and my own room is a pale grey prison.

She groans as she collapses onto the mattress, and my attention snaps back to her. I don't want to go through her clothes, but she can't sleep in jeans and a blouse. Thankfully, I find some pajamas on a bright yellow reading chair. These shorts are going to be ridiculous and test my limits. I swallow hard, vowing to focus on taking care of her instead of the hardening of my cock. This isn't the time.

"Put these on," I say gruffly, tossing them at her. I turn around and wait. After a few minutes, she whimpers again.

"I need help," she whispers.

I glance over my shoulder. She's pulled on the tank top, and I'm regretting my decisions. At least the blouse kept her tits in check. Now they're practically spilling from her neckline. She clears her throat and my gaze flicks to her face. She's trying to glare, but there's tears in her eyes. I drop to my knees. At least she's unbuttoned them.

"No comments," she murmurs.

"No promises," I breathe as I gently pull down her jeans. As soon as they're off, I drop them next to me and slide the shorts on. "Hips up."

It's not easy to get them fully on without looking, but somehow we manage it. Gently, I push the hem higher on her thigh to examine the mark on her leg. I'm sure an hour ago it was a nasty bruise. It's faded now and I press on it. Instead of jerking away from my touch, she leans into it.

"You've got two options, Kira. Either I get an ice pack for this or I massage the muscle. Which one are we going with?"

I pull my hand away, and she moans, "Don't stop."

Gritting my teeth, I rub her hip. If she keeps making those noises, I'm going to have a hard time containing myself. Focusing on her thigh doesn't help since her skin is soft and supple. The muscles underneath are tight, though. I should ask her where she went, if she was running from something—or someone.

"Who was chasing you?" I ask as I knead her flesh.

"Don't know. Animal," she groans, and my stomach flips. "Harder."

I stand and place one knee on the bed next to her as I work the tension from her muscles. She gasps and I lighten my touch. Her fingers wrap around my wrist and our eyes meet. Her throat bobs as she swallows.

When her tongue darts out to lick her bottom lip, I realize how fucking screwed I am. Images flash through my mind of those same lips wrapped around my cock, of my hands gripping her curves, of my tongue blazing a trail along her skin. I shake my head and rip my gaze away.

"Where does it hurt?" I rasp, desire clear in my voice.

"Higher."

She pulls my hand up, under her shorts to her hip, then she turns on her side and lets go. My heart skips a beat as I dig my fingers deeper and another moan leaves her. After a few minutes, I relax and brush my palms over the red spots I've left behind. She rolls onto her back again and presses her lips together.

"More?" I ask, almost choking at the strain of keeping my hands from wandering.

"Can you look at my shoulder?"

"You hit your shoulder, too?" I growl.

"It wasn't as bad as my leg." She props herself on her elbow and whips her tank top off.

My breath stutters in my chest as her tits spill out. She didn't need to take it off for me to see the injury. Maybe she didn't want me to feel weird being the only one shirtless. It's ridiculous, but it's the only thing I can think of without my brain conjuring images of her writhing underneath me. She drops back once more and points to her shoulder.

"You can't see it, but it hurts a little."

My mouth waters as I fix my gaze on where she's pointing. I brush my fingers over the spot and she shivers. There's nothing there, but I didn't expect there to be. If she wants more, she's going to have to speak up.

I should turn around and walk away. My hand has been just fine the last week and it'll be fine tonight as well. She might be starring in every one of my fantasies, but I shouldn't act on them.

"And here," she says, pointing at her jaw.

My hand lands next to her head, and I swoop down, skimming my lips over her neck. Her back arches, pressing her tits into my chest. My fingers slide up her side, scattering goosebumps along her skin, and she shivers again. When my thumb reaches the underside of her breast, I stop.

I lean close to her ear and whisper, "Where else?"

"Higher," she moans, her fingers sliding into my hair, and she grips the strands.

She yanks my head back to her neck, and I kiss my way across her soft skin. She hooks her thumbs in my waistband and shoves them down. Her fingers dance across my hip bones, and goosebumps erupt across my flesh. I didn't realize how sensitive the small strip would be. If she keeps it up, I'll lose all semblance of control. Her hands fall away from me, and I freeze, swallowing hard.

I close my eyes and murmur, "Do you want me to leave?"

"No."

"Do you want me to keep going?"

When she doesn't answer, I pull back and gaze into her eyes. Desire swims in the golden depths, and a flush washes across her cheeks. I've never seen a more beautiful sight. She captivated me the first time I saw her. While I've been hoping we get to this point, if she turns me away, I'll leave. My hand works just fine.

"I don't want you to stop. I want it all."

"Not sure if you know what you're asking for, sunshine."

Determination floods her face and her hand grabs the back of my neck. She yanks me closer and our lips brush, sending an electric pulse through me.

"Make me see stars," she whispers.

Our mouths crash together as a whirlwind of emotions coils around us. She shoves my sweatpants lower, leaving my underwear behind. The back of her hand brushes against my cock, and I groan. She does it again and I pinch her nipple, making her jolt. She can play all she wants, but she'll be in for a surprise.

I fit my knee between her legs, and she grinds into me. I can't do much with my pants around my thighs, and I rip my lips from hers. Her cry of frustration as I roll over her has me chuckling. We'll never get anywhere if I'm not able to move. I'm halfway through shucking them off when she straddles me. Her nails dig into my chest and I kick my hips up. She yelps as her pussy slides closer to my face and I lick my lips.

My pants bunch around my ankles, but I hook my hands behind her knees and pull her closer.

"Grab the headboard, Kira," I say gruffly, and she scrambles to obey.

I shove her shorts to one side and groan when I find her without any panties. Her scent washes over me and my mouth waters. I thought it would take us longer to get to this point. Now that we're here, it's overwhelming. My tongue darts out and I flick her clit. Her legs tremble in my hold and I do it again.

"Stop teasing me," she hisses.

I dig my fingers into her supple skin, and I yank her body onto me. She cries out and rocks against me as I taste her. I suck her clit between my lips. She shudders and I lap at the wetness gathering at her core. I could happily live right here for hours if she let me. When she pushes up, I try to follow her.

"More," she whispers, and I flip her onto her back next to me. The move is uncharacteristic for me and I freeze, wondering what the hell just happened.

Her hand slides between her legs and my mouth waters, the taste of her still on my tongue. I cover her body with mine and capture her lips. With her hand trapped, she can't touch herself anymore. It's probably for the best. When she comes, it'll be on my cock, not her hand.

"Take them off," she moans into my mouth.

I heave myself onto my knees and shove my underwear down. As soon as they're off, Kira's hand wraps around the base and I groan. She only gets one stroke in before I drop to my forearms. I kiss my way down her body. I sink my teeth into her ribs, right below her breast. She jumps, grabbing my hair and yanks me up. I grin as she scowls.

"What are you doing?"

"Finding my favorite spots on your body." I raise an eyebrow. "Got a problem with that?"

Her eyes widen and she shakes her head. Running my hands over her body, I make note of every twitch, inhale, and whimper. When I reach her stomach, her fingers clench in my hair and she tenses. I move on to her hip bones, running my tongue along the crease. I sink my teeth into her skin, and she whimpers. Switching to the other side, I give it the same attention.

"This one," I murmur into her skin. I grip the backs of her thighs. "And these."

"Are you—" She gasps, arching her back. "Are you counting them?"

"Perhaps. I've got a dozen already. If you're good, I'll tell you about them."

She grabs my hair and tugs. "Stop teasing me." Her snarl comes out more like a plea.

It takes me a minute to respond as I wonder if she'll end up begging by the end. In case this is all we get, I want to take my time. I have no intention of rushing anything. I'll worship her body, soaking up every moment.

"Condom," I murmur against her skin.

"No need," she moans, and her legs snap around my head.

In my haze, I take her at her word. I remember something about shifters being different, but my mind is fuzzy on the details. I trust her regardless.

My tongue darts out for one more taste of her before I nip my way to her neck. Her knees fall open as I settle between her legs, my cock nudging her opening. She jolts, forcing me deeper, and I groan. I slide my fingers into her hair and kiss her as I plunge into her. I freeze as she gasps into my mouth. Her back arches as she rolls her hips, but I need a minute—just a small measure of time to absorb the shifting inside of me.

Her nails digging into my back focuses the world again and I ease out of her, then bury into her once more. She whimpers as I do it again. When I keep up my slow rhythm, her begging begins. At first it's a soft appeal for me to go faster, which turns into a demanding cry. I sink my teeth into the soft juncture where her neck meets her shoulder.

I push onto my hands, surveying the mark I've left behind. She doesn't seem to notice, too engrossed with the sight of my cock disappearing into her. I roll my hips and her breath catches in her throat. I gaze at her body, committing the sight to memory. Kira isn't the first woman I've been with, but she's the most captivating. She's intoxicating in a way I've never experienced before.

When I pull out of her, it's with a grunt. Her greedy pussy didn't want to let me go. My cock isn't entirely happy about it, either. Her eyes fly open, betrayal flashing in their depths. Skimming my hands over her body, I track the flush to her breasts.

"On your hands and knees," I growl.

She scrambles to obey and glances over her shoulder. "See? I can be a good girl." She smirks and I return it.

"Such a good girl," I murmur, then seize her hips and thrust inside her.

Her forehead drops to the mattress, and a muffled sob leaves her. I dig my fingers into her skin and surge into her over and over. She twists the sheets in her fists, and I slide my hand around her waist. As I circle her clit, her pussy ripples around my shaft. I knew once I had her in this position, I'd lose control.

"Come for me," I grit out.

Her body shudders underneath me, and I let go. Stars explode behind my lids and euphoria explodes within my chest. Holding her tightly as she pants, I realize how hard it'll be to walk away. I won't be satisfied with only one night with her.

I ease out of her and drop to the bed before tugging her close. As she cuddles into my side, a feeling of contentment washes over me. Hopefully she'll agree to more, because I doubt I'll be able to let her go anytime soon.

Chapter 10:
No-Strings-Attached=Rules

Kira

Sunlight filters through my window and I groan, throwing my arm over my face. I never forget to close the curtains, but after last night, I'm not surprised they're open. I burrow deeper into the covers and push my ass into Chase. He grunts, tightening his hold around my waist.

I probably should be embarrassed sleeping with a man I just met. One who is staying in my house. And is friends with my younger sister. Not to mention someone who definitely won't be sticking around. Add in that he doesn't seem the type to commit. With his happy-go-lucky vibe, it's a very bad idea.

I can't bring myself to care. I tried hard enough to keep him at arm's length and not want him. It didn't work. Oh well. Now we can get on with him doing that thing with his hips again. We'll set some ground rules and deal with the consequences later. One of those rules will definitely include pretending we're not sleeping together. No one else needs to know my business.

"Stop wiggling," he mumbles, sleep lining his voice.

His fingers dig into my side, then slide to my breast and cup it. A shiver ripples through me when his thumb brushes across my nipple. As much as I'd love to roll over and jump his bones, we have things to discuss. I grip his wrist and pull his hand away. He grumbles under his breath, but I'm determined.

Scooting around to face him, I wait until our eyes meet. "We need to talk."

He smirks, blinking sleepily. His arm loops around my waist, and he pulls me closer until his forehead rests on mine. When his leg pulls mine between his knees, I realize he's trapped me. Not that I mind as long as he actually talks to me.

"How are you up so early?" he murmurs, then brushes his lips across my cheek.

"You didn't close the curtain."

His head pops up and he glances over his shoulder. He untangles his body from mine and jumps out of the bed. The room plunges into darkness, and I sigh. He dives back between the sheets and wraps himself around me once more. He's so warm, I'm not about to complain.

"What do you want to talk about?"

"Ground rules," I gasp as he sinks his teeth into my neck, then kisses the mark he's probably left behind.

He hums as he forces me onto my back and kisses his way down my naked body. His tongue flicks my nipple and I moan, all thoughts of rules and proclamations fleeing in the wake of his touch. The discussion can wait until he's done. Or rather, when I'm done.

He releases the bud with a pop and glances up at me, grinning. "I'm waiting."

"What?" I choke.

He licks my nipple, and my eyes roll back in my head.

"List your rules. Is this okay?" His fingers slide between my legs and swipe between my folds.

"Not those kind of rules."

He hums again, abandoning his pursuit to suck on my other nipple. "Focus, sunshine. What's your first rule?"

"Don't tell my mom," I whimper. His head whips up, and he rolls off of me. "What the hell was that?"

He throws his arm over his eyes. "I'm not going down on you when you're thinking of your mother."

I slam my palms on the bed and growl. "I wasn't thinking of her. However, if she knows you're going...doing *that*, she'll think we're going to ride off into the sunset. It'll be a whole thing neither of us wants."

He presses his lips together, and I wince. I don't want him to think he's not good enough, but I really can't deal with the rumors. I have to live here afterward. Once the dust settles, I'll be left with the pieces of my parents' broken hearts. As much as they all wanted us to stick around Moon Cove, they hoped we'd find our mates. When I told my mom it was absurd to assume they'd just wander into our tiny-ass town, she cried. I'm not about to do that to her again. She's disappointed in me enough.

"So this is something you want to continue? Not a one-night thing?" he asks finally.

"Oh, yeah. Of course," I mumble as I dig my fingers into the comforter to keep myself from punching him.

"That wasn't exactly an answer, Kira."

I clear my throat and throw back the covers. He grabs my wrist when I try to slide from the bed. His grip isn't enough to hold me hostage, or I might actually punch him. He tugs and I end up pressed to his side, his fingers still gripping me. His arm slips around my waist and his scent overwhelms my senses. It'll take me weeks to get the smell of him out of my sheets. I don't know how to feel about that.

"Sunshine, I'm not about to force you to do something you're not into. But the way you're talking makes me think you want to keep this thing between us a secret. And while I don't have a problem with that, I highly doubt we'll be able to. Then again, I'm not really used to any of this."

My head snaps up and I glare at him. "Explain."

He grins, swooping down to capture my lips in a quick kiss. "It's been a while since I've woken up next to someone. I've been subsisting off one-night stands for...a long time. Since Gladys hasn't talked about past relationships when it comes to you, I assumed you were in the same boat."

"What do you mean *when it comes to me*? What did she say?" I've mostly tuned her out when we're at dinner or escaping to the kitchen with Dad. She could have given him my entire history and I wouldn't know.

"Oh, I know all about Gemma's love life now. Not that there was much to tell. I think your mom just needs someone to talk to who isn't your dad. And she can't talk to you. So, I just became the default. She doesn't talk about you, Kira. She expects you to tell me."

"This is just sex, Chase. Nothing more, nothing less. Things will work a lot better if we go into this not expecting any grand declarations at the end."

His lips twitch and I tense. "No strings. Just sex? You think we can pull that off?"

"Of course we can. It's not like we're in a relationship and trying to hide it. That never works."

"Definitely doesn't work. Also doesn't work when you're trying to pretend you're in a relationship when you're not. Jake and Gemma tried that."

I prop myself on my elbow. "Excuse me? Gemma did that? My sister?"

He laughs, the sound filling my chest. It's like I'm breathing in his joy. I've never felt anything like it before. Emotions ping-pong through me, setting my veins on fire. I don't know what to do with it.

"To be fair, they weren't very good at it, but it did keep Marcy away from Jake. She was relentless in her pursuit of him. Something about liking the strong, silent type." A lightness dances in his eyes when he talks about them. I didn't notice it before.

The urge to ask him about, well, everything, sits on the tip of my tongue. I want to know what Gemma is like now. I want to know how they met and developed a relationship. I want to ask him what Whispering Pines is like. Keeping my mouth shut isn't easy. The more I know about him, the harder it'll be later.

"You know, we could be friends," he murmurs, brushing my hair out of my face. "Wouldn't be the worst thing in the world."

"I don't have friends. I don't need friends. And being friends just complicates the whole no-strings thing." The words come out robotic. This conversation is nothing new. Whenever I've hooked up with someone, they always want to stay friends. Or meet up again. I haven't had a long-term relationship since high school, and I'm not entirely sure those count.

"Except you have Vincent. He's your friend, isn't he?"

There's something in his voice I can't quite place. "Not really. He was Alissa's friend, mostly. When she left, he decided to take it upon himself to make sure I was shifting and eating. I think he thought I'd fall apart or something. Which was ridiculous. Alissa and I weren't inseparable or anything. It's not like she died. She just moved into the mountains. I was literally just there."

"That's where you went last night?" The tension in his body eases, and I tilt my head.

"Uh, yeah." The more I think about his offer, the less I'm willing to put up a fight. "Listen, I'm not a very good friend. I don't know how to be. I was a bitch in high school. Then everyone left, and I was still a bitch. Now I just keep my bitchiness to myself. At least for the most part. So, if friendship is something you need to do this, you can back out now. I won't be offended."

He gives me a look. "Really? You won't be offended if I turn down the opportunity to—"

"Don't finish that sentence," I grumble, rolling onto my back.

He laughs and covers my body with his own. "Question. Why no condoms?"

"Oh, uh, because most don't need them. Our shifter sides take care of any diseases."

"And babies?" he asks, his lips gliding across my jaw. This conversation would be easier to follow if pleasure wasn't racing through me.

"Different kinds, different rules," I gasp as he nips at my neck. "Can't get pregnant."

He lifts his head. "At all?"

I roll my eyes, wondering if he's going to stop. "Not without me partially shifting."

He grins, swooping down to kiss. "Not going to complain about that."

He kisses me again and I'm lost in him once more. It doesn't take long before I'm hot and bothered. It'd be impossible with how his hands skim across my skin or his lips find every sensitive spot. It's as if he has a map of all the right places to work me into a frenzy.

By the time he's making his way down my stomach, my back is arching and needy noises fall from me. I'm not used to this, but I'm not ready to examine why he's the one to elicit such a response from me.

"What's the next rule?" he murmurs into my skin.

"Uh, don't get at-t-tached," I stutter out when his breath ghosts across my clit.

My fingers slide into his hair, and I try to force his face closer. He's a lot stronger than I am in this position. He chuckles and his tongue darts out. I whimper, biting my lip to keep myself from begging.

"I'm definitely going to struggle with that one, sunshine."

My mind scrambles as I try to focus on his words instead of the pleasure coursing through me as he plays. When they finally do, a tiny voice in the back of my head screams to question him. It's soon drowned out by my moan as his lips wrap around my clit. He sucks, sending another burst of pleasure through my body. I don't care what happens as long as he doesn't stop.

He hums, releasing the small bud with a sigh. "How the hell am I supposed to not get attached to *this*?"

His finger slips inside me, then two, and I buck my hips. Slowly, he thrusts into me and I glance down, finding his smirk firmly in place. I'm sure I'm not in a flattering angle. I tip my head back and close my eyes. He grips my chin, never breaking his rhythm.

"Hiding? Not like you, Kira," he says, and our gazes meet.

"Double chins aren't exactly sexy."

His fingers curl inside me, and I gasp.

"Don't tell me what I find sexy."

He doesn't give me time to respond before he swoops down and kisses me. It's demanding—consuming. By the time he breaks away, I'm dazed. I writhe under his touch, my orgasm hanging just out of reach. I'm not usually into spicy times this early in the morning. There's something about him, though.

His tongue finds my clit again and his fingers surge into me harder and faster. I glance down and find his eyes fixed on me. The sight of him between my legs sends me flying over the edge into oblivion. Pleasure overwhelms me and I shudder out my release as he slows. When my soul returns to my body, he presses a kiss to my clit. He tugs his hand away and I jolt, a soft cry leaving me.

When he pops his fingers in his mouth, licking them clean, I'm lost. I don't know what the hell is going to happen, but I am not going to regret what we're doing. He's exactly what I need to tear me out of the abysmal routine I've found myself in. I'll enjoy what little time we have. I deserve it. At least I hope I can convince myself I do.

Chapter 11: Tree Fucking

Chase

The last thing I wanted to do tonight was to be dragged into the forest. Yet here I am, standing in front of Kira while she explains for the tenth time how to shift. My gaze slides down her body, wondering if I could distract her from this nonsense. She seems to be partial to my head buried between her legs. I'm pretty fond of it as well.

A whole week hasn't diminished my need for her. In the quiet parts of the night while her soft breaths fill the room, the doubts creep in about the future. That's usually about the time I wake her up with my cock. She doesn't seem to mind that either.

"Are you even paying attention?" she demands, propping her fists on her hips.

"Of course, sunshine. Pull the magic from within and shift." I smirk as she rolls her eyes.

"If you don't focus, we'll be here all night. And I have to work tomorrow."

I spread my hands wide and grin. "Then let's just call it and go home. I'll tire you out enough that you'll feel refreshed in the morning."

"You can't avoid shifting, Chase." She tilts her head. "And don't think you can distract me with your dick."

I huff, crossing my arms. "We could always try."

She steps back and drops her arms to her sides. From the look on her face, I doubt I'll be able to convince her. She's determined to get me to shift without the new moon forcing me into it. Forget the fact I've never been able to. Forget the fact I have no idea how. Kira thinks if I just concentrate enough, it'll just happen.

"Stop stalling," she snaps.

"What happens if I succeed? When I transformed—"

"Shifted."

I roll my eyes. "When I *shifted* in front of Gemma, I almost tried to eat her. What's to say that won't happen here? I doubt you'd enjoy my fangs sinking into your flesh as much as you like my—"

She holds up a hand. "Stop. You've been a shifter for almost a year. Logically, you should have more control when you're in your other form."

"Logic doesn't have much to do with magic," I mumble, running my hand through my hair.

"If you didn't have any control, you would have made your way into town and raided the garbage at the very least. You're more in tune with your cougar than you think."

"Bold words for someone who's never seen me shifted," I grumble.

An image of me half-shifted and hissing at her flicks through my mind. I'd rather she not watch me struggle with this. We'll both end up pissed off and it'll kill the vibe we've been in the last week.

Kira said she doesn't know how to be a friend, but I haven't seen any evidence of that. Every so often she snaps at me, then looks guilty as shit. I probably should tell her how much I like it. I open my mouth to tell her how much I enjoy her bossing me around, but she sighs and I wait.

"Okay, don't take this the wrong way, but..." She grimaces and shakes her head. "Maybe taking off your clothes will help."

I grin and grab the hem of my shirt. "If you wanted me naked, all you had to do was ask, sunshine."

She scowls, gesturing for me to hurry up. She doesn't have to tell me twice. Slowly, I tug my shirt over my head, and she licks her lips. If she keeps doing that, we won't be doing any shifting tonight. My hand falls to my belt and the clinking of my buckle echoes through the night. I whip the leather through the hoops and toss it at her feet.

"This isn't a striptease, Chase." Even as she says it, her cheeks redden.

I pop the button and inch the zipper down before I answer. "Doesn't mean you can't enjoy the show."

Despite the frown on her face, desire sits heavily in her eyes. I wiggle my hips, trying to be seductive as I push my jeans down. It's not easy. I don't know how dancers do this. Their bodies move in ways I don't think I'm capable of. It might have a lot to do with the type of pants, though. When I reach my knees, I almost tip over and she giggles.

"Do you need some help?" she asks, and I glance up.

"Offering to get on your knees for me, Kira?"

She presses her lips together, and I hold my breath. "Not a chance, pookie."

"Pookie? Seriously?" I laugh and kick off my jeans.

"You're calling me sunshine again. Thought you'd need a little pet name too." The corner of her mouth tips up and a full-body shiver hits me.

She glances away, and I snap the elastic of my underwear to gain her attention. My hard cock makes it difficult to take off my boxer briefs in an alluring fashion. It doesn't seem to matter since her eyes are glued below my waist. I wrap my fingers around my shaft and stroke my length steadily.

"Knock it off, Chase. I'm not sucking you off in the forest. You realize there are a shit ton of other shifters out here, right? Any one of them could stumble from the woods and catch you manhandling yourself." Her expression doesn't match her words.

I stalk toward her leisurely, and she shuffles away until her back hits a large tree. I cage her in with one hand above her head. Her heavy panting hangs between us and I duck, burying my face in her neck.

"Are you sure the idea of getting caught doesn't have you begging for my cock?"

Her breath stutters as I slide my hand behind her neck. She leans into my touch and her nails dig into my chest. For someone so hell-bent on getting me to shift, she's very easily distracted. Her need feeds my ego, though. I stroke myself, attempting to ease the ache. It doesn't help. The only thing that will help is sinking into her heat.

I skim my free hand down her body and grip the waistband of her shorts. I shove the fabric down and groan. I slide my fingers along her pussy and wetness coats my hand.

"No underwear? You're playing with fucking fire, sunshine."

She moans in response, and I rub her clit, needing more from her. She whimpers when I dip inside her core, and she spasms around my fingers. I pull them away and focus on the small bud again. Her body moves with me and her eyes fall closed. Her shorts falls from her hips and pools at her feet.

"Do you want my cock?" I murmur.

When she doesn't answer, I drop my hold on my length to encircle her throat. She gasps and her eyes fly open. Desire sits in the depths, silently begging me to give her everything. I need her words, though.

"I'm going to need an answer, Kira. Beg me to fuck you."

She swallows hard and my fingers flex against her skin. Using my thumb, I tilt her chin up and raise an eyebrow.

"P-please," she stutters softly.

I brush my lips against hers. "That's a start, but not good enough. Tell me what you want."

Her hand wraps around my wrist and pushes my hand into her throat more. "Harder. I want...I want you to fuck me against this tree. I want to feel the bark digging into my back."

When I tighten my hold, she moans my name and it might be the sexiest thing I've ever heard. I slide my free hand under her ass and haul her onto her tiptoes, then line my cock up with her entrance.

"Are you sure you want it rough, sunshine?" I ask through gritted teeth. My tip slips into her and I almost lose my grip on my control.

"Do it," she growls, her eyes flashing in the darkness.

I slam into her, our moans mingling as they take over the night. Her legs wind around my waist, holding me close to her. It's not the easiest angle with my fingers still around her throat, but we find a rhythm quickly.

I pound into her, relishing the feel of her quivering around my length. Still, I restrain myself, not wanting to hurt her. Her nails dig into my shoulders and the tang of blood fills the air.

"Faster," she gasps. "More. Give me everything."

My movements become erratic as I thrust into her, losing all semblance of control. She cries out as her pussy pulses around me. Watching her come might be the highlight of my day. Her face goes slack, bliss taking over her features.

Her body stiffens, and then she writhes within my grasp as if she can't decide whether or not she wants more. Sometime soon, I plan on tying her to the bed and making her come over and over until she's begging me to stop.

I plunge into her harder, fucking her through her orgasm. She coughs and I loosen my grip, dropping my hand to her tit. Her nipples strain against her shirt and I pinch the nub. She jolts in my hold, then whimpers. I drop my hand to her ass to seize both cheeks in a bruising grip. Faint red marks in the shape of my hand grace her throat, and a bolt of possessiveness rolls through me. Leaning forward, she moans as she attempts to ride my cock.

My teeth sink into her pulse, the need to mark her more permanently overwhelming my better judgement. My stomach tightens and I grunt. I don't know if she realizes how close to the edge I am, but her hand drops between us and she rubs her clit. Her knuckles graze the base of my shaft with every thrust. Seconds is all it takes for me to erupt and she shudders with me.

The night falls quiet around us other than our gasps. I imagine if there were any other shifters around before, they've long since fled. The thought has my cock hardening again, but I slip free from her heat.

As much as I would like to spend all night right here, we have other things to do. Plus, my stamina overshadows her own. I wasn't a slouch before in the bedroom, but my shifter side seems to have enhanced certain parts—my drive in particular.

Kira's legs unwind from me, and I step back. It isn't as easy to let her go as it usually is with others. I crave her in a way I've never felt before for any other partner. It should freak me out and have me running for the hills. Instead, I keep coming back. Even now, I want her again.

I want to cover her body in marks like the one on her neck. I want the scent of her arousal and mine filling the air as it drips down her thighs. I want her warming my cock with her greedy little pussy. I shake my head and suck in a sharp breath.

"Dammit, Chase. You're supposed to be shifting," Kira mutters as she grabs her shorts and tugs it on.

My chest tightens and what I thought was an afterglow snaps to attention. Kira's gaze meets mine and magic swirls within me. This must be what she's been talking about. I grin as I attempt to focus my energy.

My vision blurs and I'm pretty sure I pass out for a minute. When I come to, the world expands around me. For once, I don't feel like I've been shoved down into the deepest parts of my mind. My cougar feels separate, not melded to me like Kira says hers is. At least we're occupying the same space, though.

"Chase?" Kira's soft voice wraps around me, and I pull in her scent tinged with fear.

She shuffles from one foot to the other, and my ears perk up. Slowly, I pad toward her, then crouch near her feet. My muscles vibrate with the need to do something—anything. The shifter side of me wants to flee and hunt. I need her to know I'm still here, though. I'll be proud of myself later.

Setting my chin on my paws, I gaze up at her and wait. Gradually, she sinks to her knees and I huff. Of course she's getting on her knees now that I'm essentially a cat. Her fingers glide across my fur, hesitantly at first, then more confidently. A rumble rolls through me and my head tips up. I don't know what it is, but it almost sounds like purring.

This whole experience isn't easy to deal with. And I don't know if I like it. I may have been able to shift voluntarily, but I might not want to repeat it.

Chapter 12: Feathers and Fucking

Kira

Chase, because it is Chase shining from those glowing eyes, shakes his head. When he rubs his jaw against my hand, then my leg, I realize what he's doing. Our scents won't mingle, no matter how much he marks me. None of that would happen unless we were mates. We've established that's not possible, which is definitely for the best. Neither of us needs extra threads tying us together. I'm already worried I'm getting too attached.

He mewls before whipping around and taking off into the forest. My heart hammers in my chest, worry warring with the need to stay put. He doesn't need me following him, especially as a wolf. He may have been himself just now, but that would change in an instant if I shifted. I wouldn't blame him. He doesn't have the control needed to accomplish something like that.

I've had years to adjust to being around different kinds of shifters. When Chase asked about fights at the school, I deflected the question. I didn't want to send him running for the hills, thinking he was on the same level as a twelve-year-old when it came to his control.

When I was a kid, no one shifted before they went through puberty. It made sense—our human side was transforming and so was our shifter side. They went hand in hand. In the last decade, though, children have been shifting younger and younger. Hell, the Peterson's kids are only five and they just learned how. It's part of the reason Alissa left. No one believed her when she said the world was changing. No one believed her when she mentioned the goddess. Something happened when she was younger that pushed her into the lore of shifters. I never figured out what it was, though.

I push to my feet and gather Chase's clothes. I doubt getting naked actually helped. My ego wants to believe it was us sleeping together. The rational part of my brain dismisses the idea. He most likely focused enough to be able to do it on his own.

My nose wrinkles when my thighs stick together. I'm regretting going without underwear. I actually didn't think he'd be able to shift and was hoping to entice him. To be fair, I didn't imagine he would fuck me in the middle of the woods against a tree, but I'm not complaining. A wave of desire crashes over me and I shake my head.

A hissing sound erupts from the area where Chase disappeared, and I freeze. I don't know if it's Chase or someone else. With Moon Cove being a shifter community, there's more wildlife in the area. The vast forest surrounding us helps, too. Running wouldn't be smart. Shifting wouldn't be smart. Climbing wouldn't be smart. I'm definitely screwed no matter what I do.

I clutch Chase's clothes to my chest so I don't lose them when I shift and dredge up the magic within me. As I shift, a flash of white light blazes through the small clearing. My wolf attempts to take over to force me to run. She's nothing if not protective. The magic fizzles out as a single white feather floats to the ground. My jaw drops open as I fixate on the scene. A low whine leaves me, though I'm not sure if it's me or my wolf.

I take one step toward it, and it vanishes in another flash of light. Blinking away the spots in my vision, I shake my head. Seconds later, a cougar bounds into the clearing. My muscles ease, instantly knowing this is Chase. I'm not going to examine why I know that too closely. It's just because we've been spending a lot of time together lately. My tail swishes across the ground. I want to ask if he saw the feather, but we can't communicate like this. If we were fated, we'd be able to.

Chase slows as he comes to the center of the area and sniffs at the area. I don't know what the hell to do any more than I did thirty seconds ago. He could have been drawn to this spot because of the infusion of magic still flaring through the night. His shifter form could take over at any minute and I'd be in the shit. I honestly don't know if I'd be able to take him if need be.

I whine and duck my head. It's not in me to be submissive. Even now, my wolf is fighting me. She may understand why we can't attack him, but she doesn't want to stick around either. I've been trying to ignore her for the most part, which is usually easy. The longer I sit here watching him, the less I want to run. My wolf settles in the background, content to let me lead the way.

Chase's gaze whips up, glowing eyes focusing on me. All recognition—all of *him*—is gone. My hackles rise and a low growl erupts from my throat. My wolf stirs within me, ready to take over at a moment's notice. When a howl from behind him rings through the night, Chase bounds after it.

I shake out the tension in my muscles and turn to disappear into the trees. Nothing good can come from following him, no matter how much I want to. Even if Chase isn't in control, he'll be able to take care of himself. If he finds another shifter, they'll be able to deal with him without hurting him. They'll sense whether he's a shifter or an actual cougar.

As I lope into town, I don't bother to shift. Hopefully Chase will have enough sense when he comes back not to either. It may be late, but there's probably one or two people still up and they'd get a free show. I don't know where the clothes go, but magic takes care of them, even if we're holding them. He probably doesn't realize that, though. It's just another thing I'll have to teach him.

I slow as I reach my backyard and sniff. A familiar scent floats along the gentle breeze, and I shift before making my way to the front porch. My father sits on the swing, his head resting against the back as he dozes. I clear my throat, but he doesn't move. Sighing, I settle next to him and watch the stars overhead.

"Did he shift?" he asks softly, and I jolt, sending the swing into motion.

"Yes. Though there were some...complications," I murmur.

"Well, you don't smell like blood, so why don't you elaborate?"

I sigh again, not sure how much to tell him. Clearly, I won't be divulging our tryst in the woods. If I don't, though, I won't be able to tell him what Chase's trigger was. Here's hoping the appearance of the feather will overshadow his questions.

"He was able to shift voluntarily. It wasn't half bad, and he was aware when he fully shifted. I don't know what set him off, but he made a noise, then took off into the trees. There was a white light." I rest my head against the swing as well and close my eyes, then recount the rest of my night.

"Sounds like the goddess was trying to tell you something," he says when I'm finished.

"More likely it was for Chase. He did come back when it appeared, so he couldn't have gone far."

Dad chuckles lightly. "Perhaps you should open your mind a bit more, Kira. You're meant for more than this. I always knew it. Maybe it's time to put yourself first, hmm?"

He kisses my temple, then stands. I bite my cheek to keep the tears at bay. He never did say more than needed. I could deny it, say I've put myself first plenty, but he wouldn't engage. He said his piece and now he'll go home.

"Love you, Dad," I whisper as he tromps down the stairs.

"Love you too, pumpkin."

Part of me wants to call out to him, have him stay until Chase gets back. Dad has a way of making everything be okay with only his presence. I'm not a little girl anymore, despite his nickname for me. I swipe at the tear that escaped as I watch him make his way across the lawn.

He turns around and walks backward. "By the way, you might want to take a shower." He taps the side of his nose and grins before turning away.

My knees snap together, and I groan. Of course he could smell Chase all over me. For fuck's sake, Dad knew the entire time. Why did I think I could keep our fling a secret? Ridiculous. I doubt Mom knows and Dad won't tell her.

I shove from the swing and stomp into the house as I run through the times Chase and I were out and about together. Maybe the others will assume it's because he's staying at my house and not because we're sleeping together.

I take my dad's advice anyway and take a shower, letting the hot water ease the tension in my muscles. I thought I'd care more about people finding out. They'll assume we're dating, but that's not as scary as before. Maybe it'll stop the sidelong glances we get whenever we're out.

Once I dry off, I check the clock. It's only been two hours since we went off into the forest. Chase said he was usually out for a whole day when he was being forced to shift. It's not the new moon quite yet, though it's fast approaching. We won't know until next week if his cougar will bust his way through again. There's just so many things I don't know about made shifters. Plus, they each develop at different rates, according to Vincent.

I glance at my reflection and jolt. "Chase? When did you get back?"

He runs his hand through his hair, then he scratches at his bare chest. "Just now. We should talk about that shit in the forest, but I need something first."

He doesn't sound like himself. There's an edge to his voice—a hesitancy I haven't heard since the first night we slept together. I spin and cross my arms over the towel wrapped around me. Just when I thought maybe this thing between us might be okay, he's going to throw the whole thing off. I keep my eyes fixed on his face. The last thing I need is to be distracted by his dick...again.

"Get on with it then," I snap.

His nostrils flare as he stalks toward me. I yelp when he seizes my waist and deposits me on the counter. His mouth crashes onto mine and I melt underneath his touch. A gasp leaves me when his fingers find their way between my legs. I'm already wet for him. For some reason, I'm *always* wet when he's around. I whimper as he tugs his hand away, leaving me empty and aching.

He rips his mouth away and buries his face in my neck. "I need you."

He thrusts into me, and my response turns into a gasp. He groans, sinking his teeth into my neck. I tilt my head to give him better access as he surges into me. The low burning desire sitting in my gut flares to life. When his fingers find my clit, I wrap my legs around his waist and arch my back. Heat floods my system and I spasm around his cock. He doesn't slow and I whimper as stars explode behind my lids.

"Such a good girl," he mumbles into my skin. "Taking my cock so well."

I shudder, leaning away from him, and he grips the back of my neck to hold me in place. His hand slide into my hair and he twists the wet strands in his fingers. When he tips my head back, a moan leaves me. As much as I want to deny how much this turns me on, I can't. He's playing with fire, though. One of these days, I'm going to be the one holding the reins. I wonder if he'll bend to my control as well as I bend to his.

He surges into me, then stops, and I whine. He shushes me as he tugs on my hair, a delicious burn spreading across my scalp. I bite my lip to keep from begging him to move, though I know it's what he wants.

"Chase," I gasp, rolling my hips to gather any type of friction.

He chuckles, forcing my head back and pressing a kiss to my pulse. "I'm not even close to done with you yet."

Chapter 13: Purrplexed

Chase

I should be reading, but my mind keeps straying to last night. Shifting on my own is something I'll need to unpack, but that's not what's distracting me. Naked Kira is one thing. Fresh out of the shower Kira wrapped only in a towel was a whole other level. I couldn't have walked away if I wanted to. Which I most certainly did not. I kept her up way too late, though she wasn't complaining.

She's infiltrated every corner of my mind. Most of the time, she's a welcome distraction from dealing with this shifter thing. Right now isn't one of those times. Having a boner while sitting across from her father isn't very respectful. Not that he knows I'm currently imagining his daughter naked. If he can read minds, I'm screwed. It doesn't help she's in the same building.

"Chase," Ben grunts, and I glance up. "You haven't turned the page in ten minutes. Something on your mind?"

I clear my throat and heat rushes to my cheeks. "No, sir. It's just a little hot in here."

We're stuffed in an office in the back of the general store with one small window. Summer doesn't want to let go, and it's stifling in here. Here's hoping he takes the bait.

He shakes his head, and a smile plays on his lips. "If that's what you'd like to go with. Perhaps you'd like to talk instead of reading a boring history book?"

He pushes to his feet, already decided, and I follow him out the door. Gladys yells from behind us, but I'm pretty sure she's talking to Kira. We don't interact much while she's working. Especially after I almost kissed her goodbye the other day. I had to play it off like she had something on her face. Thankfully, no one was paying any attention to us.

"Would you like to talk about shifting last night?" Ben asks as we wander down the path leading to their house.

"I'm still processing everything. Did you grow up in Moon Cove?"

He nods. "I did. Born and raised. As was my father and his and his before him. We're very much rooted in the formation of this community. It's evolved, but largely the same. Many moons ago, the goddess sent my ancestors here and they established the town. It was smaller then and much more...exclusive."

"What do you mean?"

"Ah, well, shifters didn't always live well together. Most kept to their territories and their own kind. Once humanity started encroaching on the various areas, shifters merged together for protection. Several hundred years ago, though, there were only wolf shifters around here. My family came from up north, and my wife's came over from Europe."

"Gemma mentioned extra abilities? I don't have to worry about being able to fly or something, right?" It's been one of the many fears plaguing me over the last year.

He chuckles and steers us toward the lake. "I doubt it, though we won't know until you've fully settled. You're like a toddler, in a sense. You'll have to learn how to be at peace with your cougar before anything else can develop. One thing at a time. The moon will guide you if you let it."

I scowl, though I glance away so he won't see. "The moon doesn't seem to have much interest in me."

He sighs and rubs his hip. Kira said he's been having issues with an old injury. She didn't say what happened, and it isn't my place to ask. He eases down on the bank and pats the grass next to him. I plop down, letting the breeze from the water wash over me. I miss being home. Kira's place is nice, but it doesn't beat waking up to the sun rising over my own private lake.

"The moon led you here, Chase. It guided you to Whispering Pines long before you needed. It allowed you to find Jake and, eventually, Gemma. Perhaps you should stop blaming the moon for misleading you and search for why you're fighting fate."

I grit my teeth, unwilling to admit he's right. I never wanted this in the first place. When I found out Jake was a shifter, I thought it was cool. He didn't give me many details, but I figured out a lot just by watching him. It was one of those wild things I could gawk at without truly being a part of it. Now that I'm in the thick of it, I no longer think it's cool.

"Is Gladys your fated mate?" The question pops out before I can rethink it. "Sorry, is that rude?"

He laughs as he leans back on his hands. "No, it's not, although others might disagree. She is my fated mate. I was lucky enough to find her. Not many are these days. I'm honestly impressed Gemma found hers in Jake, especially since he's a bigfoot shifter. They're rare even for us."

"Do—" I cough, gathering the courage to ask what I really want to know. "Do made shifters have fated mates?"

He turns to me, raising his eyebrows. I continue to gaze out across the water. It's blinding, but preferable to meeting his stare. He'll assume I'm talking about Kira. Unless he still doesn't suspect we're anything more than reluctant roommates. He's a smart guy, though. Despite what Kira thinks, he'll know there's something between us.

"A shifter is a shifter, Chase. Once someone shifts for the first time, they're just a shifter. There is no distinction between the two." He holds up his hand when I try to interject. "I understand we've called you a made shifter. And it may not be the opinion of everyone. However, there's no fundamental difference between the two."

"Except you just said finding your fated mate was rare."

"It is. But it's not going to be any easier or harder for you because of the way you became a shifter."

"What does it feel like?" I mutter, trying not to wince. My father and I never had a conversation like this. He told me to wrap it up and treat my partners with respect.

He tips his head back, contemplating my question. I appreciate that he's not brushing it off or answering right away. The longer he takes, though, the more worried I get. Finally, he smiles softly.

"It feels like coming home. Not everyone sees it right away, but with Gladys, I knew. The moment she stepped into my world, everything was brighter. Everything made sense."

"Jake and Gemma didn't know right away."

"No, I suppose they wouldn't have. Gemma was searching for a place she belonged. She's been lost for a long time. I don't know your friend well, but from what I hear, he's a bit of a recluse. And as a bigfoot shifter, he's bound to be a little standoffish and assumed he'd never find a mate. Sometimes it takes a bit for us to find ourselves before we can accept someone else. I imagine if your fated is out there, you'll find them exactly when you're meant to. Just don't let the opportunity slip by because you're afraid."

He sprawls on his back and closes his eyes before folding his hands over his stomach. I doubt I'll get more from him, so I follow suit and one by one my muscles relax. I didn't realize how wound up I was.

Nothing could have prepared me for what I'd find in Moon Cove. It's more than meeting Kira. It's more than learning from Ben. It's more than being able to shift by myself. It's the entire community.

I want to experience more of it. I didn't plan on staying through the festival. In fact, I was going to go home once the film crew showed up. The last thing I'd want is to ruin everything for them. As someone who can't control their shifts, it didn't seem like a good idea. Now I might actually get to stay. And if that means more time with Kira, all the better.

After a while, I realize I don't know a lot about Ben. We've been meeting for a bit now and he rarely opens up. With his comment about mates and the little personal history he's talked about, I might be able to learn a little more. He didn't say much about the extra abilities some other shifters have.

"Kira said not everyone could partially shift. Is that from your ancestors?"

He hums and I peek at him from the corner of my eye and spot a small smile. "I suppose it could be, although the goddess could merely bestow those extra gifts at her own discretion. We don't know for sure. Then again, both Gladys and I descended from a line of dire wolves long since lost to time."

"Why would dire wolves have magical abilities?"

He chuckles. "I said a *line* of dire wolves. While the remains of actual dire wolves have been found, they'll never recover those of our ancestors. Once a shifter passes, our bodies aren't left for those on this plane. Magic dissolves our shifter forms, and the goddess absorbs our souls to pass along to the next generation of shifters. What's left behind is merely our human form. You'll never find the bones of what humans call supernatural creatures."

"So I have the soul of another shifter living inside of me?" The thought gives me the creeps. What if they're the ones who prevented me from moving forward? What if they're the ones controlling my shifts and forcing me to black out?

"It's a theory. None of us will truly know until the goddess takes us. And even then, we may not be aware. You don't have to worry about being someone else's skin suit."

I snort, running a hand down my face. "Well, I wasn't worried about that *before,* but shit, I might be now."

He bursts into laughter, a boisterous sound that echoes across the lake. He's usually so reserved it takes me a minute to recover before I join in. It's a welcome reprieve from the morbid conversation.

I don't know how any of what he's teaching me will equate to being a shifter. I don't live in a community like Moon Cove. It seems like a lot of useless information I'll never need. We never touch on the mechanics of how to shift or the rules about protecting shifters from prying eyes. Telling Ben all that seems like a recipe for disaster, though. Not to mention being incredibly disrespectful.

The only thing I've found helpful in actually shifting is Kira. Or rather, fucking her. There must be some kind of magic in joining with another that calls to the magic within me. I wonder if it would work with anyone else. I have no desire to test the theory or talk to Ben about it. He may suspect we're sleeping together, but I don't need to confirm those suspicions.

"Why don't you take those books home and read there? I have other things to do this afternoon," Ben says, breaking me out of my thoughts.

He pushes to his feet and we make our way back to the store. Once he's loaded me up with enough material to last a lifetime, I say my goodbyes. Kira won't be back for several hours. I don't have anything else to occupy my time, so I settle in on one of the various beds in the living room to read.

My mind wanders as I do and I end up spending more time than I should fantasizing about all the things I'd like to do to Kira. I don't know how much time we have left, but I'm determined to make the most of it. She's quickly becoming essential to my days, not to mention my nights. Convincing her to come with me to Whispering Pines seems like an insurmountable task. With each day, though, the prospect becomes more and more appealing. I don't know if I'll be able to let her go.

Chapter 14: You've Got to be Kitten Me

Kira

I scowl at Chase, silently raging at him for the soreness between my legs. Two days isn't enough time to recover from our activities. We may have gone a little too hard. I can't bring myself to care. Chase is a breath of fresh air. Apologizing for finding something beyond my doldrum existence isn't in my nature and I refuse to do it. I'd still rather my mother didn't find out about us, though.

I huff from the kitchen and Chase's lip twitches. He's buried in a book, sprawled across one of the beds I should probably haul out of here. I squint at the cover, trying to read the title. Dad keeps handing him more every time they meet. I'm glad he's distracted since he seems to have an insatiable appetite. Doesn't help that Mom has been calling me off work the last few days. I wonder if Dad told Mom about us. I hope not.

"Spit it out, sunshine," Chase murmurs as he turns the page.

I'm not going to complain about the soreness. "When are we going to talk about your shifting?"

"Whenever you want. Although, I imagine the feather appearing overrides whatever I remember." He still doesn't bother looking at me.

"Neither of us knows anything else about the feather. Dad's looking into it, but we'll just have to wait. So, shifting it is. What do you remember?"

I lean against the small island and cup my mug of tea. Even if Dad does find out something Alissa doesn't know, it won't change anything. It's not a problem we need to deal with. The goddess will do what she wants to do. No amount of digging will change her mind. I'd like to know *why* the feather shows up, but I doubt I'll get my answers. Maybe there's another made shifter about to appear.

He clears his throat, pulling my attention back to him. "I remember you. I could smell your fear. Want to explain that?"

I nod, hiding my smile behind my mug. "I wasn't afraid of you. I was worried you were going to attack me if your cougar had shoved you down too deep. How long were you aware of what was going on?"

"The whole time. At least, I think so." He snorts and closes his book. "Hard to tell when I didn't have a watch."

"It'll get easier now that you know what it's like. Want to try again?" As soon as the question is out, I know I'm in trouble. A glint enters his eye and a rugged grin takes over his face.

"So it *does* turn you on imagining getting caught. You could have just said that, Kira. No need to hide behind this shifting nonsense."

I give him a deadpan look, though heat curls in my gut. His nose twitches and he inhales deeply before shoving off the bed and stalking toward me. I straighten and set down my mug.

"Do *not* give me that look, Chase. I'm still recovering from the last round," I say gruffly.

His response is a feral smile as he prowls around the counter. I shuffle to the side, keeping the island between us. We're in a stand-off, each waiting for the other to make a move. He feints to his right, then swings to the left. I shriek, dashing away. I don't even make it to the stairs before his arm slides around my waist and he lifts me off my feet.

"Put me down," I squeal, and his chest rumbles with a laugh.

I giggle as he hauls me toward the bed in the living room. He drops me onto the mattress and his book bounces with me. It smacks me in the head and I yelp through my cackling. Chase's fingers run over my face and into my hair as he searches for an injury.

"I'm fine," I gasp, knocking his hands away.

"I'm sorry."

I laugh again. "Chase, I'm okay. I promise."

He scans my face, searching for any hint of pain. He won't find any. I close my eyes and relax, waiting for him to decide I'm fine. He sighs, then lies next to me on his side. His arm loops around my waist and tugs me against his body. Our breathing evens out, syncing up. I swear if our heartbeats do the same, I'm going to have to cut him off.

"You know, I'm surprised you're a cuddler," he murmurs, his lips brushing my temple.

I hum, not willing to answer. The truth is, I'm *not* a cuddler. Usually, I kick out whoever was in my bed or I'd leave soon after. Some partners were clingy and wanted to chat afterward. I didn't think it was a big deal since we'd never see each other again. With Chase, it never occurred to me to leave. I could say it's because I was in my own house, but I could have sent him back to his room. For some reason, I've fallen asleep. The closest to walking away was the other night when he shifted.

"No snarky comments?" Chase chuckles, and his fingers skim along my side, dipping under my shirt.

"You want me to admit you're rubbing off on me?" I snap upright and point at him. "Don't even think about it."

He grins and I lie back down. His lips brush against my temple again and his hand resumes its path along my skin. I should be worried I'm getting in too deep. It hasn't even been that long and I'm already in over my head. Part of me screams to run as far as I can—go hide out in the woods with Alissa. The louder part doesn't give two shits. It'll be fine.

I pick up the book and gaze at the cover. "*This* is what Dad gave you? Is he trying to bore you to death?"

"He said the lore was based in history and if we don't know about it, we won't understand anything. He was pretty adamant this was important."

I scoff and toss it aside, then roll into him. His forehead rests against mine, our breaths mingling. We should go back to our previous conversation. Or go out and try to shift again. Instead, I bask in the comfort I find in his arms and wonder how the hell I'm going to get myself out of this mess I've created.

Sweat drips down my temple and I swipe it away with my wrist. The scent of freshly tilled dirt wafts up and I inhale. Slade laughed when I said I was planting a garden. He didn't understand why someone would do it when they weren't a farmer. Digging in the soil, watching the plants grow, eating the food I've grown with my own two hands—I couldn't describe to him how it felt. It became something I cling to.

I've been working at my parent's store since I was a teenager and while I don't mind it, I needed more. I craved something that was completely my own. Several hobbies came and went before I settled on gardening. Painting gave me a headache. Reading is great until my shoulders start hurting. Wood carving was too dangerous. I attempted to knit and ended up stabbing myself one too many times. I don't even know how I accomplished it. Alissa bought me a camera one solstice, but all the pictures were shit. There were others, but none of them stuck around. When winter sets in, I won't be able to do this either, so I'll switch to reading until it's time to plant again.

I huff as the hot sun beats down on my neck. I thought it'd be turning cooler by now, but summer doesn't want to let go. The temperature at night is dropping at least. I glance up at the house, wondering if Chase cranked up the air conditioning. I didn't expect to fall asleep earlier. When I woke up, I didn't know where I was. Not that I cared. Chase was reading with me sprawled across his chest. He smiled down at me, and I hightailed it out of there. Hopefully, he didn't notice how tense I was.

Shit is getting out of control. I didn't care while we were cuddling, but the more I think on it, the more I worry I really am in too deep. No one's ever made me feel truly safe like he does. Which makes no sense, given what type of shifter he is. When he smiled at me, so comfortable and relaxed, I freaked out. We established boundaries. I can't be the one who weaves threads between us. He'll be blindsided and I'll end up heartbroken.

This is exactly why I didn't want to be friends. I knew the lines would get blurred. Instead of talking to him, I ran to the garden to work up a sweat. I have to do something with my hands or I'll end up saying something I regret. I don't want to end our arrangement. My head just needs time to screw itself on straight and remember why I gave into him in the first place.

"Let the moon guide you," I whisper as I stab my spade into the soil. Weeding isn't my favorite thing, but it needs to be done.

I used to hate when Mom would spout off the old adage about the moon. She used it as a cure-all for all life's problems. When I was younger, I would complain to my friends about it. They all heard the same thing and understood my frustration. Now that I'm older, there's a layer of peace that comes with it. It absolves me of worrying about a future—a fate—I might never understand.

"You want to go out to dinner?" Chase calls from the upstairs window.

I lift my hand, though whether or not I'm agreeing, I have no idea. I'm not particularly hungry. Or maybe my head's just too full of other things to register my stomach. I'll have to shower if we're going into town. My parents are working tonight anyway, though I'm starting to wonder if they're making up shifts. Ever since I talked to Dad on the porch, he's said they're working. Festival preparations are ramping up, though. Not to mention there's a production crew coming soon.

As I finish the row, I wipe my brow again and stand to survey my plants. They're doing well this year. I'd have more if it weren't for the Peterson kids. They learned to shift and decided the only food they want is from my garden. It's annoying, but their giggles are pretty cute. One of these days I'll catch them with the hose, but it won't be today.

My ears twitch as Chase tries to sneak up behind me. I don't know if I have it in me to pretend I'm not in a terrible mood. I wouldn't have cared before. Ignoring him isn't an option, and he doesn't deserve that, anyway. It's not his fault I'm in the doldrums and confused as shit.

His fingers skim across the back of my neck. He doesn't say anything as I continue to attack the dirt, though there's no weeds left to pull. When his lips press against my temple, I pull in a shuddering breath. Whatever happens, I just need to center myself. I'm perfectly capable of compartmentalizing my emotions. I can be his friend and sleep with him at the same time without muddling things. Everything will be fine.

Chapter 15: Here, Kitty, Kitty

Chase

"Where do you want to go tonight?" I call to Kira.

She disappeared into the shower ten minutes ago. I don't know if I'm the cause of her bad mood, but hopefully she'll even out once she's fed. I dig in my bags for appropriate clothes to wear. The pants I wore when I got here are nowhere to be found, and I'm starting to think Kira stole them. Keeping my things in the spare room seemed like a good idea at the time, though I sleep in Kira's bed every night.

When Kira doesn't answer me, I wander into the bathroom. She's rinsing her hair, her form wavering behind the frosted glass. Every time I see her, I'm mesmerized. It's been a long time, if ever, since I've been this smitten with someone. I don't know if I could have gone through with no strings attached like she originally wanted. It would have been fucking hard to turn her down.

Her hands run down her curves, then up her arms. With her eyes closed, it's as if she's putting on a private show just for me. I'd feel awkward if this was the first time I've watched her shower. I've made it a habit of sneaking into the bathroom and surprising her. My cock hardens when her palms skim over her tits. My mouth waters at the memory of her skin under my tongue.

I take off my shorts quickly, suddenly glad I never found my pants or shirt. When she turns, I open the door as quietly as possible and slip in behind her. She jolts, then melts in my arms as the spray hits my back. Her head rests against my chest, and I brush my hands across her wet skin. She hums when I roll her nipples between my fingers. I duck my head into the crook of her neck and scrape my teeth across her pulse. She shudders in my hold, as usual.

"How wet are you for me?" I murmur.

"Why don't you check?" she says, though the challenge comes out with a gasp.

I chuckle and walk my fingers over her stomach, which quivers under my touch. Slipping my hand between her legs, I groan when I'm met with her desire. I'll never get used to this—having her in my arms, ready and willing. We should get going. I don't know how late the diner stays open. As much as I want to feast on her, I don't want her to go hungry.

"Should I make you come before we go to dinner?" I ask. She's already riding my hand as I stroke her. "Or should we wait until after?"

"Both," she whimpers.

"Greedy little thing, aren't you?"

She scoffs even as her palms smack against the glass in front of her. She grinds her ass into me and I groan. Gripping her hips, I hold her still. If she keeps it up, I'll end up coming all over her back. She glances over her shoulder, a challenge resting in her eyes. If I give her a chance, she'll start making demands. I wouldn't complain, though.

I thrust inside her and she arches her back, her hands sliding down the wet glass. I use the new angle to plunge into her again and again. Her moans swirl around me, urging me on. No matter how many times I'm with her, it still overwhelms me. My back tightens and I grit my teeth. I slip my hand around her waist and rub her clit. Her body jolts in my hold, and she gasps as her pussy spasms around me. I plunge into her one last time, groaning as I come.

She shivers, quivering around my cock, and I grunt. After a minute, she straightens and I slip out of her. The spray hits the back of my neck and I spin, ducking my head under the water. She slides around me and uses her ass to push me back. I chuckle as I smack her ass. It doesn't take long for me to harden again, but we need to get going. I expect her to say something, but she closes her eyes. She might not mean it as a dismissal. Then again, I did interrupt her shower.

"I'm going to get dressed," I murmur, pressing a kiss to her shoulder.

I step out and dry off before making my way to the spare room. Eventually, I need to figure out a way to get her to open up. Fucking her every time she shuts down won't always work. The more time we spend together, the more I want to be around her. I want to learn everything about her—be there for her. It's probably too soon to be this attached. I don't care.

Her shadow passes in front of my door, and I follow her into the bedroom. Leaning against the frame, I watch as she grabs her clothes. I'll wait as long as necessary for her to open up if that's what it takes. She needs someone who won't walk away.

"I don't want to go to the diner," she says as she pulls on a shirt.

"There's that place by the general store. You like the food there?" Getting her to decide where to eat or even *what* to eat is like pulling teeth. I can't figure out if it's because she truly doesn't know what she likes or if she doesn't want to make a decision.

"I usually stay away from it. The film crews are always there and it's annoying when they start asking questions. Like I'm some spectacle to be gawked at because I live in a town known for supernatural shit." She tugs her shorts on, and I realize she's wearing my shirt. It shouldn't have the effect on me that it does. Possessiveness rolls through me, and my mouth waters to taste her.

"They can gawk at me if they want, but I didn't think they were in town for another couple weeks."

I slide my hands under her shirt and up her sides. Her forehead hits my chest, and I wrap my arms around her. She's been bouncing between sulky and needy. Not that I mind. Whatever's on her mind will either work itself out or it won't. We're not to the point where she'll talk to me yet. I wish she'd talk to me, though. It's what friends would do. The lines between us have blurred and I'm desperately hoping it doesn't turn on me.

"They should be here within a week or two. We can go there. I just don't want to see anyone right now. They'll have not-so-subtle questions and sidelong glances, and I just don't want to be under a microscope anymore."

"Is that why we're not going to your parents? Because they see too much?" I murmur into her hair.

"No. They're busy tonight with friends. But also, yes. It's just a lot of pressure. I knew they'd talk about us. The whole damn town does it whenever someone comes through."

My fingers flex and I try not to tense. I doubt I'll achieve a casual tone, but I try anyway. "So when people come to Moon Cove you…"

I don't know how to finish the sentence. It's none of my damn business who she slept with before. And I shouldn't care whether she had this arrangement with them. I wonder how many times the town's whispered about her behind her back, betting on when she'd settle down. Which isn't fair in the slightest. None of them talk about Slade and his future. Her oldest brother, Alister, isn't the center of the gossip mill.

"You what?" she whispers.

"Never mind. It's not important. Let's go to dinner. If anyone says anything, I'll just shift in the middle of the dining room, and you can make a run out the back."

She snorts and tips her head back, resting her chin on my chest. "You'd blow the entire community's cover. I have a feeling they'd run you out of town."

I bite my cheek and force a smile as her words remind me of Gemma. Now isn't the time to bring up her sister. The last time I tried didn't work out very well. We're in a different place now, but I'm still not going to ask her what happened between them. It's none of my business. Gemma told me her side. If Kira wants to leave it in the past, so be it. I'm not going to be able to drag it out of her.

She sighs and steps out of my arms. "Ask me, Chase."

I could pretend I have no idea what she's talking about. She'd call my ass out on it, though. And she doesn't deserve for me to treat her like she's not smart enough to figure it out.

"What happened with Gemma?"

She huffs as she drops onto the bed. "That's not the question you want to ask, but fine. Gemma had just been put in the rotation to shift for the cameras. One of those silly supernatural documentary companies was in town during Samhain to 'catch' a mythical creature. Alissa thought it'd be funny to play a prank on her that wasn't all that funny. I'm sure Gemma thinks I was involved, but I wasn't. I didn't know Alissa was going to do it. Gemma shouldn't have rushed. She should have waited, but she was a teenager. None of us should have that responsibility on our shoulders. Hard to change tradition, though."

"And telling her she wasn't good enough?" I ask gruffly. As much as I like Kira, Gemma is my friend. She's mated to my best friend.

She rolls her eyes. "Is she still harping on about that?"

"She said you told her you're the better daughter," I murmur.

"Oh, yeah," she laughs. "Forgot about that. Although, I said I was the *perfect* daughter—not better. I was like fourteen and a bitchy teenager. She told me I'd die alone once, too. I figured that was just sister stuff. Didn't realize she cared about that shit."

I sink onto the bed next to her. "I don't think it was just that one thing. It was a lot of little things built up. Probably wasn't just you."

"Mom has a lot of opinions, which she voices very effing loudly," she grumbles. "Gemma got out, though. She paved the way for the rest of us."

"She got out because of Slade. But she was running away."

She nods slowly and twists her fingers together in her lap. "I told her she wasn't good enough so she wouldn't come back. She wouldn't have listened if I'd helped like Slade did. She deserved more than what this town has to offer."

I inhale sharply as the pieces fall together. "So, telling her not to come home was—"

"If she came back, she'd never leave. Especially when she was struggling. Every time she was homesick at college. Every time she moved. Every time she lost a job. Every single time, I told her the town remembered so she wouldn't get trapped, again."

"Like you?"

She shoots to her feet and heads out the door. Talking about Gemma was one thing, but I shouldn't have pushed her. I knew she would shut down if I asked. Kira's hiding from herself and she's not ready to deal with it. Not yet anyway. And certainly not to me. Maybe we'll get there in the future. Or maybe I just blew this whole goddamn thing up.

She stomps back into the room and glares. "You don't know shit about me. Stop thinking you do. You don't get to walk in here and demand answers to questions you don't know anything about. I'm perfectly content where I am. Just because—"

I hold up my hand, and she falls silent. "Why don't you stop before you say something you'll regret? If you're not ready to talk about it, just say so. If I'm not the one you want to open up to, say that. Don't start insulting me because I asked a question. Now, are we going to eat?"

"Eat? You're thinking about food when we're in the middle of a fight?" she cries, throwing up her hands.

I smirk and slowly stand. "Didn't realize we were fighting, sunshine. You know what that means, right?"

She scowls, narrowing her glittering eyes. "Why don't you enlighten me?"

"Means you kind of like me."

I grab her hand and tug her out of the bedroom. She sputters behind me, but doesn't disagree. The longer this goes on, the deeper I fall. Which might be exactly what I've been waiting for.

Chapter 16: A Total Cat-tastrophe

Kira

Being at the restaurant in the tourist part of Moon Cove sets me on edge. Other than my parent's store, I rarely come here. We've separated the town, but it's not enough for me personally. At least the magic keeps them out of our areas. If there were tourists wandering down Main Street, I might lose my mind. Our community would probably die, honestly. Doesn't mean I like this part of town.

"Relax," Chase breathes. "No one is looking at you."

"Oh, I know that," I mutter. "They're looking at *you*."

I didn't even realize there were so many single women in Moon Cove chomping at the bit to flirt with someone. It happens when the film crews come into town sometimes. Usually when we have other shifters, though, they're more reserved. At least, I thought they were.

"Aw, don't worry, sunshine. I've only got eyes for you." He grins, his blue eyes twinkling.

He pops a fry in his mouth, then nudges the plate toward me. When we went to the diner, I knew Harriett was fucking with me by bringing me a salad. She has strong opinions about my thighs. She's smart enough not to say anything about it. Here, there's no reason my food didn't come out. The server said it was a mix-up. I don't know if I believe her since her eyes were focused on Chase the entire time she was talking.

"They can flirt with you all they want."

His smile dims, probably thinking I was referencing our unattached arrangement. I wasn't. We may have said no strings attached, but he wouldn't go after someone else. Especially right in front of me.

It hits me how much I trust him. Maybe it's because Gemma vouched for him. Or because of his relationship with Dad. Or even the respectful way he talks about Mom. Regardless, he does only seem to have eyes for me.

"I wouldn't do that," he growls.

A shiver rolls through me, and I swallow. "I know. Which is why they're free to shoot their shot."

His eyebrow rises and his smirk reappears. "Is that so? Careful, Kira. Another compliment tonight and I might get a big head."

I grab one of his fries and stuff it in my mouth, trying to hide my own smile. In just a few weeks he's infiltrated my life, and I don't know how to handle it. I haven't smiled or laughed this much since...ever. Not truly. I've never been secure enough to be vulnerable in front of others. I may not have been the oldest, but I was the one everyone looked up to. Shifting before my older sister Sloane was ultimately my downfall.

"I think with everyone hitting on you, you'll be just fine," I say as I push my morose thoughts away.

"You won't be if we don't get some fucking food in you." He glances around, searching for our server.

"It's fine. I can wait." I can't. I'm slowly wasting away here. My stomach is attempting to eat itself. My blood sugar has turned on me and after all I've done for it. Betrayal at its finest.

"You really can't. Your attitude tanks with your blood sugar like they're on some fucked up rollercoaster made up of only drops," he mutters, and I snort. He glances at me, concern lining his eyes.

I grab my glass and take a sip. "I was just thinking my blood sugar has betrayed me."

"Is that a thing?"

"No idea, but it sounded right in my head."

"I'm going to find someone," he grumbles.

He's out of his chair before I can tell him to leave it be. I sink farther into my chair. I doubt he'll make a scene, but I don't want to make a fuss. If the slight of not bringing my food was personal, I'd rather Chase not know about it.

There are a lot of things I did in high school I'm not proud of. Some people in town are still hurt by what I did. I don't blame them. I just don't want Chase's view of me to change because of the choices I made fifteen years ago.

This is part of the problem with never leaving a small town. No one forgets a goddamn thing. It's hard to grow out of your past mistakes. It's why I pushed Gemma away. I needed her to become more than the girl who fucked up. She was meant for more than Moon Cove had to offer. I wish I had half of her bravery. I'm stuck in this place and I made the best of it. With Chase coming into my life, I realize I might not be as content as I thought.

Chase plops back into his chair and smiles. "Okay, so apparently they gave your food to another table accidentally. Then they forgot to make it. So, I told them not to bother and we're going somewhere else."

"Chase, there is nowhere else unless we go to the diner."

He holds up his hand. "It's fine. We're not leaving. They said they'd bring it out in five minutes along with extra desserts. And since the only thing we really wanted was the desserts, I figured that would be good enough."

Three minutes later, true to their word, the server comes out with my food. They set a new burger and fries in front of Chase as well. I'll never be able to come back here, but that's fine.

As soon as the manager steps out of the kitchen, I realize what actually happened. Crystal never was my biggest fan. She wanted to be the most popular girl in school and thought I was competition. For some reason, I cared back then and had no problem going head-to-head with her. It was petty shit that shouldn't matter after all these years. No one dumped blood on someone or slept with the other's partner. There was no huge blow up where we pulled each other's hair and permanently disfigured the other. Just snide remarks and low-blow comments. I apologized a few years ago, but apparently that wasn't enough.

Crystal smirks when our eyes meet, and I sigh. When she makes her way over, I hunch over my pasta. Maybe she'll only speak to Chase and leave me out of the conversation. I glance toward the kitchen and see a guy I went to high school with. He was quiet, but we were friendly. He mimes eating, then gives me a thumbs up. Thank the goddess he made sure no one tampered with my food. I'd like to think Crystal wouldn't stoop that low.

Crystal leans against the table, facing Chase and says, "I'm so sorry for the mix-up. Hopefully, everything looks good now? How is it tasting?"

"Given the fact I'm not the one who was missing their food, perhaps you'd like to turn around and address Kira instead."

I've never seen Chase so stern. There's an edge to his voice and not a hint of a smile. He's more serious than I originally thought, but nothing like this. He honestly looks like he could tear Crystal's head off. A shiver runs down my spine and I straighten.

Crystal clears her throat and slowly spins, flipping her dark hair over her shoulder. "Kira."

"Crystal. It's fine. Thank you." I barely get the words out before a low growl erupts from Chase. "Chase, stop it."

Crystal's eyes bounce from me to him, then back again. She's a shifter and should know the signs of someone riding the edge. The last thing we need is Chase shifting in the middle of the goddamn restaurant. Especially in this part of town. We might be able to play it off as a stunt for the upcoming festival. Except it'll be harder to do that in a building.

"She should apologize," he hisses, and he crosses his arms over his chest.

Crystal turns to me, her eyes widening. "I'm sorry it took so long for your food. Will we need a cleanup?"

It's been a minute since we've had to call my dad in to clean up someone's messes. He's good at pacifying humans. Mom says it's some leftover remnants of a gift from the goddess. I think it's just him. Most of our clean-ups revolve around the kids now since they're shifting earlier each year.

I press my lips together as I gaze at Chase. He raises an eyebrow, and I realize he isn't as close to the edge as I thought. He's just pissed. Most shifters, especially new ones, aren't able to control their shifts when their emotions are running high. It's probably the reason he was able to do it voluntarily the other night. I'm not about to risk it, though.

I shake my head. "I think we'll be fine. Just some to-go boxes. I think we've overstayed our welcome."

Chase leans forward as if he'll argue, and I glare at him until he sits back with a huff.

"We shouldn't have to leave."

Crystal hightails it back to the server station, and I lean over the table.

"We most certainly do. But if she doesn't bring the dessert, I'll let you lie in wait for her out back and you can hiss at her when her shift is over."

I smirk as he narrows his eyes, muttering, "We deserve this shit for free."

Crystal comes back and we're outside in less than five minutes. She didn't make us pay, but Chase doesn't seem pacified. I don't understand why he's so upset. I ate enough of his fries I'm not hangry anymore. I'll still devour the pasta when we get home. Or maybe just the dessert. Maybe both.

"It's not a big deal, Chase. Shit happens in a kitchen," I mutter as we walk back. "And I got food in the end."

"You think I'm pissed about the food being late? Fuck, Kira. I'm not an asshole."

"I don't think you are. You're like the furthest thing from an asshole."

He switches the bag from one hand to the other and laces our fingers together. "How do you know Crystal? I know that's a strange question, given the fact you live in a small town."

"We went to school together. Didn't exactly get along." I hold my breath, hoping he'll drop it.

He grunts and his fingers flex on mine. "You two cross paths a lot these days?"

"Uh, no? For a small town, we don't frequent the same places, usually. Most of the locals don't come into the general store or the restaurant. We stick to our side unless we're going to work. We don't have the same friends, either. I think the last time I saw her was at the summer solstice, but we didn't talk. Why?"

"She made some comments I didn't particularly like," he mutters.

I doubt they're anything I haven't heard before. Gossip travels fast, especially when people think they know who you are. I'd rather not have him recount the things Crystal thinks of me. It's embarrassing enough given my past.

"I'm sure whatever she said was deserved. I wasn't very nice in high school and neither was she."

"This definitely wasn't beef from high school," he growls. "She kept saying you'd never be able to hold on to the prize, and you'd fuck it up. Something about running off. It wasn't particularly flattering."

I let out a sharp laugh, and he scowls. "Chase, they weren't talking about *me*. I mean, they were, but she thinks she's got a chance with you. Honestly, I have to live here after you go home, so maybe don't start shit, hmm?"

He sighs, shaking his head. "We'll see about that," he mumbles as he tugs me along.

I make a note to talk to Dad about how he's acting. His reactions are wildly off base given what happened. Tonight has been ridiculous and weird.

I glance at the night sky and spot a sliver of light left. The new moon is tomorrow, which definitely explains his volatile reactions and my own morose thoughts. Like the full moon and toddlers, the new moon affects shifters in strange ways. Hopefully, we'll both even out in the next couple days, and we can go back to normal—whatever that is for us.

Chapter 17: No, Seriously. Fuck the Moon

Chase

One minute I'm convinced Kira is about to throw me out and the next I'm about to strangle her. I don't know what the fuck is wrong with me, but I'm hiding from her. I've run around the lake twice now and I'm dripping in sweat. Wiping the wetness from my brow with my shirt, I try to catch my breath.

Last night was a fucking shitshow. She was in a bad mood and I thought once she ate we'd be fine. Instead, my feelings were all over the place. Crystal's comments about Kira were the final straw. Not only did they forget her food and make excuses, but Crystal kept running her mouth. I see now that Kira was right, and it wasn't about her at all. I'm used to getting hit on. For some reason, I didn't expect it to affect me so much.

I might be in too deep. Kira didn't act jealous and that might have pissed me off, too. Which is ridiculous since we're not dating. I shouldn't have any expectations of her. The longer we do this, the further I fall. And I'm fucking terrified. I tuck my shirt in my back pocket and shake out my hands.

"Chase?" a woman calls, and I close my eyes. I'm pretty sure it's Crystal, and I don't have the fucking energy for her.

I turn anyway and force a smile. "Hello, Crystal."

She giggles manically, her hands fluttering by her sides. "How wild to run into you here. Doing a bit of exercise?"

Her eyes dip to my chest and I wish I would have put my shirt back on. I glance over her head and find a gaggle of women loitering by a group of benches overlooking the lake. They keep stealing looks at me, then whispering to each other. I wonder if they planned this.

"Uh, yeah. Good day for it," I say, hoping she'll take the hint.

"Well, you clearly aren't a stranger to exercise. I'm sure it must be hard to not be able to do it." She shoots me a sympathetic smile, though I have no idea what she's talking about. I was literally just jogging.

I could let it go, but I'm afraid it'll only come up again if I don't address it. "What do you mean?"

"Oh," she gasps, then bursts out laughing. "I'm sorry. I just assumed you weren't able to have your normal routine. You seem like you work out *a lot*."

I don't know if she's telling the truth or if it's something like last night. When I overheard her gossiping about Kira, it took everything in me not to react. Kira doesn't need me to fight her battles, but I'm not one to sit idly by while people bad-mouth her.

"I'm perfectly content with my routine, thanks. Was there something you needed?"

"I just feel so bad about last night. What a fiasco!" She giggles again, and it grates on my nerves. "If you want a redo, I'm off tonight. We could go for dinner or maybe a late-night picnic?"

My brows pull low, and I almost blurt out that I'm taken. Kira's comments lately stop me. The words "once you leave" have left her mouth more often lately. It's another thing grating on my nerves. We may have started this as a fling, but we're clearly more than that.

I never saw myself settling down, more so because I never met someone I *wanted* to spend an extended amount of time with. I've been waiting for someone who fills the empty parts of me. Most people would think it's too soon to know whether she's the one, but I'm to the point where I'm done fighting the feelings inside me. We might not be fated mates, yet something led us to each other.

"I'm busy tonight," I say gruffly, realizing I never answered Crystal.

"Of course. Man like you must be busy. Tomorrow?"

"I'm busy every night."

Her face sours, and I wonder if I'm about to get an earful on decorum or some shit. She glances over her shoulder, then huffs as she faces me.

"It's her, isn't it?" she sneers. "She got her claws into you before the rest of us even knew you existed."

I cross my arms, and a drop of sweat slides down my neck. "I'm not a piece of meat to be fought over. I'm capable of making my own decisions, Crystal. Regardless of my involvement or lack thereof with Kira, I'm not in the market to date."

Her eyebrows rise, practically disappearing under the hair swooping across her forehead. "Yeah, of course. I didn't mean it...I'm sorry."

"Apology accepted. Anything else?"

"Can you tell Kira I'm sorry?" She presses her lips together, obviously working through something. "I kind of fell back into some things. Those are my friends from high school and we just...you know."

I don't know what she's talking about. I don't keep up with anyone from high school. We had superficial relationships, anyway. Once we were no longer forced to be in the same place, we didn't keep in touch. We didn't have anything in common other than the fact we were all rich. Once my parents passed away, I was gone.

Bouncing around the country didn't help with finding new people to hang out with. It wasn't until I settled into Whispering Pines that I felt like I'd found a place to belong. Then I spent the next several years wearing Jake down enough to be my friend. I knew we were meant to be friends. Now I wonder if it was so I'd eventually meet Kira. The goddess was apparently playing the long game.

"Perhaps you should talk to her yourself. Might be best to put your energy into helping with the festival instead of dredging up old rivalries."

She nods, then wanders back to her friends. Concerned looks are passed around and I turn away, ready to run another circuit around the lake. My phone buzzes before I can get going and I pull it out. I scowl and shove it back in my pocket, then take off. Both Gemma and Jake have been calling for the last couple days. I'm sure they're worried I'll spontaneously shift and attack someone in the middle of Main Street. I haven't answered them, mostly because my shifting is all they talk about nowadays.

With my mood soured, I make my way back to Kira's. I probably shouldn't since I don't want to take my shitty attitude out on her. It's not Kira's fault I'm so out of whack. I thought once I shifted, I was out of the woods, so to speak. No one told me I'd feel like I was going through puberty again.

I slam through her front door, then grimace. Kira doesn't yell at me, so I'm pretty sure she's not home. I shove the heavy wood closed softly and make my way to the shower. Unfortunately, the hot spray does nothing for me other than clean my body. I used to be able to wash away my emotions. They'd swirl down the drain along with the suds. Those days are long gone, apparently. Ever since I became a shifter, showers haven't been the same.

It's not until I'm back downstairs that I notice the note on the counter. Kira went off to her parent's store for inventory. She's hiding from me, and I don't blame her. I've snapped at her more today than since we met.

My body itches, magic flowing just under my skin. If the moon or goddess or whatever forces me to shift tonight, I might black out. Since I don't know these woods, I might end up doing something I'll regret and be completely unaware of it until morning. The thought sets me even closer to the edge.

I'd ask Kira for help, to keep an eye on me, but I don't want to hurt her. Still, I need to tell her...something—warn her, if nothing else. I'm hoping I can bring myself to actually do it. Prowling toward the general store, I mutter out excuses I could give her. By the time I get through the back door, I'm no closer to coming up with what to say.

Kira should be in the storerooms, yet she's nowhere to be found. I stomp down the hall and almost run into Ben coming out of a room. His hand shoots out to steady me and an involuntary hiss leaves me. Instantly, I regret it and stumble back.

"Whoa there, Chase," he says in a soothing tone. He studies my face, then gestures behind me. "Why don't we go outside? Enclosed spaces aren't great for you right now."

I want to argue as annoyance bubbles in my gut. It's not worth it. He'll think he's right no matter what I say. I pivot and stalk back out the door. My head twitches as I step outside, and the scent of dill invades my senses. I search for the source, slowly scanning the area. Ben's hand lands on my shoulder and I jump. He drops his light hold on me and I spin to face him.

"Have you shifted since the other night with Kira?"

I shake my head. "I figured once would be good enough."

"After the first voluntary shift, we do it again and again until we're comfortable."

I grit my teeth, my eyes darting everywhere but his face. "Well, no one fucking told me that. And I'm the furthest thing from comfortable."

"Clearly," he sighs. "I'm sure Kira didn't want to push you at the time. She probably thought the same as you—that the other night would be enough to appease the moon."

"Fuck the moon," I snarl, throwing my hands in the air, then running them through my hair.

Ben's expression darkens, and I realize I've pushed him too far. I thought he had an endless well of patience. Then again, I haven't done anything to piss him off. I step back, ready to run. I shouldn't have come here. I should have waited at the house for Kira. Hell, I should be deep in the woods where I can't infect anyone with my vitriol.

"I'm sorry," I breathe, then turn and take off.

Ben calls after me, but I don't slow. He shouldn't have to sit there and deal with my toxic behavior. I knew this whole trip was a waste. Maybe other made shifters could handle turning. They probably have no issues beyond finding a safe place to shift. Something must have gone wrong when the goddess picked me. I wasn't good enough then and I'm definitely not good enough now.

As the trees swallow me up, the light extinguishes around me. The darkness matches my mood, and I welcome it. I've spent my entire life making up for things out of my control. For years I've put on a facade of being happy and unaffected by everything. People only saw my parent's money and didn't notice how fucking lonely I was.

Becoming a shifter hasn't changed that feeling. In fact, I'm more isolated now than I ever was before. Even Kira doesn't want others to think we're anything more than temporary roommates. Every time we're out, she puts space between us. If someone makes a comment, she's quick to correct them. I convinced myself we had something more when she was clear from the start we were nothing more than fuck buddies. Hell, she didn't even want to be friends. I forced her into it.

"Fuck me," I breathe, coming to a stop to lean against a tree.

I wanted more with her. It didn't matter to me if we were fated mates or not. Being destined to fall for someone wasn't even something I knew about a year ago. Regardless, I thought we could turn this fling into an actual relationship. I don't know why since we live so far away from each other. And I doubt she's willing to move to Whispering Pines. As much as she's complained about her life here, I don't know if I'd have enough time to convince her to come with me.

"I wouldn't want to go with me either," I mutter.

Despair crashes through me. Between Kira slipping through my fingers and my failure at being a shifter, I'm tapped out. I can't fucking do this anymore. I wish I could quit. If I could reverse whatever the goddess did, I'd seize that opportunity with both hands. Jake told me it was a gift, but gifts should be returnable.

My chest tightens, and I brace my hands on my knees. My breath comes out in short gasps, and magic invades my body. With each inhale, my lungs burn and my vision blurs until I feel the pull coming over me. My bones crack, the sinew twisting with each change. I close my eyes as I morph into my shifter form.

This is about the time I usually black out, and I wait for the sweet calm of darkness to take me. When nothing happens, I open my eyes and peer through the trees. A pure white wolf peeks at me from behind a trunk, and I crouch, my tail lashing through the air.

When I shifted with Kira, I couldn't feel my cougar. Ben talked a lot about being one with my inner animal. I dismissed most of it since I've never felt what he was saying. Now, it's like another version of me has taken up residence in my head, nudging me to accept him. I'm more concerned with the other animal across the way who's currently dipping their head, almost in a greeting.

My tail swishes through the brush, tangling on a branch, and I glance over my shoulder. Hissing, I attempt to shake it free. I swear it's longer than before, though that's ridiculous.

A howl splits the night, and I whip my head back around. The white wolf turns and saunters off through the trees. I don't know why, but my cougar nudges me to follow. If it was a real wolf, they probably would have attacked. Maybe. Aggression tactics in wolves aren't my strong suit, though I should probably read up on it.

Reluctantly, I pad after the animal, hoping I'm not about to get myself in a mess of trouble, or worse—killed.

Chapter 18: Dark Watchers

Kira

The storage room I'm stuffed in is stifling. Mom said I didn't have to do the inventory today, but I need something mindless to keep me busy. Chase's rollercoaster of emotions didn't stop after we got home. I thought after a good night's sleep he'd be better, but nothing really changed. As soon as I told him I was going to the store, he took off for a run around the lake. He didn't even kiss me goodbye, which is all I've been thinking about since he left.

When did I start expecting him to act like a boyfriend? I can't pinpoint the exact moment, and it's bugging me. The closer we get, the more the lines between us blur. It sets me on edge. I don't want my heart involved in this. It'll make everything messy. Or rather, it'll leave *me* a mess when he leaves. So, I went to the other end of the spectrum and kept commenting about when he goes home. It was word vomit. I couldn't stop even though his eyes tightened every time I did it.

Muttering to myself, I throw the stack of kitchen towels back into a pile. They have a silhouette of a bigfoot stamped on the front with various sayings. Mom says they've been flying off the shelves. I cringe every time I think about it. I wonder if Jake cares about these things. Some shifters don't like what we do here. They avoid our type of community at all costs—something about profiting off our existence. I never did understand why they had a problem with it. What we do might be exhausting, but it keeps our town running. Without the tourists, we'd have died out long ago.

"Maybe they wouldn't care if they got a cut of the profits," I mumble, then begin to count them again.

If I don't get the count done soon, I'll end up doing it tomorrow, and I'd rather spend time with Chase. Tonight is the new moon and I'm worried he's going to shift again. With the way he's been acting, I wouldn't be surprised if he's forced into it. I thought him doing it voluntarily the other night would help, but we won't know until the new moon passes.

"Kira?" Dad's voice floats from the doorway, a hesitancy lacing his tone.

"Yeah?" I set a stack of ten towels aside and pick up some more.

He clears his throat, and I grit my teeth. If he doesn't spit it out, I'm going to end up snapping at him. Then he'll scold me, and I'll feel like I'm fifteen again. My parents have done so much for the community, for our family, for me. They don't need my shitty attitude to pile onto their stress. I made their lives hard enough when I was in high school. Every day I try to make up for it, but it's never enough.

"We have a problem," he finally says, and I glance over my shoulder.

"What kind of problem?" My muscles bunch and there's an uptick in my pulse. Whatever he's about to say isn't going to be good.

His brows pull low, concern swimming in his eyes. It's the same look he had when he told us about Gemma being caught shifting all those years ago. It's the same look he had when Alister said he was taking to the high seas—whatever that means. It's the same look he had when we woke up and Alissa was gone without a trace. I hate that look.

"Chase and I were speaking. He was clearly riding the edge, and I made a mistake, Kira." His words are measured as if he's afraid I'm a ticking time bomb or something.

I set another ten towels next to the pile, and I sigh. "I'm sure you're fine. Like you said, he's been a little wired with the new moon."

I struggle to keep my tone flippant. My fingers tingle as I fight the panic rising within me. I have no idea what mistake Dad could have possibly made that would warrant him coming to me. With the way Chase has been acting lately, though, I assume he overreacted.

"He yelled at me, Kira. He doesn't strike me as the type of guy to do that often."

I pull in a deep, calming breath. "What did you say to him?"

"It's not important, Kira. Although, after our interaction, he apologized. And then he took off into the woods."

It takes me a minute to process his words.

"What do you mean, he took off? Into the woods?" I cry, dropping the stack and leaping to my feet.

Chase might be grown and capable of taking care of himself as a human, but as a shifter, he's no better than a teenager. Volatile and explosive, new shifters aren't able to control their emotions, which feeds directly into shifting spontaneously. And with Chase only doing so once on his own instead of the moon forcing him into it, I doubt he's in control right now.

Dad blocks the doorway, a serious look in his eyes. "I wouldn't go after him, Kira. He's obviously going through his transition. If you interrupt that, it could have dire consequences for both of you."

"He's not ready. What if he's out there and hurt?"

Dad's nostrils flare and he shakes his head. "I won't stop you, but he's capable of taking care of himself, Kira."

"Why the hell do you keep saying my name?" I snap as I rub my sweaty palms over my hips.

"Because you're riding the edge, and I'm pretty sure you don't realize it, dear. Just take a deep breath and think this through," Dad murmurs in what he probably thinks is a soothing voice. It's not. It only sets me more on edge.

"Let her go, Bennie. Let the moon guide her," Mom says from behind him, and he glances over his shoulder.

I can't see her around his frame filling the doorway, but after a minute, he nods and steps aside. I rush from the storage room, past my father. Mom latches onto my wrist, halting me as I pass her. She gives me a look I can't decipher, then lets me go.

The heat hits me as I rush outside. The sun has almost set and I'm sure the temperature will drop. It's been getting colder and colder as of late. I barely make it to the boundary, and between one step and the next, I shift. A snarl bursts from my throat when Crystal yelps as I pound past her. For once she's by herself. It's not uncommon for her to be surrounded by her friends, yet she's sitting on a bench by the lake. I don't have time to question why. Whatever issues we have aren't important.

I push myself harder as I round the water, hesitant to enter the forest. He could be anywhere by now. I doubt Dad came and got me right away, thinking I'd chase after Chase. If he's even a little bit aware while he's shifting, I need to find him. It'll be my fault if he gets hurt. It'll be doubly my fault if he hurts someone else. There are harsh penalties for a transgression like that.

I backtrack toward the lake and check the outcropping. Lights pop up across the water as the sun dips below the horizon. I turn away, determined to find him. Maybe I should have put a tracker on him. Then at least I'd know in what general vicinity to search.

I end up in the clearing we visited before. There are too many scents to be able to pick up on his, and I'm too wired to do a more thorough scan for his specific one. I'm sure it's my imagination, but I swear I smell him by the tree he fucked me against. A shiver rolls through my body and I shake out my fur.

Glancing around, I sniff one more time. When nothing stands out other than pine and the hint of autumn, I lift my head. A mournful howl leaves me, more my wolf than me. She hasn't been too forceful when it comes to Chase. Now, despair crashes through me, but it's not mine.

I'm sure it would be a strange feeling for a human. Dealing with conflicting emotions that aren't entirely your own is completely different. Shifters have years to learn how to cope. Especially since their shifter sides manifest earlier than the first shift. I can't imagine what it's been like for Chase. All of this shit was just dropped onto his lap without warning. And I left him to figure it out alone.

Dad told me to help him with the practical side of things, and I let him down. I thought if I got too close, I'd end up liking him. Turns out that was a moot point. I could blame him, but I didn't put up much of a fight. Should I be freaking out just because he went off to shift by himself? Probably not. Yet I can't convince myself everything will be fine.

I shrink into a ball in my mind, letting my wolf take over. Maybe she'll be able to narrow down where he is. We end up wandering through the woods for a while, until my paws are sore and my lungs burn. Night fell long ago and without the light of the moon to guide me, I'm at a loss. I'm wallowing, though I can't bring myself to give up.

My wolf has taken me farther than I thought when we come to another clearing. It's one I've never encountered before, but that's not unusual. This forest is vast, taking up hundreds of acres. It's a prime location for a shifter community for that reason alone. Tipping my head back, my eyes travel along the ridges of a mountain jutting from the landscape. A shiver rolls through me, apprehension making me take a stumbling step back.

A dark shadow occupies one of the outcroppings, silently observing the trees. As I scan the rest of the rock face, I find two more watchers. I've never seen a dark watcher before. They're known for sticking to their area far south of us. Some say they're harbingers of evil, others an omen of discontent to come. Even others assume they're guardians for the goddess or spies. I never gave them much thought. Alissa was obsessed with them for a while. She gathered every piece of information she could dig up. I never asked her what she found. We were too wrapped up in our own lives and she was my annoying little sister.

I hide within the trees, my eyes fixed on them. I'm about to turn away when one of them moves. Then again, they might not. It's more of a feeling of their eyes on me, the weight of anxiety suffocating me. I drop to my stomach and let out a whine. My wolf wants to run, but can't. Not with the heaviness of their stare blanketing me.

After what feels like a lifetime, they vanish in a puff of smoke and the weight is gone. It takes even longer to regain my strength and stand. I stumble into the trees, weaving through the trunks without a clear path forward.

I could go home, wait for Chase to show up. I could hang out by the border at the lake and hope he appears. Or I could go to Alissa's and ask for help. She probably won't have much more success than I've had. She'll know about the dark watchers, though. If they're an omen about my future with Chase...

I correct my course toward her place. It'll take me a while to make my way to her. Maybe I'll get lucky and find Chase along the way. I'm too tired and confused to do more beyond talking to her. I'll have to trust that Chase will find his way back to me unscathed. Too bad my faith isn't all that strong.

Chapter 19: Effing Purrfect
Chase

My muscles ache as I unwind from the fetal position. The wood planks underneath me aren't the most comfortable, and I sit up. I definitely don't know where the hell I am. Night has fully fallen and stars glitter overhead, though I have no idea what time it is. The last thing I remember was following a white wolf through the forest.

"Hey, you. You're finally awake," a woman says, and I glance to my right.

She seems familiar, but I can't place why. Her dark hair blends in with the shadows along with her black clothes. She sips from a mug, the steam curling around her face. I probably should be worried I woke up on some random woman's porch in the middle of the night, but this is pretty on brand for my life.

"How did I get here?" I say gruffly, then clear my throat. I assume she's a shifter, though I suppose she could be a recluse like Jake.

"You walked. Well, padded? I dunno a lot about cats. Especially your kind of cat. Then you curled right up on my welcome mat and took a little catnap." She snorts at her own joke.

Definitely a shifter. "And I turned into a human...when?"

She waves her hand around, gazing at the forest. "Sometime after you fell asleep. Doesn't matter. It's a good thing the goddess had the foresight to keep us clothed when we shift or this would have been *really* awkward."

I chuckle, propping my elbows on my bent knees and drop my head in my hands. My head swims as I attempt to remember why I ran off in the first place. Oh right, because I yelled at Ben and thought I wasn't good enough for, well, anything.

"Are you the wolf?" I mumble as I rub my temples.

"One of the wolves, but if you're asking if I'm the white one, yeah. You have no idea who I am, do you?"

I peek from under my arm at her. "You seem familiar…"

Her lips twitch. "I'm Alissa. Probably doesn't mean anything to—"

"Kira's sister? Well, that makes sense."

"Ah, so she told you about me?" She takes another sip, then nods. "My reputation precedes me. Which is totally something I would have wanted when I was younger. Now I just want to be left the hell alone."

I push to my feet too quickly. My body sways, and I grab onto the railing to steady myself. I never am fully functioning when I come out of a shift. The other night, I stumbled around the woods for a while before I was able to make it back to Kira's. It's never fun, though I doubt it'll ever change.

"Where do you think you're going?" Alissa snaps.

"I'm not one to overstay my welcome. Sorry about sleeping on your porch."

I take one step and crash to the ground, missing all the steps on the way down. Groaning, I push to my hands and knees.

"Well, that wasn't smart. Why don't you come inside and have some tea?" She stands and makes her way to the door, then mutters, "Or maybe whiskey."

I push to my feet and follow her inside the small cabin, still a little unsteady. From the looks of it, there's only one room other than the bathroom. Kira said she lives alone, so it's probably perfect for her. I stop two steps in while she stomps into the kitchen and fixes me a drink. My eyes widen as she pours a hefty dose of liquor into the tea. Drinking it while in my state might put me on my ass.

"How long have you lived here?" I ask as she hands me the mug, then retreats to the kitchen again.

"About six months. But we're not here to talk about me." She leans against the counter and tilts her head.

"I don't even know *why* I'm here," I mumble.

I take a sip and force myself to swallow. The liquor burns its way down my throat, leaving fire it its wake. Too bad she doesn't have a plant I could toss the rest into. I'd rather not offend another member of the Livia family. I've got a hefty list started already with Gemma, Kira, and Ben. Gladys probably won't be very happy if she finds out I'm sleeping with her daughter. I'm not exactly a catch in the shifter community.

"Duh. The moon led you here. You did follow the moon, right?"

"There is no moon tonight. And I'm not entirely convinced it'll guide me anywhere other than straight into trouble."

I shouldn't lay all my problems at her feet no matter how much she nods along. Except talking to Ben is like consulting with an oracle, and Kira doesn't want to dig our relationship any deeper. I was trying to encourage her to open up. Maybe it's a good thing she hasn't really. It'll make it easier when I leave. Which is exactly what she's been telling me the entire time. My heart aches at the thought, but I can't keep pretending any of this will get better—that *I'll* get better.

"Ah, so you're at that stage of the process. Well, I can tell you how you're feeling is completely normal. You're essentially going through another form of puberty. You're fighting your shifter side, but really, it's just you fighting yourself. If you spent some time in your other form, you might make some actual progress."

"I don't want another side of me. I don't want to get to know them. I don't want to be like this. So, unless you can magically make me normal again, I doubt there's much you can do for me."

She presses her lips together as if she's holding back a lecture. I don't fucking care. Being in Moon Cove hasn't helped me become a better shifter. The only good part has been Kira.

"Were you happy? Before, I mean. Were you content with your life?"

"Yes," I snap, though it's not entirely true. She raises an eyebrow and I glance away. "My life was my own. I could do what I wanted, and I wasn't forced into something I didn't need or want."

"That's not the same thing as being happy, but that's fine." She lazily waves her hand and sighs. "What was your childhood like?"

I march forward and drop the mug on the counter. "I'm not having this therapy session with you, Alissa. You may think you know me because Kira mentioned me, but we're strangers. I'm not going to open up and tell you all the deep, dark secrets of my past."

"Fair enough," she says, and I turn for the door. "Although..."

My forehead hits the wood, and I grit my teeth. "Although what?"

"Shit's not going to get any better by running away. You'll go back to wherever the hell Gemma moved to, hole up in your house, and pretend the rest of the world doesn't exist. The moon will continue to force you to shift every new moon, and it'll only get worse and worse. Those episodes you've been having—"

I whip around and snarl, "How the hell do you know about those?"

She gives me a look. "Seriously? You're not the first made shifter, Chase. You're not even the first made shifter who tried to ignore what was happening. Actually, I'm impressed you were able to go this long without completely losing it. Some end up in their other form for years, forgetting their human half. Doesn't mean it goes away, though. Do you really want to lose who you are just because it's hard?"

"I don't like feeling like this," I admit, dropping my chin to my chest.

"No one does. I don't think you have a problem being a shifter. I think you have a problem because the choice was taken from you. If you would have been given the option, would you have chosen this life?"

I don't answer, mostly because I'm not ready to admit it out loud. When I found out Jake was a shifter, I thought it was amazing. It was a world I never knew of and while I wanted to learn everything, I also didn't want to push him. So, I waited. It took Gemma coming and my transformation for him to even tell me what type of shifter he was. If I had the choice back then, I would have jumped at the chance. Anything for something new to happen in my dull life.

Alissa steps in front of me, her hand twitching by her side. "We could wait until you actually admit it, but we both know the answer. Instead of fighting the inevitable, why don't you focus on what you *can* choose now?"

Kira's image pops into my head, a slight smile on her lips. If I could, I'd choose her. If I was in any position to offer her something more than she has here, I'd give it freely. I'd give her everything her heart desires, except she won't tell me what she wants.

Staying in Moon Cove isn't an option for me. I have a house and friends. I help with the summer camp. And I'm an outsider here. Kira would be just as much of an outsider in Whispering Pines. Asking her to put herself in that position isn't fair.

"I appreciate you trying to help, Alissa, but I'm going to go. I need to apologize to your dad. And probably Kira," I mutter.

I turn to leave and open the door, then jerk back, almost running into Alissa. Kira slowly lowers her hand, clearly about to knock, and confusion swims in her eyes. She opens her mouth once, then twice, then snaps it shut.

"Hey, K. Fancy seeing you here. The moon guide you too?" Alissa calls, laughter tinging her voice.

Kira leans to peek around me, then straightens. "So, normally I'd probably assume something nefarious was going on here, but I'm guessing she lured you here in her wolf form?"

"Who uses words like nefarious?" Alissa mutters. "Get out of the way, Chase. Something will probably jump out and eat her, and then we'll have to explain shit to the parents."

I step out of the way, and Kira sweeps past me. The urge to just walk out overwhelms me. If I run away now, I'll never recover from it. Forget about Kira forgiving me. Maybe it's better to deal with this now rather than later. Not in front of her sister, though. I just don't know if I can keep up this charade of a fling with her. I'm starting to fall for her, and soon it'll be too late for my heart.

Slowly, I close the door and stand next to it instead of joining them in the small living room. There's no place for me to sit, anyway. I'm perfectly content letting them catch up without interruption. After a good ten minutes of them whispering back and forth, I wonder if I should have left when I had the chance.

I clear my throat and they both glance at me. "I'm going to go. Kira, I'll see you at...your house."

Her eyebrows pop up, and she purses her mouth. Alissa's gaze bounces between us, though she doesn't say anything. I don't know why I'm lingering. I don't expect either of them to protest or beg me to stay. I'm not someone important in the grand scheme of things. Just a temporary guest in their world. I wish the same could be said for being a shifter.

I make it out the door and off the porch before I remember I'm miles away from Moon Cove. It'll take me forever to get back to the town unless I shift. The thought of going through the transition again so soon sends a chill down my spine. For the first time since I became a shifter, the cougar within me stirs. I've felt him when I'm in my other form, but never while human.

He nudges me, and I shake my head as if I can dislodge him. He hisses in my head, then nudges me again. It's like having an annoying voice in the back of my mind who won't shut up. There's almost a physical reaction within my body when he knocks around in my body. I wouldn't be able to describe it to someone who hasn't been through it.

Magic swirls around me, or rather, within me. I fight against it, but my cougar hisses again and I squeeze my eyes shut. For some reason, he doesn't take over, letting me come to grips with what's happening. I don't know if this is what the others have been talking about, but it's painful. My breath stutters in my chest as my lungs seize, and I brace my hands on my knees as I struggle.

It's not worth it. Even if my cougar takes over and I black out, it'll be better than this. Hopefully, he'll leave the sisters alone. A growl echoes within me as if he's offended by the mere thought. I let go, allowing him to do whatever the hell he's going to do.

The door opens behind me, and I glance over my shoulder, but I've already shifted. Kira's face falls and she whispers my name. It's the last thing I hear before the darkness takes me.

Chapter 20: Definition: Shitshow

Kira

"Go after him," Alissa whispers harshly. When I don't move, she shoves me onto the porch and slams the door.

Chase doesn't even twitch, tracking my movements as I stumble to the railing. I bite my lip as I wait for him to do something. Before when he shifted I could tell he was in control. Now, I'm not so sure. If he attacks me, I'll be forced to defend myself and I don't want to do that. I didn't care about that when I searched for him. I do now, though.

"Chase?" I say under my breath.

He slinks around and faces me, his muscles rippling under his fur. It's probably the worst move, but I shuffle down the stairs. He freezes, one paw still in the air. His tail lashes back and forth and I focus on it. I could be wrong, but I swear it's longer than before. When he moves again, I inhale sharply.

I plant my feet on the ground, holding onto the banister in case I need to make a quick escape. When he's inches away, I hold my breath. His shoulders drop and I close my eyes, bracing for teeth or claws or something. Instead, his head bumps into my hand, nudging me. I exhale, my lids fluttering open, and he nudges me again. I expected his fur to be rough, but he's soft, almost silky. As I run my fingers behind his ear, a rumbling noise erupts from him.

My wolf perks up, answering his purring by whining with affection, though it's only in my head. Clearly, she's warmed up to him. She struggles against my hold and magic rushes through my veins. I try to suppress the urge to shift, but

I'm quickly losing my grip. My wolf doesn't seem to care that he's a cougar. Or that he could probably take our face off with one swipe of his claws. Or that he could take a chunk out of our hide with his teeth. She just wants to be closer to him, and I don't understand why.

When I can't resist the pull any longer, my body morphs, shrinking and yanking at various muscles. Usually, it's a seamless transition for me—a blink between one step and the next. It's almost as if my wolf is prolonging the transformation to give him time to run. He doesn't, merely sitting on his haunches until I'm done.

I crouch while my wolf pushes toward him. She could easily take over if she wanted. I've had years cultivating a relationship with her, though. She'll let me handle things as I see fit until we're in danger. If Chase would accept and work with his cougar, he could have the same connection and have more control. He's just so damn stubborn.

I shake out my fur, trying to slough off my own guilt. He might be stubborn, but I haven't tried nearly as much as I should have. I was so concerned with how close we were becoming and what that would mean for me.

A whimper escapes me and I swear he smirks. Which isn't possible since he's a goddamn cougar. Cats do *not* smirk. I drop my head, trying to rein in my wolf, and then Chase bumps into me. It isn't until he nips at my jaw that I react. I pounce over him and take off for the trees.

Even for my wolf it was too much. As much as I want to give into him and his bid for affection, I can't. We shouldn't even be shifted together. We're supposed to be enemies, staying out of each other's way. Clearly, our inner beasts didn't get the memo.

He probably doesn't understand the meaning behind his nipping. He probably thinks it's perfectly normal. Until we're human again, I won't know for sure. I'm not about to risk it, though.

The trees flash by as I race through the forest. He pounds behind me, easily keeping pace. I'm surprised he hasn't overtaken me. It's not until we're halfway home that I slow. I pant as I lope toward the small stream bubbling along without a care.

Chase leaps over the water and lands on the other side with ease. He settles across from me, lapping at the water. A shiver rolls through me when our glowing eyes meet. I'd think his cougar was challenging me if it wasn't a look that's all Chase. I don't know how to explain it, but it's him shining from the cat.

Maybe he is challenging me. Chase certainly likes to boss me around in the bedroom. Bastard. If he thinks we're getting frisky in these forms, he's lost it. I swipe at the water and douse him. A hiss erupts from him, and I tip my head up as I prance away.

I make it three steps before I freeze, my hackles raising as a chill of magic rolls through the forest. My ears perk up, and I desperately search for the source of unrest. It's not another shifter, but it's something. It's almost like the magic when the white feather appeared, yet darker. Chase's body leans into mine, his tail whipping against me.

A shadow shifts downstream, almost floating, but never truly moving. Chase steps toward it, and I growl at him. Apprehension floods my system for a second time tonight, and I retreat a step. Yipping at Chase quietly, I silently beg him to follow me. I turn and dash into the forest once more. Thank the goddess he trails me, allowing me to take the lead. No way am I'm fucking with the dark watchers.

I didn't even have a chance to ask Alissa about them. She was too busy cussing me out for not letting Chase in. She said a lot of things in a very short amount of time and none of it made me feel better. I thought out of anyone she'd understand why I'm keeping him at a distance. My excuses didn't fly with her. I don't blame her. Most of them were pretty pathetic.

It's not until we come to my spot overlooking the lake that I slow. My muscles ache with the tension and fatigue of running so much tonight. I never put this much effort in when I'm shifted. Then again, I don't usually have to go chasing after rogue shifters and encounter mythical legends. I'll have to tell Dad about everything. Not tonight, though. The rest of the night will include me collapsing into bed and nothing else.

Chase shifts slowly, and I glance away. When I was learning, I never wanted someone to watch me. It was embarrassing since it took me a while to figure out how to do it quickly. Others didn't seem to have the same issues—especially Slade, who thought it was hilarious to throw pebbles at me while I was learning. Looking back, it was funny, but not when I was fifteen.

"You going to shift or am I walking back by myself?" Chase asks, exhaustion lining his voice.

I gather the magic left behind from his shift and close my eyes. When I open them again, I sigh and run my hands through my hair. He doesn't bother looking at me, merely turning to make his way down the small path curling around the edge. I plop down on the outcropping and my stomach flips. I thought we'd come to some sort of understanding. Pretty ridiculous since we were both shifted at the time.

From the corner of my eye, I track his progress, but he's stopped. He crosses his arms over his chest as a sharp wind gusts through the trees and sends his hair fluttering.

I huff, wondering if he's standing guard or something. "You can go. I don't need a watchdog."

"I'm a cougar. Not a dog," he snaps.

"Finally claiming it?" Bitterness sweeps over me. I don't know how the hell we got here or how to get out.

He doesn't respond, but I don't expect him to. I hate this, even though I knew it would happen. Every time I get involved with someone, shit goes south. And it's usually my fault. I'm not conceited enough to think all of Chase's reservations stems from me. Then again, I'm most likely the root of a lot of the problems. Helping him with shifting was the one thing my parents asked me to do, but I danced around it.

"I can talk to my parents," I murmur as my heart cracks. I didn't think it was possible, yet here I am, fighting back tears.

"About what?"

"About what happened tonight, moving in with them, the dark watchers...take your pick."

He makes a sound in the back of his throat. "I don't understand half of what you just said, but I'm not moving. You want to kick me out of your bed, so be it. But I'm not fucking leaving."

I push to my feet, my muscles protesting, and plant my hands on my hips. "Bold of you to assume you have any say in who stays in *my* cabin."

He steps into my space, his arms crossed over his chest, brushing me. "Stop running, Kira. You think you're the only one going through shit? You think everything revolves around you?"

"What the hell are you talking about? I only offered because you clearly need somewhere else to stay. Hell, I'll get you a room at the hotel if that's what you want."

"You're who I want," he roars.

He grabs my upper arms and goosebumps erupt along my skin. I expect him to shake me, push me away, pull me close. Instead, he drops his hold on me and paces away. He mutters under his breath while running his hands through his hair. I don't know what the hell I'm supposed to do. We're clearly not on the same page.

"This was supposed to be no-strings," I whisper. I cling to the rules we set, if only to protect myself. Before it was stubbornness on my part. Now it's just plain fear.

"Tell me what those things were—at the creek."

Apparently, we're not going to talk about his little outburst. "I think they're dark watchers. They usually are seen down south. I was going to ask Alissa more about them, but we didn't have a chance."

His nostrils flare and he glances away. "What are they?"

"Omens? Harbingers of death? Guardians for the goddess? No one really knows."

"Why'd you run away?"

I huff, shaking my head. "I didn't fucking run away. I got the fuck away from them. Two very different things."

"I wasn't talking about at the creek. At Alissa's, you ran away from me. Why?"

"Can we not have this conversation? I'm tired. I'm cold. And I'm hungry. The last thing I want to do is hash out a bunch of things that won't matter in the morning."

"What the hell happened out there, Kira? What the hell is happening to me? You dodge questions left and right. You won't open up to me. You start to tell me shit and then clam up. Where the hell do I stand with you?" The remnants of his voice echo across the lake as he falls still, but his eyes aren't fixed on me. They're trained over my shoulder.

He holds up his hand when I tense. Like hell am I turning around. He wiggles his fingers at me, and I slowly shuffle toward him. If a dark watcher is behind me, I might just get dragged to whatever form of hell the goddess has thought up. Dad thinks our souls are recycled, but I never gave it much thought.

When I reach him, he wraps his arm around my waist and slowly eases us backward. A low growl erupts from behind me and my mouth drops open. I shove at Chase's chest. Not that it does any good. He's not about to let go of me when he thinks there's a threat around.

"Knock it off, Slade," I call over my shoulder.

My brother yips, laughing at his little prank. Chase still doesn't let me go until Slade takes off into the forest. I didn't even know my brother was sticking around. He's usually gone by now, only sticking around town for a day or two before dashing off to the next adventure. An ache builds in my chest, cutting off my breath.

"Let's go home. We'll deal with everything in the morning," Chase says, exhaustion lining his voice as he drops his hold on me.

I want to argue or make up or tell him off. Instead, I follow him silently. We're halfway around the lake when he takes my hand. As his palm presses into mine, a sense of calm ripples through my body. I'm too tired to worry about it. We'll deal with everything in the morning, just like he said.

Chapter 21: Switch-a-roo

Chase

I thought I'd sleep late after last night's antics, yet the sun is barely kissing the horizon when I open my eyes. A sliver of light pierces through the gap in the curtains, and I huff. Reaching toward the fabric, I'm careful not to disturb Kira, who's fast asleep on my chest. With a twitch, the light cuts off, and I sigh as I settle back.

Kira burrows into me, her nails digging into my side. The last thing I want to do is talk about yesterday. I close my eyes, soaking in her warmth. Something happened between us while we were shifted. She's not willing to admit it. Not yet. But there was definitely something there. I felt closer to my cougar, closer to her. Or maybe it was her wolf. Whatever it was, she was intoxicating.

Whenever I shifted around Gemma, it was terrifying. The split second before I blacked out, I felt the need to rip out her throat. I refused to be around her during the new moon after that. She kept wanting to try again, but I refused. Jake would have thrown me into a tree and broke my back or something. He's crazy protective of her, even more so since they discovered they're mates.

With Kira, though, it was as if I was coming home. Which is ridiculous. Ben gave me a book on mates, fated and otherwise, and none of them mentioned cougars being with wolves. Our species are just too different to attract one another, apparently.

Not that I should be hoping she's my mate. There are too many obstacles standing in our way. The most obvious being my inability to shift properly. Last night was a fluke. Two or three shifts where I'm still fighting my cougar doesn't mean I'm improving.

I close my eyes and run my fingers through Kira's hair. I push the doubts from my mind and soak up the remaining time I have with her. When her leg slides over mine, my cock twitches. She has a habit of rubbing her knee along my crotch while she's sleeping. Usually, I'd wake her up, but this morning feels different. I didn't even know if she'd let me sleep in her bed last night. When I tried to go into the spare room, she snarled at me.

"Go back to sleep," she whines. "You keep tensing up."

I hum, skimming my palms down her back. I force myself to relax, hoping she doesn't wake up more. I'm not ready to let her go. My hopes are dashed when she rolls away, all the way off the bed. Her feet hit the floor and she stomps off to the bathroom. Sighing, I sit up and scoot until I'm propped against the headboard. I had grand plans for the slats built into the wood. I wonder if we'll get to use them.

Kira stumbles back into the room, dark rings under her eyes. She's limping, though that could be from tiredness. She didn't seem injured last night. Not that she'd say anything if she was.

"Why are you awake? It's freaking early," she mumbles, then collapses next to me.

I flip the covers over her and she whines. When I try to slide out of the bed, her hand finds mine and she tugs. I settle back once more and rub my thumb across her skin as she laces our fingers together. I focus on the feel of her instead of the plethora of things we need to discuss. It'd be so easy to ignore it all. Kira probably wouldn't mind. She seems to have a tendency to sweep things she doesn't want to deal with under the rug.

She squeezes my hand. "I don't want to talk."

"You can go back to sleep," I murmur.

"I don't want to sleep if you're not." She sighs, untangling our hands and rolling on her back to stare at the ceiling.

I scoot down and loop my arm around her waist. I don't expect to do anything except doze, but darkness pulls me under. Maybe it's her warmth or just being near her. Whatever it is, I'm not complaining. My sore body matches my exhausted mind. I would have been a wreck the rest of the day, if not longer, had I not. By the time I wake again, my head is clearer and my muscles have relaxed.

Kira stretches next to me, a whine coming from her as she does. She mumbles something I don't catch, but I'm not about to ask. She's not a morning person on the best of days. Talking to her before she's had caffeine is never a good decision. The delay will help me figure out how to fix everything. Or let go if need be.

"I'm going to take a shower," she says before stumbling toward the bathroom.

"Yeah, okay," I mumble. Not that she hears me through the closed door.

I swing my legs off the bed and drop my elbows on my knees. I flip open the curtains and wince as the bright light hits me. Usually there's not a lot of activity on a Monday morning. Kids are in school and adults are at work. Today, the lake is overrun with several families picnicking along the edge. The path running behind Kira's cabin is packed with people jogging back and forth.

Pushing to my feet, I run my hand through my hair, then make my way to the bathroom. Normally, I just barge right in while she's showering. Today I knock and hope she doesn't cuss me out or worse—ignore me.

"What?" Kira calls over the spray.

"Is there something going on?"

"Get in here. I can't hear you," she shouts.

I open the door slowly, leaving it cracked instead of walking in. "What's going on in town?"

"Stop letting the warm air out," she shrieks, and I sigh, stepping inside. "What the hell are you talking about?"

"There's a bunch of people at the lake and others rushing around. What's going on?" I try not to peek at her. It'll only make it harder to resist her. All it takes is a look or her scent and the need to fill her overtakes my common sense.

"It's two days before the production crew comes. Showed up a little earlier than expected. The town comes together and gets all the rest of things in order. Oh, and a lot of people want to live it up these last couple days. Most of the businesses on Main Street are closed unless you can catch someone. Mom will probably be calling and asking for help." Her wavy form ripples behind the glass and I step back, averting my eyes.

I clear my throat and shake my head. "Help with what?"

"They always put on a whole potluck for the town. People bring dishes and there's yard games and shit." She opens the door and pokes her head out. "What the hell are you doing?"

I glance at her and my resolve crumbles. She yelps as I rip the door from her grip, then cup her face, my lips crashing into hers. The spray hits me as I crowd her against the wall and she moans as her fingers grapple with my underwear. They're already soaked, but I'm too busy tasting her to worry about it.

Running my hands down her body, I devour her. When I reach her hips, her nails graze up my back. I let go of her and struggle to remove my underwear while my tongue sweeps into her mouth.

She grabs my sides and spins us around until she slams me into the wall. I'm not about to argue if she wants to take control. She knocks my hands away and drops to her knees. This shower is definitely not large enough for these types of activities. Her feet hang out of the shower, the door swinging wide open.

There's no way I'll be able to fully block the water. I grab the spout and shove it down. At the same time, she frees my cock and leaves my underwear around my thighs. Her nails dig into my skin while her other hand grips the base of my cock. A moan leaves me, and I jolt when her lips wrap around the tip. My head smacks the wall and my eyes flutter closed.

Her tongue swirls around the head, and then she takes me deeper. She's barely started and I'm already riding the edge. When she hums, my hand slams into the glass beside me. Her eyes meet mine, laughter dancing in the golden depths. I grip her hair, and her lids flutter shut as she moans. Grappling with my control, I resist the urge to take over.

"That's it, sunshine. You take my cock so well," I murmur.

Her fingers slip to the back of my thighs, and she eases back slowly. I allow her to play a bit before I stop her. My fingers twist into her strands, and I tip her head back.

I raise an eyebrow. "What do you want? You want me to come down your throat?"

She swallows hard and I lose control, thrusting into her mouth with abandon. I'm teetering on the edge when she leans back and releases me. A growl leaves me even as she strokes my length.

"You're being very bossy for someone at my mercy," she says.

I open my mouth to retort, and she pulls my cock into her mouth again. I cough as she hollows her cheeks, then swallows. It's too much and not enough all at once, and I groan as I come. My head hits the wall as she laps up every drop. When she releases me, I glance down and spy a smirk dancing on her face. She licks her lips, and I expect her to stand. Instead, she strokes me slowly. Her other hand falls between her legs, and I pant.

I silently thank the goddess for gifting me with a quick recovery time as my cock hardens once more. I don't know how long I'll be able to last watching her touch herself, though. When her mouth parts, releasing a moan, I can't take it. I seize her wrist and her gaze snaps to me.

"Up," I grit out.

She scrambles to her feet, then shakes her head. I turn off the water and grab her around the waist. Her body against mine sends heat flowing through my veins. I guide her out of the shower and spin her around.

"Hands on the counter."

She glances over her shoulder and smirks. "Thought I was in charge?"

"You want to take control?" I ask and drop my hands to my sides. "Be my guest, sunshine."

She huffs, then grips the edge of the counter. I don't move, waiting for her to tell me what to do. I stroke my shaft to ease the ache building inside me. She wiggles her ass, and I grit my teeth. If she keeps enticing me, I'll end up taking over.

"Chase," she snaps, then drops her head. "Please."

"You wanted to be in control, Kira. Tell me what you want." I cross my arms to stop myself from reaching for her.

I catch her reflection in the mirror as her nostrils flare. When she glances up, desire mixed with frustration dance in her golden eyes. I smirk, waiting for her to voice what she wants.

"I want you to own me," she growls.

As I step closer, her body trembles in anticipation. I grip her hips and ease into her. She spasms around me, forcing a grunt from me. She does it again, probably on purpose. I thrust into her hard and fast. Ecstasy cascades down her face as she tumbles over the edge, yet I don't slow. Her chin drops, hiding from me, and I slide my hand into her hair. Gripping the strands, I tug her head up and a moan falls from her.

My orgasm builds and my movements become erratic. She pushes back with each thrust, her whispered pleas driving me on. She cries out and her back arches. I follow her into the whirlwind of euphoria rocking through me. I cover her body with my own as I roll my hips, wringing every last drop of pleasure from her.

I flex my fingers in her hair as she drops her forehead to the counter. If we stay like this for long, I'll end up taking her again and again. From the way she's wiggling against me, I doubt she'd mind.

When her eyes meet mine in the mirror, I realize we won't be getting to the many conversations we need to have anytime soon. She's too overwhelming—all my common sense flees. Everything else can wait until later. I'll soak up every minute with her until then.

Chapter 22: Chocolate and a Fifth of Whiskey

Kira

We shouldn't have slept together…again. At least not until we deal with what we're doing here. I'm not about to string Chase along if he's caught feelings. And I'm not about to admit my own threads tying me to him.

When Chase leaves, I'll deal with my heartbreak the way all women in my family do—with a block of chocolate, a fifth of whiskey, and a long-ass run in the woods. It's the way our mother taught us, though it might not be the healthiest of options.

"We should talk," Chase murmurs from behind me and I jolt. Why the hell is it so easy for him to sneak up on me? No one else is able to.

"Not the time, Chase," I hiss as I wash another plate. There are always more dishes, even when we have a dishwasher.

"Except we're the only ones in here. Your mom is busy directing others and your dad is helping set up. So, let's start with what you want."

His arm brushes my side as he reaches around to grab the plate from my hand, his chest pressing into my back. My breath hitches and warmth spreads through me. I'm definitely not having this conversation with him while I'm fighting off the urge to throw him on the table. Right now, I'm not sure whether I'd ravish him or punch him.

"I want to finish these dishes," I grit out.

"Hmm." His lips brush my shoulder. I shouldn't have worn a tank top. The more skin he has access to, the less likely I am to resist him.

The back door opens and he smoothly steps to the side, pretending like he's been drying the plate the entire time. I glance over my shoulder as Mom steps into the kitchen.

"Oh, you two don't have to do the dishes. Kira, can you cut up the fruit? Chase, I would love if you could bring another table from Sloane's room. It's the first door on the left at the top of the stairs. Actually, Kira, you might need to help him with it. Hard turn at the top. Also, we need to toast the rest of the garlic bread. Thank the goddess we don't have any vampires around." Mom lets out a chuckle at her own joke. I smile, then burst out laughing at the look on Chase's face.

His cheeks redden and he scowls. "I'm assuming vampires aren't real."

Mom's chuckles turn into full-blown glee. She practically skips from the room, probably to share with Dad. Thankfully, they won't spread the information to others. Unless Chase brings it up. They're nothing if not aware of jokes being funny only if everyone is laughing. It's one of the lessons they hammered into us.

"Can we pretend I didn't think werewolves and vampires were a thing?" Chase asks, running his hand through his hair.

"Sure, although we don't know if vampires are real or not, I suppose. I thought bigfoot was a myth until you confirmed Jake was definitely a sasquatch."

He grabs my hand and tugs me toward the stairs. "Except I thought others had seen them?"

"Sure, but people lie all the time. The amount of dark watcher sightings that are just some kid in a Halloween costume is ridiculous. I guess I just assumed they all were mistaken or wanted attention. Why are you dragging me upstairs?" I trip up a step and he catches me, because of course he does.

"Your mom needs another table. We're getting another table." We reach the top and he swings to the right. I tug him to the left into Sloane's old room. "I don't know how you do this."

He stumbles around the space, searching for what Mom needs. I step around the boxes and grab the one she wants. I shake it a little to get his attention, and he grins. Somehow being busy has brought back some of the light in his eyes. I'd be happy except I know I'm the reason that light was muted.

"Do what?" I ask as we struggle to get the job done.

"Huh? Oh, I mean, it must be nice to always have something to do with the town. And having family around all the time. But it feels a little stifling sometimes." He grunts as he lifts the table over his head. He'll never fit through the doorway, but I won't say anything. He'll need to figure it out.

"It is a lot," I murmur, then sigh. "Which is why it's important I stick around. Mom and Dad can't handle all of this on their own. Everyone else just left."

I slip into the hallway, and we finagle the table through. It's a good eight feet and there's a shit ton of boxes in the way. Chase kicks one and it tips over, spilling clothes everywhere. There's not enough room to swing it around or stand it on end, and we end up pivoting too much.

"You need to swing it," I snap, shoving at the corner.

"Swing it where?" he snarls, wildly gesturing at the stuck table. "There's no-fucking-where to swing it, sunshine. If you'd like to climb over here and do it yourself, be my guest."

"You've got to be fucking kidding me." A frustrated cry leaves me, and I yank it toward me.

"You two good up there?" Dad calls from the bottom of the stairs.

"We're fine," I yell. "Perfectly fucking fine if Chase would get his shit together."

"If Kira wouldn't keep jerking the damn thing while I'm trying to wiggle it through," Chase shouts.

Dad's chuckles ring through the house, and his footsteps fade away. Of course he didn't help us. He probably thinks this will build character or some shit. Chase huffs and I growl at him, baring my teeth. His brows pull low, studying the obstacle between us so he doesn't even see my frustration. He smacks at the legs and they rattle. He does it one more time, probably for good measure.

"Can we just get this shit done? I'm hungry." I cross my arms over my chest.

"You're always hungry. You need more sugar in your life," he mutters, still staring at the table.

"What the hell is *that* supposed to mean?"

He rubs his chin and tilts his head. "Your blood sugar drops too quickly because you're not eating enough cake. Just a theory, though."

"Well, can we get this done with so I can go eat some damn cake?"

He rolls his eyes, then grabs his end and shoves it hard. The corner of the table slams into my stomach and my breath whooshes out of me. I latch onto the railing, hoping I don't fall down the stairs as I groan.

"Shit. Shit, shit, shit." Chase vaults over the table and his foot catches one of the legs. He falls in slow motion, arms pinwheeling as he crashes to the ground.

I'd laugh if I wasn't fighting for my life to breathe. He crawls toward me and wraps his arms around my legs as he apologizes. I tip toward the wall and smash into it, then slide to the floor. He's still clutching my ankles as if I'll roll away if he doesn't. He ducks his head and his shoulders shake.

"Stop. Fucking. Laughing," I wheeze, pressing a fist to my chest.

"What in the world are you two doing? I asked you to get a table, not wrestle. You know what? Don't answer that. Whatever is happening up there, I don't want to know," Mom calls, and she rushes back outside.

"Great. Now your dad thinks we're at each other's throats and your mom thinks we're bedroom wrestling," Chase mutters.

I bury my fingers in his hair and brush the strands from his forehead. "She's used to the random crashes. And Dad's used to the shouting. At least they used to be when we were growing up. I'm sure they're outside giggling at our antics, remembering the good ole days."

"You guys had fun, didn't you?" he asks, sorrow lacing his tone.

"Yeah, we did. We had our fights and said shit we didn't mean, but I liked growing up in a big family. Sometimes I wish..." My head hits the wall as I cut myself off. I don't need to burden him with my desire to go back in time. I could do things differently, fix my mistakes, and maybe they all wouldn't have abandoned me here.

"Tell me," he whispers.

I bite my lip as an ache forms in my chest. "I wish things were different, is all."

"They still could be."

"Nah. They're off living their lives. They don't need me busting in and ruining everything for them. Plus, it's not like I can leave this place. Mom and Dad need someone here to help them. I'm all they have left." I sound pathetic, but I can't infuse a false sense of joy into my voice.

"And who do you have?"

I clear my throat and untangle my hand from his hair. "I don't need anyone. I'm fine just the way things are."

I make the mistake of glancing at him then. His eyes flash with hurt before he drops his hold on me and pushes to his feet. I didn't mean to offend him, but it seems like that's all I do these days.

Besides, he's leaving. I don't even know if he's sticking around for Samhain. Dad's been hinting about Chase being the one who shifts for the production crew. I doubt he's said anything to Chase, and I'm not going to breathe a word.

"You're lucky, Kira. Growing up with all these people around who noticed you. That shit doesn't always happen."

He dusts off his hands on his shorts and swings around to wrestle the table the rest of the way through the door. I want to ask him what he means. I'm too scared he won't answer. We have enough things standing in our way. Adding another one doesn't seem like a good idea.

"You don't talk about your family," I blurt out, then squeeze my eyes shut. "Sorry. Forget I brought it up."

"No, you're fine. Only child. Parents are dead. Nobody else." He messes with the table a little more, though I don't think he's doing anything of importance.

"Except Jake and Gemma," I murmur, pushing to my feet.

His head pops up and he glances over his shoulder. "Gemma is your sister, Kira. Not mine."

"Technically, yeah, but she acts more like your sister than mine. And Jake has been in your life for years. They're your family, Chase."

Grooves appear between his eyes, and he turns away. "We need to get this downstairs before your mom comes back."

I clear my throat and step forward. "You want the bottom or the top?"

He snickers. "I'm up for either, though today I think I'll take bottom."

"I'll keep that in mind." I say it under my breath, but he still chuckles as he positions himself on the stairs.

He cusses more than a couple times on the way down. At one point, the table slips from my grip and cracks him in the chest. I end up holding the thing with my entire body while he catches his breath. He didn't appreciate when I pointed out it was payback.

"Mind the sideboard," I call when he swings the table around the corner.

He stops suddenly, and I run into one of the corners, swallowing a yelp.

"The what?"

"The sideboard," I gasp.

"What the hell is a sideboard?" His head swivels around, and I point to the low cabinet sitting against the wall. "That's a hutch."

"No. *That's* a hutch." I point toward the piece in the living room displaying all my mother's knickknacks.

He grumbles, picking up the table again. We end up making it outside with little fuss. He doesn't seem to want to snarl at me anymore. I'd take it as a good sign, but now I'm just worried I messed up again. Bringing up his family wasn't the smartest idea. I don't even know why I did. It's not like I want to know more about him or his past. This is just a fling. If I keep telling myself it's only temporary, maybe my heart will believe it.

163

Chapter 23: Son
Chase

Ben claps me on the shoulder, his grin firmly in place. I smile back, then take a swig of my beer. I've been nursing the same one for the last hour. No one seems to notice. I swear most of the town is here, celebrating one last hurrah for summer. Or the last night of freedom, if Kira's to be believed.

She's been avoiding me since we brought the table out. She slipped back inside to finish prepping the food when Gladys put me to work out here. Every time I try to find her, she disappears. It's as if she's afraid to be seen with me. My stomach flips every time she dodges me. I shouldn't have tried to start the conversations we desperately need to have. And I definitely shouldn't have said anything about my family. It wasn't the right time. There never seems to be a right time.

"What do you think?" Ben asks, gazing at the crowd.

"What do I think about what, sir?"

"Our little celebration." He lifts his hand to someone, finally releasing me from his hold. "We've been having these since the kids were little. It's one of those traditions."

I take another drink to buy myself some time. While I think it's nice, there's too many people. Everyone's nice and welcoming, but I've been having the same small talk for the last three hours. My feet hurt and my head aches and I'd love nothing more than to go home. I've socialized enough, in my opinion. Leaving without Kira isn't on the agenda, regardless of how she's treating me.

"It's great," I say, infusing my voice with more vigor than I feel.

He gives me a look I can't decipher. "Perhaps you should take Kira home. She's fading fast. Never did like these big events."

"She looked like she was doing fine."

His hand lands on my shoulder again and he leans in. "So did you. You did great tonight, son."

Ben saunters away, oblivious to the dark chasm I'm falling into. My vision darkens at the edges, and I suck in a sharp breath. Gladys's voice rings through the air, but it's as if she's calling to me through a tunnel. The beer bottle slips from my numb fingers and drops to the grass. I focus on my breathing, trying to center myself once more, but it doesn't work.

Warm hands cup my cheeks and a sense of peace ripples from the contact.

"Chase," Kira whispers. Or maybe shouts. I can't be sure. "Chase, just breathe."

The darkness recedes, and Kira's face fills my vision. I focus on her instead of the crushing weight sitting on my chest until my muscles ease and my lungs expand. Concern swims in her eyes as her gaze searches mine. I swallow hard, wrapping my fingers around her wrists to keep her close. She's the only thing grounding me to the present.

Her thumbs brush my skin. "Are you okay?"

I nod, not trusting my voice. It was as if my entire brain shut down when Ben called me son. Never in my life has someone addressed me like...like they knew me the way a dad would. My father wasn't cold, per se. He had plenty of good qualities. They merely lent more toward the business side of things rather than the paternal. He provided, gave me stability, and set me up for life. There was no affection, though. Only pride. Ben's words repeat on a loop in my head as I fixate on Kira.

"Chase," she murmurs, and my fingers flex, holding her close just a little bit longer. "Are you about to shift?"

"No," I breathe. "No, I'm okay."

"Let's go home, then." She tugs away from my grip and drops her hands. I catch her mother's concerned gaze over Kira's shoulder. I don't have it in me to reassure her. Thankfully, no one else seems to have noticed my little hiatus from reality.

I follow Kira as she weaves her way through the crowd. At one point, I almost bump into one of the tables laden with food. Kira snatches at my hand and guides me around it. I'm not about to tell her I tripped over a divot in the lawn. I'm just glad she's acknowledging me in public.

Her cabin comes into view, and I breathe a sigh of relief. I don't want to be cooped up inside, so I tug her toward the chairs on her porch. Clutching her hand still, I sink into one. She doesn't protest, thank the goddess. I'll have to explain what happened or she'll think the worst. My head tips back against the seat and I close my eyes.

"Do you need to shift?" she asks, and I squeeze her hand.

"It wasn't a shifter thing. No magical outburst or epiphany," I murmur.

"Then what was it?"

"Your dad said something that threw me off." I don't know how to explain. Kira grew up with him. I don't know if she'll realize the gravity of his words.

"What did he say?"

I bite my cheek, hoping a bit of pain will help me keep my shit together. "He noticed I don't do well with crowds after a while. Told me I did good tonight."

"Okay..." she pulls out the word, probably sensing there's more.

"He called me son." Silence meets my declaration, and I wonder if I should have kept it to myself. "It's not that big of a deal."

"Clearly it is if you reacted the way you did. Mom thought you were going to have a panic attack. Or that you would end up shifting in the middle of the party."

I peek at her from under my lashes. "Did your dad notice?"

"I mean, he was smiling when we left. I wasn't really paying attention to anything but you."

"You'll have to do damage control tomorrow," I mutter, realizing the bind I've put her in. "You can just tell them I'm still learning or some shit."

"What? Why the hell would I do that? You're doing much better than you were. You've shifted several times on your own. I'm not about to lie. It's none of their damn business what's going on with you. Or us, for that matter. They can go stalk a dark watcher for all I care." She huffs as she glares out into the night.

A smile creeps up on me, easing the remaining tension in my muscles. "You sure you're okay with people gossiping about us? We're practically living together. They'll come up with all sorts of things."

"Oh, shut up," she grumbles, tugging her hand from mine to run her fingers through her hair. "I may have found that I don't really care what they all think. I know I said I wanted to keep this quiet, but it's not like that's possible. Like you said, we're practically living together. I'm sure they already think we're dating."

I pick my head up and my face splits into a full grin. "Dating, huh?"

She rolls her eyes, her hand waving away my words. "Seriously, you're going to piss me off and then you won't get laid."

"You remember the resistance you put up the last time you were angry, right?" I smirk and she huffs.

We may not be able to fuck our issues away, but it's a good way to kick the can down the road. If Kira had a choice, we'd pretend our problems didn't exist until I went back to Whispering Pines. I've been waffling—wanting her and wanting to protect her, regardless of her needing it. The jury's still out on whether I'll ever be good enough. I don't know if it was Ben's words or something else, but I'm done ignoring the parts of me screaming for her. Whether or not she recognizes the connection we have doesn't matter. She'll discover soon enough that there's more to this than tumbling into bed together.

My knee jiggles as nerves overtake me. "What happened at Alissa's? Why'd you run away?"

"Do we have—"

"Yes. Because you've been avoiding it all day."

"Me? *You* avoided it this morning when you busted into my shower," she snaps, and I chuckle.

"Touché. But you did refuse to talk about it while we were doing dishes."

I grin as her face reddens. One of my favorite things is riling her up. Her nose scrunches and her cheeks go pink. I don't really care if she brushed me off earlier. She jumps up and paces across the porch.

"We were in my parent's kitchen," she says through gritted teeth. "Did you honestly think I was going to spill all my wants and desires when anyone could have walked in?"

I push to my feet and step in front of her. She huffs, spinning away, and I grab her waist. I pull her back to my chest and dip my head until my lips skim along her soft skin. She melts into me, just like she always does. Might not be the best idea to get so close to her when we're trying to actually discuss shit. I'll end up fucking her against the door for everyone to see.

"We're not in your parent's kitchen anymore. So tell me, sunshine, what do you want?" I whisper in her ear, and her body trembles in my grasp. "Just one itty-bitty want."

"I want...I want..."

I straighten, hoping it'll help her focus. She could cop out and say she wants my cock. I wouldn't put it past her. It's not what I want, though. I want to know why she ran away, why she refuses to open up, why she's so effing scared of change. Pushing her might not be the best way.

I drop my hold and step back. "It's okay. We'll talk about it later."

She faces me, deep grooves between her eyes. I reach up and smooth her skin. She heaves out a deep breath and her lips purse.

"I'm sorry," she whispers, glancing away.

"You don't need to apologize. We'll go back to the way things were. No strings." I smile softly even as my chest aches.

Her lips part, but no words come out. My stomach tenses as magic builds in my gut. I crack my neck and shuffle back.

"Chase?" Kira's hand stretches out and I lean away.

"I'm fine. Just...I think I need..."

My body morphs, shifting while my cougar takes over. Not completely, but enough to shove me to the side. Before I know it, I'm blinking up at her with glowing eyes. Kira yelps, stumbling away. My cougar attempts to force us forward while I hold him back. I don't want to scare her. It wasn't like I was trying to shift.

A soft yowl leaves me, and Kira squeezes her eyes shut. My cougar whines in my head, but I don't know how to reassure him. It's not as if I'm going to attack her. He just wants to be closer to her. For some reason, he thinks if she smells him everything will be fine—all her walls will crumble.

"So, I'm not entirely sure what you want me to do right now. Do you need to frolic under the moonlight? Make a sacrifice to the dark watchers? Raid the leftovers back at the party?" She winces as she crouches. "I can't exactly go walking in with a coug—what the hell is that?"

Her gaze is fixed over my shoulder, and I glance behind me. The night is quiet, barely a breeze rustling the gold and orange leaves on the trees. My tail whips through the air as I face her once more. The end slams into the chair and I startle, leaping off the porch and hissing.

Usually, I'd be embarrassed, but my cougar takes over, scanning the area for threats. I prowl back up the steps and wind my way around Kira's legs. She's not exactly short, but my head sits above her elbow. I force her toward the door, hoping she'll take the hint and hide inside.

"Chase, stop. Nothing's out there. You need to shift. Now," Kira says as her hand skims behind my twitching ear. If she's looking to distract me, it's working.

My tail swishes back and forth, heavier than I remember. I push my head into Kira's stomach, silently begging her for something. My cougar is curled in the corner of my mind and purring. He's no fucking help, of course. I mentally flip him off. It's a strange sensation to know he's there, yet I'm unable to describe what it's like to have another entity residing in my head. I doubt anyone other than another shifter would understand it. Not that I'm about to go spouting off about who I am now.

"Kira?" Slade calls from behind me, and I tense. "Why the fuck is a sliver cat marking you?"

Chapter 24: Cryptids Galore

Kira

I scratch behind Chase's ears as he purrs at my feet. He refuses to shift, though I don't blame him. Slade started yelling shortly after he showed up, and it took a bit before Chase would stop guarding me. As it is, Slade's on a chair at the foot of the porch while I'm stuck by the door with Chase between us.

"Tell me again why you think he's a silver cat? He looks like a cougar, Slade. And he's been shifting for a year. Made shifters don't just morph into cryptids after they've already been changed." Exhaustion winds its way through my voice, and Chase lifts his head and his glowing eyes find mine.

Slade runs his hand through his hair. "Sliver. Not silver. I told you, Kira, I don't know. Alissa might. Or Dad. Since you refuse to call either one of them, you'll have to figure that shit out on your own. Or I'll do it after you leave."

Chase hisses at my brother, and I snort. At least Chase is still in control or I'm pretty sure Slade would have a few more scars riddling his body. He's got quite a few for being a shifter. We heal fast, but Slade found a way to get around all that when he was younger. He always said he lived hard so he could die easy. I still don't fully understand what he means.

"We'll tackle that last comment later, but what the hell is a sliver cat?"

He sighs, dropping his head in his hands. "For fuck's sake, Kira. Fine. I will explain again. A sliver cat is like a ball-tailed cat."

"Which doesn't fucking help," I murmur.

"Shut up and listen," Slade growls, and Chase's muscles bunch. I shush him, running my hands down his fur.

I raise an eyebrow at Slade and his fingers curl into fists. "Continue, Slade. Without the extra sass, please."

"They look like cougars. Sliver cats are a lot bigger, though. Usually, their tails are like over ten feet long. They have a ball on the end, hence why they're like ball-tailed cats. One side is smooth, one side has spikes. They hang out in trees and smack their victims, then pull them into their nest to eat them." He narrows his gaze at Chase. "He hasn't beat his tail against his chest, right?"

"I don't even think he *knew* he had a ball on the end of his tail until tonight. He didn't *have* one until tonight. I thought it was longer, but I wasn't really paying attention. Why does any of this matter? So he's a sliver cat. You practically shoved Gemma at a bigfoot shifter. They're both cryptids." I don't want to accuse Slade of being a hypocrite, but he sounds like a freaking hypocrite.

"Because they're dangerous," he explodes, jumping from his seat, which tips on its side.

Chase springs to his feet, the hair on the back of his neck standing on end. He snarls at Slade, who stumbles back and trips over the chair. A burst of laughter erupts from me, and I slap my hand over my mouth. Apparently sliver cats are protective. The thought warms me. Then I remember his comment about going back to no strings and a chill rolls down my spine.

I tilt my head and run my hand down Chase's tail until I reach the ball at the end. It quivers in my hold, but there aren't any spikes. Chase's ears twitch and a shudder ripples under his skin. I glance at Slade, and he scowls as Chase curls against me with his head in my lap.

"He sure seems real fucking dangerous. I'm so terrified right now," I deadpan.

Slade rights his chair. "And what happens when his shifter form takes over? Sure, he seems fine now, but he could switch at any minute."

I pull my lip between my teeth. He's not wrong, especially since I don't know the first thing about sliver cats. I was worried before since we didn't know how

Chase would react if his cougar was in control. Talking to Alissa is my first order of business.

Slade might know more about cryptids than anyone else, but it doesn't make him an expert on everything. He's quick to jump to conclusions until something comes along and challenges his perception. I'm sure it's kept him from getting killed. Doesn't help me now, though.

"Do you think he's completely morphed into a sliver cat? He doesn't have spikes," I murmur.

Slade drops into the chair and tips his head back. "I have no idea. Ask Alissa. Now, can we talk about where you're sleeping tonight?"

"I'm sleeping here. And so is Chase," I say, and his gaze meets mine. "I'm assuming you're going to be staying at home?"

"That hasn't been either of our homes for a while, Kira."

My hand stalls on Chase's head, though he doesn't seem to notice. "Then where are you sleeping?"

"Mom and Dad's. Just because it's not home doesn't mean I'm not crashing there."

"If it's not home, then where is?"

The corner of his mouth tips up. "Haven't found it yet. And neither have you."

I narrow my eyes, then glance up. "Uh, what would you call this?"

"A house, Kira. That's not a home." Slade's gaze dip to Chase. "And you know it."

He pushes to his feet and shoves his hands in his pockets. I'm surprised he's not arguing about Chase staying here. Then again, he doesn't usually get involved in the first place.

"Don't go gossiping about Chase to anyone," I snap.

"I swear to the goddess, Kira...fine. I won't tell Mom and Dad. But I still don't think you should be here alone with him."

"And I think you should keep your snout out of my business."

He huffs, rolling his eyes. He lifts his hand, and I sigh as he disappears into the night. I wonder if Chase wants to run. He's been dozing for a bit now. I wonder how much he'll remember of Slade's and my conversation. If his cougar—cat, whatever—was in control, I don't know what he noticed.

"You going to sleep at the end of my bed? Or are you going to shift back?" I ask, and he stretches.

He's definitely longer than he used to be. He almost takes up the entire width of the porch. His coat still looks like a cougar, though. If I didn't see his tail, I'd think he was just a big mountain lion. I wince as his claws come out. He yawns, his fangs glinting in the moonlight. I'm definitely not scared of him, but he isn't really aware of his new body. He almost took out the railing, the chair, and my ankle when Slade showed up.

I shove to my feet, my wolf stirring in my chest. She's been oddly silent through all of this. I'm not about to dive into that mess. She's been quiet for a while, letting me deal with the bullshit littering my life. I'm no closer to figuring out what the hell I'm doing than I was when Chase showed up. When I decided to get my shit together, I don't know. I was perfectly fine with the way my life was before he came to Moon Cove.

At least that's what I thought. I wouldn't have said I was happy. The night before Alissa left, she asked if I was. I didn't have an answer for her. I mumbled something about being content, but she didn't look like she believed me. Or maybe she was thinking about herself. I knew she wasn't happy here. None of my siblings were.

It wasn't that they didn't love Moon Cove or growing up here. There's just so much pressure to stay. In school, our teachers taught us about shifters who were exposed. They talked about the dangers of being caught. When Gemma had her incident in high school, they used it as a cautionary tale. I used to hide at the top of the stairs, listening to our parents talk about what it would mean for the family. Everything is safer in Moon Cove. The goddess protects us here.

Out in the world, though, was adventure. It was freedom. It was something *more*. One by one my siblings flew the nest, and I was the only one left. Abandoning my parents isn't an option. But this doesn't feel like home anymore. Slade was right—it hasn't felt like that for a long time. If only I could follow in my sibling's footsteps and find what I was looking for. Slade makes it seem easy, but who will my parents turn to when I'm gone?

Chase's head butts into my stomach and I jolt. I shouldn't be hanging out on my porch worrying about things I can't change. Moon Cove may not be home, but I can't leave. And I can't ask Chase to stay. He has a life back in Whispering Pines. Which is why this will never work out between us. We're too different—on separate paths that happened to converge at this moment in time. I wanted to enjoy this little slice of happiness. I wanted to live in this dream and pretend it was reality.

"Borrowed time," I whisper, shaking my head as I push inside.

"What's borrowed time?"

I yelp and spin around. "What the hell, man? This whole sneaking up on me thing is *not* going to fly. I don't even know how you do it."

"I wasn't sneaking. You told me to shift back, so I did." He gives me a lopsided grin.

"Do you remember anything?" I ask, even though I don't want to get into it right now.

"Oh, the whole Slade threatening to take you from me? Oh, and your defense of me? Yeah, I remember the important bits, sunshine." He kicks the door shut, a glint entering his eye.

I narrow my gaze as he crosses his arms, and ask, "What's with the look?"

"Nothing you need to worry about yet. Why don't we go to bed?"

"Yet?" I shake my head. "It doesn't matter. How much did you hear and understand?"

He sobers, though his grin stays in place. Most would probably think he's fine, but with the tightening around his eyes, I know he's not. I should drop it and let him deal with shit on his own. Didn't I just decide to relish this time and deal with the rest later? And here I am, pushing him to open up more. Then again, I should be able to separate teaching him and my feelings. I can't. Not even a little bit. What the hell is wrong with me?

"I heard it all. I heard I'm not a cougar shifter, but a cryptid. I heard I'm a sliver cat, though I don't know what the hell that is any more than you do. I heard when Slade told you to get away from me. And when he tried to get you to leave. Oh, and I heard when he said I was super dangerous and you shouldn't be alone with me." His body twitches, and I wonder if his tail would be lashing back and forth if he was shifted.

"We can talk to Alissa or Dad, if you want. Or you can. Whatever. I'm going to take a shower. Remember"—I point at him—"don't go out the windows. I'm not replacing the glass because you turned out to be a cryptid."

I'm halfway up the stairs when he chuckles, and I turn to glare at him. "Don't even think about ambushing me in the shower again."

He laughs as he holds his hands up in surrender. The glint is back in his eyes and I rush upstairs. Hopefully, I'll have time to wash my hair this time before he busts into the bathroom. His footsteps pound after me and an uncharacteristic giggle erupts from me. Worries of the future fall away as he growls behind me. We'll deal with it all tomorrow.

Chapter 25: Oh Shit
Chase

I probably should have figured out where the hell I was going before we shifted. Alissa's cabin in the woods doesn't show up on a map. Not that I can carry that while shifted. Glancing over my shoulder, I make sure Kira is still in sight. I shouldn't be leading anyway, but she refuses for some reason. She keeps circling back as if she's making sure no one is following us.

She's probably worried about Slade. He's been showing up the last couple days. Not that we've talked to him. We've been studiously ignoring everyone. It helps that the production crew showed up. It gave us an excuse to lay low. We probably should talk about where we go from here. With what I've figured out, I'm not entirely sure what we should do. I'm content to ignore the future for now.

Leaving in a few weeks won't be easy. My nose twitches as I pull her scent into my lungs. Before, I merely smelled some type of floral, but now there's fresh-tilled dirt and a hint of honey. Every time there's something new—another layer to her I've uncovered. I whip my tail through the air and knock a dead branch from the tree above me. If the thing gets much longer, I'm going to end up strangling myself with it.

Kira growls as she brushes against me. I gesture with my head for her to take the lead, and she shakes her fur out. I have no idea what that means. One of these days I'll have to read up on wolves and their movements. Even if she won't come back to Whispering Pines with me, the information will help me deal with

Gemma. We'll have to test the theory with someone other than Kira before I go home. My cat howls in my mind, and I dip my head, then shake it vigorously. He's been a little bitch ever since we morphed into a sliver cat.

Alissa's cabin comes into view and I huff, my breath hanging in the air. I didn't realize the temperature had dropped enough to see it. Alissa lifts her mug from her spot on the porch in greeting. I wonder if this is all she does. Then again, her cabin is stuffed with books so she probably reads a lot. As much as I enjoy my solitude, I don't know if I could go weeks without seeing another living being.

I should shift so I don't scare her, though the process still isn't pleasant. At least I'm not blacking out anymore. Nor am I in excruciating pain. Kira mentioned it could get better the more I shift. Which would be fine except with us cooped up in her small cabin, it's been a struggle. I found myself suddenly very grateful for the many beds stuffed in her living room, though. I was able to actually stretch out, which was nice.

"You two stalking me?" Alissa calls, and Kira huffs. "Don't get me wrong, it's nice to have a little company, but I get the feeling you're only here for information."

Kira shifts and twists her fingers together. "I figured you wanted to be alone. You *did* run here in the middle of the night without a word to anyone."

Alissa scoffs, then kicks her feet up on the railing. "Fair enough. You going to shift, big guy? I honestly don't think you'd fit inside as you are."

"It might take him a bit. He's still getting the hang of it," Kira says as she climbs the stairs. She drops into the chair next to Alissa.

"Is he bigger? I swear he didn't look like—oh. Oooh. Now I get why you're here."

"Yeah, there's been some...developments. Slade freaked out—wanted me to run to Mom and Dad's house. Something about him being dangerous because he's a—"

"Sliver cat," Alissa murmurs, pushing to her feet and makes her way to me. "I've never seen one before."

When she gets close, I snap at her outstretched fingers. She yanks her hand away while Kira busts out laughing. When I lope toward Alissa, she scrabbles back, her head whipping back and forth between Kira and me. I wanted to mess with her, but I don't want to scare her.

Gathering the magic within me, I nudge my cat curled up in the corner of my mind. He doesn't move, content to let me play. I growl at him, but the sound reverberates through the night, and Alissa squeaks while racing for the porch.

"Knock it off, Chase," Kira calls as she saunters down the stairs.

"Kira, I don't think he's in control."

"He's fine," she says nonchalantly, waving her hand.

She drops to her knees in front of me. I don't have a way to tell her it's not me, it's him. She smiles and her hands cup my cheeks.

"See? You're not scary, are you?" She drops her hands and glances over her shoulder. "He's him."

My cat finally decides to wake up and I shift, though I'm on my hands and knees. "The baby talk was a bit much, sunshine."

I push to my feet as she does. Alissa lets out a string of curses, then stalks into the cabin. I look to Kira for some direction. She sighs, her shoulders drooping. When she faces me, though, she smiles. It's not like the other ones—slightly forced and tired. It's softly radiant, like the sun piercing through the clouds after a rainstorm. It catches me off guard, and I suck in a sharp breath.

"Are you okay?" she asks, her brows pulling low.

"Yeah, sorry. Yeah." I run my hand through my hair. "Are we supposed to follow her?"

"Not entirely sure. Maybe we shouldn't test our theory tonight, though," she mumbles.

"What theory?" Alissa asks when she steps back outside with a stack of books.

Kira clears her throat. "We're just trying to figure out if Chase will stay in control around other shifters. We can ask Dad, though."

"Knock it off, Kira. The whole good girl act doesn't fit you well."

I lean in, my lips brushing Kira's ear as I murmur, "You're my good girl and fit perfectly."

Her elbow lands in my stomach, and I double over. She didn't hit me hard, but her elbows are bony. Kira saunters away from me, her hips swaying more than usual. If we weren't at her sister's, I'd throw her over my shoulder and fuck her against a tree again. The thought has heat flowing through my veins, and I swallow hard. I wonder if it's normal to want someone as much as I want her. It's not exactly something I can ask anyone. I don't even know how to describe the constant need she elicits in me.

"Uh, Kira? Did you break him?" Alissa asks, and I shake my head.

"Chase," Kira hisses, and I step toward them.

"I'm fine. Let's get this over with."

I don't really care what Alissa's books have to say. Honestly, I know everything I need to know. Whether I'm a sliver cat or a cougar doesn't really matter. Now that I'm no longer fighting with my shifter side, I'll be able to learn from him. We'll work on whatever we need to together. It hits me then and my feet stutter. I came to Moon Cove to learn how to shift without being a danger to anyone else. I've accomplished what I needed. Everything else I can learn at home.

My gaze rolls over Kira chatting with Alissa. She's the only reason I haven't left yet. Especially now. I don't want to leave her behind, but she's made it clear she's staying in Moon Cove. If this was a human relationship, we might be able to do long distance. I wasn't built for relationships. At least, that's what I thought. Until I met Kira.

"Chase, perhaps you'd like to be a part of this conversation? It is about you, after all." Alissa motions me forward, but I can't make my feet move. I cross my arms over my chest and wait.

Alissa glances at Kira, who shrugs. She's gotten used to the strange shit I've been doing the last few days. Or maybe she hasn't and just doesn't care. The thought sends an ache through my chest.

"Alrighty then. So, a sliver cat being followed by dark watchers might not be as bad as we think," Alissa says, thumbing through a book.

"Little flaw in your assessment, Alissa." I hold up my hand when Kira tries to interrupt. "The only time I've seen a dark watcher was with your sister. *She* has seen them twice, though. Unless there's times she hasn't told me about."

Kira scowls. "It doesn't make sense why they would show up now. I've been here my whole life. You, on the other hand, have been here less than a month. And you've morphed from a regular goddess-made shifter to a cryptid no one's seen in a century."

My head snaps to Kira. "A century? No shit?"

Alissa nods, tapping on the book. "According to this, yeah. At least that long. We thought they were extinct."

"Couldn't it just be like sasquatches?"

She's already shaking her head. "I don't think so. Bigfoots are rare and keep to themselves, but others still see them. This is more like dire wolves. Sliver cats are thought to be descended from mountain lions, or as you call them, cougars. There's no direct line known like there is from our family, though that could just be faulty record keeping."

Kira's teeth find her lip and she worries the flesh. My hands twitch with the need to ease her anxiety. I won't in front of her sister. We're still operating on the basis that no one knows we're sleeping together. I'd rather say we're dating or in a relationship. If I even think it, though, I'm afraid I'll blow my chance. Not that I have one at all.

Alissa's talking again, but I zone out, wondering how I can possibly convince Kira to give us a chance. She's perfected the art of ignoring the parts she doesn't want to think about. It doesn't help that she's wormed her way under my skin and I can't keep my hands off her. I thought being sequestered in her cabin the last few days would satiate my need to sink into her, but it hasn't.

"Well, if you think that's what needs to happen," Alissa says. "Chase, you good to shift again so soon?"

"You realize I might attack you, right?" I ask, and Kira joins her.

Alissa snorts, a smirk on her face. "As if you'd be able to—"

"He could," Kira mutters. "He's got spikes on one side of his tail now. And that shit hurts."

Alissa doesn't seem to be concerned, so I gather the magic again and shift in front of them. Alissa yelps and the noise echoes through the air, ringing in my ears. Kira's scent fills my nose once more, and I pounce away from them. I prowl back and forth on the edge of the tree line. Kira keeps wandering closer to me, which definitely doesn't help. I should have thought this through.

"Alissa, just fucking shift," Kira shouts.

Alissa rolls her eyes and in a blink she shifts. My cat shivers as Alissa's glowing eyes meet mine. He nudges my attention away, focusing on Kira. From what I can tell, he doesn't give two shits about the sister. He's too enamored with Kira. He purrs in my head, forcing us forward. It's not until I bump into Kira's stomach that he eases up. She huffs, but her fingers find my ear and a rumble pours from my throat.

Alissa's white wolf form inches closer, and I wind my way around Kira's body. Alissa freezes, then drops to her stomach and rests her head on her paws. I'm probably giving myself away, though maybe we can play it off as familiarity. We have been living together for a while now. Alissa's smart and probably figured it out already. Hell, she probably smelled it on us or something.

"Chase, it won't work if you don't go near her," Kira says as she looks down at me.

I can't pull my gaze away from her. My tail wraps around her legs, keeping her close to me. She presses her lips together as she fights a smile. I can't let her go. How am I supposed to leave my mate?

Chapter 26: Magic be Magicking

Kira

Chase took off for the trees ten minutes ago. Usually, I'd be worried, but he seemed like he needed to run. Since he morphed into a sliver cat, he hasn't had the chance. I don't know why, but over the last few days, I've been able to read him better when he's shifted. I haven't been worried about it. We have been spending a lot of time together.

"So we going to talk about all..." She waves her hand where Chase disappeared. "*That.*"

"Was there something specific you'd like to know?" I ask, then take a sip of the hot cocoa she brought me.

"Well, I'm not going to butt into your sex life—"

"Appreciate it."

"Okay, but you're sleeping with him. And he's leaving." She shoots me a look I don't want to decipher.

I take another drink to stall. I tried not to think about it. We have some time left before we have to tackle those issues. The last couple days have been bliss, though there's been a cloud hanging over everything. At least for me there has. Chase seems to be basking in finally settling into his new form and being himself. A calmness has come over him like he can see his future now. A future I'm not a part of.

"Are you coming to Samhain?"

Her eyebrow rises and she purses her lips. "Why?"

"Because if you are, we're going to need some ground rules before we talk about Chase." I don't think she'll blab to our parents, but Slade has a way of weaseling information out of us.

"I wasn't planning on it, but if you'd rather keep things under wraps, I won't say anything. Does that ease your worries?"

"Fine. We're doing the whole no-strings-attached thing. And we're sort of friends. So, I suppose friends with benefits? We haven't really talked about it lately. Although he did take me out one night. I don't think it was a date. Friends with benefits still go out for food, right? Actually, the more I think about it...we're living together. Temporarily, obviously. Is roommates to lovers a thing? You're the reader, so I figure you'd know better than me."

Her jaw drops the longer I ramble. This is why I didn't want to have a whole-ass conversation about Chase's and my relationship. I knew once I started talking about it, I'd have a hard time stopping. I've needed someone to confide in for a while. Like hell I'd open up to Slade. He's too quick with a joke, and he's a gossip. I don't have any other friends, really. They're more acquaintances who used to be friends.

"He seems to be coming into his own, though. So, he'll probably leave soon. Going back to Whispering Pines. Which has always been the plan, and I knew it was coming, and there's no reason he would stay here. Which is fine," I mumble.

"Uh, before you spiral, maybe you should breathe." She shoves my head between my legs.

"I said I was fine," I cry, struggling against her hold.

She snorts as she lets me go. "You seem like you don't want him to leave."

"We had a deal. *I'm* the one who set the ground rules. Why would I want to get tied down like that?"

Her eyebrows shoot up, and I glance out at the forest. Maybe I should go find Chase. I thought I needed to talk about this with someone, but I'm regretting it. I love Alissa. She's a bit too perceptive, though. She'll suss out some deep, dark secret I never wanted to reveal. Or she'll dig up my wants and desires, forcing me to face them.

Alissa tucks her legs underneath her. "You ever think—"

"I really don't want to talk about this."

"Course you don't. Because if you talked about it, you might have to face something you're not ready for."

I scowl, shaking my head. "It's not like we have a future."

"Unless he's your mate."

Immediately, my mind rejects the idea. Not only would it be unlikely due to our shifter forms, I'd know. I would have felt it the moment we met. At no point did I think there was something more between us. Sure, I wished we could see where this thing between us goes, but that doesn't mean we're mates. I gave up on that dream a long time ago.

Dad kept saying someone might come through I hadn't met yet and I shouldn't give up. Now that I'm in my thirties, I knew it wasn't meant to be. Most of us never find our fated mates. Mom and Dad, Jake, and Gemma—they're unicorns among shifters.

"We're not fated," I say finally. An ache blooms in my chest, resonating through me. A low tone reverberates through the trees, deep and mournful. I swear magic floats along the sharp breeze, and I wonder what the hell is coming.

Alissa scrambles to her feet and races inside. I try to follow her, but my legs won't move. In fact, I can't move at all. Anxiety bubbles in my gut as I scan the forest, hoping Chase will appear. If he's out there with whatever threw magic into the world, he might be hurt. He might be caught up in it. I don't even know if dark watchers have magic.

My heart thunders in my ears, blocking out the sound as Alissa reappears. She drops a heavy tome on the small table between our chairs and flips through the pages. I hardly think now is the time for a little light reading. I hate I can't even make the quip. It's a lost opportunity. Not that I should be worried about something as trivial as a comeback.

"Oh no," Alissa breathes, then spins around and cups her hands around her mouth. "Chase!"

She shouts his name over and over until his form bounds from the trees. As soon as he comes into sight, my body relaxes. His muscles ripple as he pounces over the railing and onto the porch. Alissa yelps as she stumbles away, and Chase knocks over her chair and the table along with the stack of books she had piled up. Nothing touches me as if he knows exactly where I am without even looking. His tail wraps around me and he crouches, scanning the forest.

"What the hell, Chase? You broke my chair," Alissa cries as she grabs the books.

"Shift, Chase, or she might beat you with one of the broken slats of wood."

There's plenty of magic for him to draw from and he shifts. There's still a disgruntled look on his face as he scans the trees. My hand brushes his arm and he whips around.

"What's wrong?" he demands.

"Nothing. Just some weird magic floating around. Alissa freaked out a little, is all. Do you need to go back out?" My eyes flick to Alissa, but she's too busy grumbling under her breath to notice.

"No, I need to know what the hell just happened," he growls and turns to Alissa.

"Uh, well. I just..." Alissa presses her lips together and shakes her head. "Maybe *now* isn't the time to talk about it. But I do have a book for you that might be helpful."

I push to my feet. "What book?"

Alissa waves her hand dismissively. "Just one about cryptid shifters and all of that. I'm sure you would find it immensely boring."

She hands Chase the thick book, and I bite back the urge to demand answers. If this really is about Chase and his new form, I should be patient. I definitely shouldn't pry into something he might not want to tell me. It still hurts she isn't willing to give me even a little heads-up. And from the way Chase is staring at the book, I doubt he will either.

"Chase, go get the rest of my table you raged your way through. It's over there in the yard," Alissa says, pointing toward the forest.

He lopes down the stairs, and Alissa rushes toward me. She envelops me in a hug, though I can't remember the last time we did something like this. It's not unpleasant, but I'm a little taken aback.

"Uh, you okay?" I murmur as she clings to me.

"Don't be afraid," she whispers.

"Afraid of what?"

"The whole 'not being able to move' thing. It's natural. And while I can't explain because it's definitely not my place, I just need you to be open. Stop denying yourself happiness." She drops her hold on me, then shoves me toward the stairs. "Go away. I moved into the forest so I wouldn't have to see people, and you two are becoming a problem."

I stumble to Chase's side and glance back at my sister. She's already flouncing her way inside, and she slams the door after her. Chase drops the broken wood next to the porch and turns.

"That was weird, right?" he asks.

"Definitely weird. Then again, Alissa and I haven't spent a lot of time together. She was too young when I was a teenager and by the time we grew up, we were too engrossed in our own lives to really notice anything else around us."

Her living room window slides open. "Seriously, get the hell out of here. Don't come back for at least a week." She slams the sash shut once more.

"Guess that's our cue," Chase mutters. "You good to shift or are we doing this the hard way?"

"Let's walk a bit first. At least get out of her line of sight before she starts throwing eggs at us or something."

His fingers lace with mine, and he tugs me toward the trees. He walks with confidence as if he knows exactly where he's going. I'm content to let him lead, at least for a bit. I open my mouth several times, but I never know how to start the conversation we clearly need to have. I settle on the one subject that's not personal. At least for us.

"Shifting seems to be getting easier."

He grunts, squeezing my fingers. I glance at him from the corner of my eye. His gaze darts around as if he's waiting for something to jump out at us. My wolf doesn't seem concerned with anything. The strange magic from before dissipated as soon as Chase appeared. The apprehension I've felt the last two times I ran into the dark watchers is nowhere to be found. I can't figure out why he's so on edge.

"Did you see something out here when you were running?" I ask.

"No," he snaps, though there's no heat behind his words.

"Well, you seem like something's eating at you."

I'm so focused on him, I don't notice the hole in front of me and my foot falls right into it. I crash to my knees, my hand ripping from his. He growls, pouncing over me, and he covers my body with his own. A low rumble rolls around me, and I yelp when a rock bites into my palm.

"Chase, stop. It's just a hole," I cry, though it's muffled.

He eases back and snatches at my wrist. He examines the wound, which is already closing. I squeeze my eyes closed and focus on shifting my sight. I should have done it when we stepped out of the circle of light at Alissa's cabin. For some reason, I forget the most mundane things when he's around. It's as if my wolf just dips when he's beside me. As if she sees it as his job to protect me instead of her. The more time we spend together, the worse it gets. She'd better figure shit out pretty quickly, though.

Chase glances up and he jerks back. "Sorry. Your eyes are glowing. I wasn't expecting that. I forgot you can partially shift."

I tug my foot from the hole and brush the dirt from my shoe. "I don't do it often unless I'm in the dark or digging in my garden. It's not actually all that useful any other time."

"Except it could come in handy if you're ever attacked. Like by a stair or a hole." He grins as he helps me to my feet. Whatever funk he was in before seems to have broken. I'm not going to question it.

"Turns out I don't need to fear the stairs anymore now that you're there to save me from them," I quip.

His grin fades the slightest bit, and I kick myself for saying anything. He doesn't take my hand this time as he walks through the trees. It takes me a second to catch up to him. I don't know what the hell is going through his head. Given the way he's reacting, I'm not sure I want to know.

Trudging after him, I keep my eyes on the ground. I don't want to trip and have him feel the need to save me again. I used to be independent. I didn't need anyone around to make me feel like what I was doing mattered. Not that I felt like it did, anyway. Praise wasn't something I sought out. I just need to remember how to function without Chase. I didn't think I was in danger of falling for him, and it happened. Feeling like I needed him wasn't even on my radar. And I don't. If I keep telling myself that, I might be able to go on with my life when he's gone.

Chapter 27: Good Boy

Chase

I shouldn't be ignoring Kira. With every step I'm hurting her, and I know it. I can't seem to make myself stop, though. If I do, I'll end up ravishing her in the trees. I'd shift and put us both out of our misery, but I'm not sure I'd be entirely in control.

My cat stirs in my head, screaming for attention. No, screaming for her. As soon as Alissa called my name—as soon as I got back to Kira—I knew something was wrong. My cat hasn't shut the fuck up since. He's been yowling for the past hour for me to shift. I can't trust that he won't take over and mount her. I don't even know if that's the right way to say it.

"We need to shift. We can't walk all the way ho—back, Chase."

My feet stutter to a stop beside a small creek. It takes me a minute to figure out this isn't the same one we came upon before. I wonder how many streams litter this mountain. I swallow hard as Kira's scent washes over me. If she comes any closer...

I crouch and splash water on my face. It doesn't help the flames burning their way through my body. My cock hardens and I bite back a groan. I don't want to hurt her feelings, but I can't take it anymore when she sits next to me and sighs. Our eyes meet in the dark and she licks her lips, a questioning look on her face.

My hand seizes the back of her neck, and I slam my mouth to hers. Her yelp is lost in a moan as I devour her, sweeping my tongue inside. When she whimpers, I'm completely lost. The next few minutes are a rush of wandering hands and clothes flying in every direction. When she falls onto her ass, a giggle erupts from her, capturing a piece of me I never knew existed.

When she tries to scramble upright, I yank her toward me. Gripping her hips, I dig my fingers into her flesh. Her head tips back as the scant moonlight reflects off her skin—a fucking vision of perfection given form. She'd never believe me if I told her how goddamn beautiful she looks in this moment.

I pick her up and slam her onto my cock, and our groans mingle together in the space between us. I'll never get used to how it feels to be inside her. No matter how many times, it's always an intoxicating experience. Her pussy spasms around my length and she whimpers, her forehead hitting my shoulder.

When I lie back, she braces herself on my chest and rolls her hips. Usually, I'm the one to take control. She melts under my touch, obeys every command I give. Tonight, I need her too much to demand anything but her pleasure. She can take from me what she needs and I'll gladly give it all. Everything I have is hers already.

"Ride me, sunshine. Take what you want," I murmur.

She rocks her hips back and forth. I keep my hold on her waist until she grabs my wrists and forces me to cup her tits. They're heavy and perfect. Rolling her nipples between my fingers, I watch her face. Desire shoots through me as a bolt of ecstasy hits her. I'll never tire of watching her lose herself in my body.

Slowly, she lifts to her knees, then sinks down on me again. Her head tips back, golden hair cascading behind her. A flush crawls up the long column of her neck and the urge to wrap my fingers around her throat has me dropping my hands to her thighs. Sitting back and letting her control things is freeing, but also difficult. Part of me wants to flip her over and bury my cock into her hard and fast.

Her eyes meet mine, and electricity fills the air. Her lips part as her pussy envelops my length again and again. I thrust into her, unable to stay still. She feels too good. She shudders, euphoria cascading across her face. A growl rips through me as she flutters around my cock.

I flip us around so she's underneath me. I forget how fast I am these days. Kira doesn't seem to notice as she arches her back. Her hands slide up my arms, and I bury myself into her, then stop. Her nostrils flare as I smirk, wondering if I can get her to beg for another orgasm. She smiles sweetly before her fingers find my throat. She squeezes and I suck in a sharp breath.

She bares her teeth. "Be a good boy and fuck me. Now."

A shiver rolls through me, and I duck my chin to my chest. "Yes, ma'am."

I surge into her as a desperate need to please her overtakes me. My muscles bunch as I thrust into her, her moans mingling with mine. As my movements become erratic, she flexes her fingers on my throat. When her hand slides to the back of my neck, I grunt. She pulls me down and our lips collide. I groan into her mouth as she pulses around my cock. Her orgasm triggers my own, and I shudder out my release.

Our harsh breathing fills the space between us and I close my eyes, attempting to slow my racing heart. I bury my face into her neck, soaking in the tranquility settling over us.

"Move," she gasps, and I rear back. "There's a rock."

She winces as she writhes underneath me. I grunt as her hips rock against me, and I pull away. She rolls to her side and curls into a ball. A red mark stands out on her skin, though it fades in front of my eyes. Once again, her scent washes over me and my cock hardens. I didn't use to be able to recover so soon. Since I met Kira, I feel like I'm constantly horny. At least when she's around. I wonder if it's a mate thing.

I lean down and press my lips to the mark. Goosebumps scatter across her skin, and I skim my fingers up her side. She huffs, turning her head to glare at me.

"If you're gunning for round two, you should think again," she snarls.

I grin, then lean down and nip at her ribs. She swats at my head and I chuckle. Helping her to her feet, I sober. The connection between us is enough to distract me, but as soon as it's broken, the doubts return.

We need more than sleeping together. More than my issues with shifting. More than our forced proximity. Every time I try to build something more, though, she pulls away. She may get sucked in for a moment, yet she always comes to her senses. Something holds her back and I'm afraid it's her family.

If that's the case, I'll lose every time. I wouldn't even show up if it was a fight between them and me. I may not know what it's like to have a family like hers, but I can see how important they are to her. Forcing her to choose would only shove her further away. Plus, I'd rather join them than take her from them. It doesn't matter either way.

Kira gathers her clothes and tugs them on. I follow her lead, swallowing all the words I want to say. She turns to me, a challenge hanging in her eyes. I shift before she can bombard me with questions I'm not ready to answer.

"Well, at least you didn't actually run away," she mutters, then shifts as well.

It takes less time to get back to her cabin than before. I almost stopped at the outcropping, but Kira ran ahead of me. When we reach the edge of the forest, she skids to a stop and shifts.

"I wouldn't go walking through town like that unless you want people asking questions," she says. "We should probably tell Dad, though."

I shuffle back into the shadows of the tree. My cat hisses at me, trying to force me to shift. He's walking a fine line between wanting to claim her and wanting to ravish her. I don't really understand the difference, but he's not exactly in the right headspace. I gather the magic and shift. My head twitches without warning, and I shut my eyes.

She turns as soon as I step from the woods. I need to get my shit together before I lose her completely. I'm fucking this up and I can't seem to stop myself. As soon as her cabin comes into view, Slade bounds around the corner. The last thing I want to do is talk to him. He clearly doesn't like me. Nothing I can do about that.

Slade grabs Kira's arm, and my feet stutter to a stop. The need to rip his hands from her overwhelms me before I remind myself, and my cat, that they're related, and she's not in danger. I'm not getting involved with their sibling spat. Their dynamic doesn't make sense to me. Then again, neither does hers and Alissa's. Envy bubbles in my gut and I shove it away.

"Chase. A word?" Ben calls from behind me.

Sighing, I pivot and make my way toward him. He's already wandering off, headed for the lake. I follow him, wondering if I'm about to get a talking to. My stomach flips, nerves running rampant through me.

"I heard I may have upset you at the party. It wasn't my intention," he says when we stop at the shore. "Don't be upset with Kira. She didn't want us to worry."

"I wasn't going to shift in the middle of the party. I'm sorry I caused a scene, sir." I tuck my trembling hands in my pockets to hide them.

"Is that what you got from that?" He shakes his head. "We were worried about *you,* Chase. I don't mean to upset you again. We wouldn't want you to hole yourself up in Kira's cabin for another two days."

He thinks I disappeared because of him. "She didn't tell you?"

"Kira merely told me it wasn't you almost shifting at the party. She didn't want us to think it was our fault, either. She doesn't tell us your secrets. And you're not required to say anything either." He tucks his hands behind him and rocks back on his heels.

"Do you know what a sliver cat is?"

When he raises an eyebrow, I continue, explaining everything we've learned. I'm surprised Slade didn't out me to them. Ben doesn't interrupt me, thankfully. I don't know if I'd get through it all if he did. I don't want to throw Alissa under the bus, or Slade, but I tell him most of what we've learned and where the information came from.

"Is Alissa okay?" he whispers, emotion making his voice hoarse.

"She seems good. Maybe a little lonely, but she did say she needed it."

He clears his throat. "If you see her again, please tell her I'd like to see her at Samhain. She's never missed one, and I'd hate for us to be the reason she stays away."

"I don't think you're the reason—"

He holds up his hands, halting my reassurances. "I'm well aware of the dynamics of my family. I'm also aware of why each of my children left. It's hard to balance keeping the community running and safe while raising kids to feel comfortable enough to make their own decisions. Gladys and I did our best, but I'm afraid some of them think we wanted them to stay in Moon Cove."

"Didn't you? Gemma seems to think Gladys wants her back so she'll stay here." I shouldn't stick my nose into their business, but I doubt Gemma will ever say anything.

He sighs, glancing over his shoulder at Kira and Slade. "We miss her. And we were worried. She was out in the world with people who didn't understand what she is. Being a shifter in the human world isn't as easy as you'd think. She insisted on going to the bigger cities, which makes things even harder on her. My wife may not have gone about it in the right way, but we just want to see her. It's hard for us to get away."

I'm not about to tell him how to navigate his relationship with his children. Hell, I'm the last person someone should take advice from on that front. The more I learn about the Livias, the more I realize how devoid of love my own family was. I was there because my parents were expected to produce an heir. Once they did their duty, I was an afterthought. At least that's how it felt. Being raised by nannies and butlers and housekeepers was normal for me.

"I appreciate you taking me in. Teaching me what I needed to know."

"I get the feeling there's more to those statements beyond mere words of gratitude. I won't push you, though." Ben turns and claps me on the shoulder. I swear if he calls me son again, I might break down.

"What about Kira?" I ask before he can walk away.

"What about her?"

"Does she want to stay here?"

He studies my face, and I struggle to keep my face neutral. "You'd have to ask her that. Although, for the right person..."

He walks away, and I duck my head to my chest, breathing through the anxiety threatening to pull me under. I shouldn't have asked him in the first place. Kira and I will need to talk—sooner rather than later. Once we do, though, I'm afraid I'll be going home much sooner and completely alone.

Chapter 28: Lone Wolf

Kira

"You going to tell me what Slade was bitching about?" Chase asks, and I sigh.

I'd really rather not since most of it had to do with family drama. Between Gemma shacking up with her mate and Alissa running off into the woods, we haven't talked about the others lately. I didn't forget them, though Slade accused me of it. He seems to think our family is falling apart. And it's apparently all my fault.

"Just family stuff," I mutter as I search through my cupboard for something to eat.

Chase's warmth presses into my back, trapping me against the counter. I expect him to box me in with his arms on either side of me. Instead, one hand grips my hip and the other wraps around my waist. His fingers dip under the hem of my shirt and skim across my skin. He kisses his way up my neck, and I tilt my head.

"You can tell me, you know. I'm a good listener."

My shoulders slump and I tuck my chin to my chest. I can't talk to Slade about this, and I wouldn't dare to put this on my parents. If I talk to anyone in town, it'll only start rumors and we have enough of those to deal with at the moment.

"Slade just told me about what the others are doing. Our siblings. You know he went to visit Gemma?"

"I didn't, though I haven't spoken to Jake lately."

I turn around and he drops his hold on me. "Why not?"

He smirks, though it doesn't take over his face like usual. "I've been a bit busy. Besides, we're not talking about me right now."

He grabs a bag of chips before tugging me toward one of the beds stuffed in the corner of the living room. It's situated by the window, letting the moonlight in. I don't know why he's so enamored with the many mattresses strewn across my space. He barely ever sits on the couch anymore. Usually I'd question him, but I doubt he'd answer. He's determined to keep the focus on me.

"Alright, spill," he says as he settles against the window and pulls me to him.

My back rests against his chest and he plops the chips in my lap. "Well, you know about Gemma, but apparently I'm a dick for not calling her. Slade isn't happy Alissa won't come home. He thinks she's going to get eaten by a bear or something. Eli, he's the youngest, isn't picking up the phone. He was supposed to come home at Samhain and stay through winter. Might not happen now. When I asked if Mom and Dad were worried, he didn't answer."

"Sounds like *he's* worried," he murmurs.

"He is, but he's being a turd about it. For some reason, he thinks I should go after Eli. As if I know where he is. Then there's Sloane and Alister, both of whom are quite capable of taking care of themselves. Slade thinks it falls on us—or rather me to save everyone."

"Where are they? Or are they in the wind like Eli?" He reaches around me and shakes the bag. As if I'd munch on them while having a conversation.

"Alister took to the high seas. Whatever that means. Maybe he wants to become a pirate." I snort, imagining him shifting while on a ship. Maybe he'll find a mermaid out there to fall in love with. "Sloane...she took a job in another shifter community. They're more closed off than Moon Cove, apparently. Slade thinks they're holding her hostage."

It's the bare minimum I can give him. Slade doesn't care whether I have anything going on here, despite his pep talk a few weeks ago. He probably thought telling me to spread my wings was a good idea at the time. Then Mom complained about something or he talked to one of the siblings and lost his shit. Either way, it's now my problem. Because I'm the one who fixes everything for everyone.

"Maybe you should call them. Then he might get off your back?" He says it more like a question rather than a statement, and I sigh.

"Yeah, sure." I scoot away from him, and he tugs me back.

"Oh no. You're not getting away with that. What's wrong with my advice?"

I snatch at the bag of chips and throw it against the wall, snarling. I yank away from Chase and spin on my knees. He holds up his hands as I glare at him. Concern rests in his eyes, and my anger bleeds away. I slump and his hands cup my cheeks, forcing me to meet his gaze. When he smiles, it's like my heart is being ripped from my chest. He's too fucking good for someone like me. Why he sticks around is beyond me. He should have run for the hills the minute we crossed paths.

"Sorry. You're right. Calling them isn't bad advice. I just doubt they'll answer me. And Slade…" I pull from his grasp and run my hand through my hair. "Slade will probably blame me, then take off again. He seems to think because he always comes back, he's doing his duty to the family. And I'm supposed to take his place when he's gone. Like an interim president or something. It's fine. I'm used to it."

"I'm going to ask you a question and I need you to really hear it before you blow up at me. Or jump my bones." He chuckles, and I give him a look. "Seems like every time we start talking, I end up buried in your pussy."

My cheeks heat and I glance away. It's one thing when he says shit like that when we're naked. It's entirely different when we're clothed. I don't consider myself a prude, but I never know what to say.

"Anyways." I pull the word out, scrambling to remember what we were talking about. "What's your question?"

He sucks in a deep breath as if bracing himself for my reaction. "What do you want?"

My mind blanks as I stare at him. "With what?"

He sighs, running his hand through his mussed hair. "Let's start with your family. What kind of relationship do you want with them? Do you *want* to be the person they run to when there's a problem?"

"No," I blurt out, then snap my mouth shut. "I don't mind it. I like helping my family. They're...they're my family. I love them. I just didn't think I'd be the one who had to keep everything together. It's hard. And stressful."

He laces our fingers together and stares at them while whispering, "Would you leave if you could?"

"I can't."

"But if you could."

I'm already shaking my head before he's finished. "You don't understand, Chase. It's out of the realm of possibility. My parents are the leaders of Moon Cove. Oh, people will tell you we make decisions by council, but ultimately, my parents are the ones they all look to. My family has run the general store for decades. We're the ones who generate the most income for the town. We're the last founding family. If we fail, Moon Cove fails."

"I hear a lot of 'we,' but no 'I.' You're not responsible for their success or failure. Why do you think you're the only one responsible for the town?"

I pull my hands away. "I never said I was. But I'm a part of this family. I'm not abandoning them because it's a little hard. You wouldn't understand."

His brows pull low, and he glances out the window. "Maybe we should make some food. You want pasta?"

He scrambles off the bed before I can answer. I don't know why he's so set on fixing me. It might not be his intent, but it sure as hell feels like it. Chase is constantly asking me how I feel, what I want, where I'm going.

Next, he's going to badger me about my hopes and dreams. He'll be sorely disappointed when he realizes I don't have any. I used to, way back when. And then I grew up and figured out dreams were for those with wings. Like Gemma and Eli going off to college. Like Alister, finally making a move. Like Slade, who never stops moving. They have dreams and they're going after them, even if they never reach them.

Explaining to Chase that I'm not like them...it would be embarrassing. It would be devastating. Because I'm supposed to be content. I'm supposed to be happy. I fucking chose this life. Gemma asked if I wanted to go with her when she left. I scoffed and walked away. I couldn't go with her then. We were at each other's throats half the time while growing up. We never would have survived being cooped up in a tiny dorm room for months on end. And she would have come home. At the first sight of hardship, she would have convinced me to bring her back, and I couldn't let that happen. I never was good at telling her no, despite what the others thought—what Chase thinks still.

I only wanted what was best for my siblings, and I did everything in my power to give them exactly what they needed. If it was at the sacrifice of my own desires, so be it. At the end of the day, at least I can say I accomplished something. I paved the way for them to go. It's a strange position to be in. Alister and Sloane are both older than me. They should have been the ones to take the reins. Alister, as the oldest, should be taking over the family business. Sloane should be the one leading the town. She would be amazing at it.

"Shit. I'm going to be fucking terrible at this," I mutter.

Chase calls my name from the kitchen, and I glance over my shoulder. "Food's up."

If he heard me, he doesn't comment, just sets the bowl of reheated pasta on the island and dishes up his own plate. We'll end up eating in silence and I'll hate every fucking second of it.

I feel like I did something wrong. Like by opening up to him, I've ruined everything. Which shouldn't matter, given our circumstances, but it does. I can feel it in my bones. Deep down, I know I'm losing him with each moment that passes by. Except I never really had him. He was a distraction from my routine. I don't believe the lie anymore.

I make my way to the kitchen and pick up the fork. I was hungry before, but now my stomach is in knots. He leans against the counter, eyes fixated on his food. The pasta was good when he made it last night. Now it tastes like dust. Regardless, I force it down before giving up halfway through. There's no reason to keep the rest, and I scrape it into the trash. He doesn't comment.

"I'm going to shower," I mutter.

He grunts, still focused on his food. I hesitate, hoping he'll say something. He doesn't, because of course he doesn't. I trudge upstairs and quietly shut the bathroom door. Our conversation runs through my head on a loop as I search for where I went wrong. Sure, I blew up a little, but it wasn't because of him. And I apologized. He didn't seem upset about my outburst.

My forehead hits the wall as the spray hits my back. I wish I was like everyone else. I'm sure others aren't taking a scalding hot shower hoping the water burns away their feelings. They all seem perfectly normal and content. They're not repeating conversations in their heads over and over until they find where they went wrong. Probably because they know what to say. They don't have to pick their words so they don't piss someone off accidentally.

Tears streak down my face, mingling with the water. I wish I could fix whatever's wrong with me. Instead, I wipe the wetness away and turn the knob. I dry off and pretend everything is fine. If I fake it long enough, eventually the world will right itself. Chase will leave. I'll take over my parent's store. I'll dig in my garden and shift when I need to and hold myself and everyone else together. And I'll be fine. Everything will be fine.

Chapter 29: Put the Claws Away, Sunshine

Chase

I should be planning when I'll leave. Instead, I've thrown myself into helping Ben get ready for Samhain. The town apparently takes things very seriously. Whispering Pines has a small-town celebration, but it's nothing compared to Moon Cove. I suppose being a shifter community helps. With the added stress of the production company in town, I couldn't let Ben shoulder it all alone.

Kira has been busy helping her mom, but I'm pretty sure she's avoiding me. After she finally opened up to me the other night, I thought we would get somewhere. We didn't and I'm pretty sure it's my fault. When she told me I wouldn't understand what she was going through, it hurt. I thought she was right and I couldn't understand the pressure she was under. Except I do. It might be different since Kira actually loves her family. Still, I get the demand of familial obligation weighing me down.

So much was expected of me growing up because of my last name. It was a given I would carry on the family name, take over the business, and walk the path my parents paved for me. Except I never wanted any of that. Money couldn't buy my parent's love, though they thought it would keep me in line. I toed the line long enough and then they were gone. The business was sold, the assets went into a trust, and I disappeared from elite society. I left everything behind for Whispering Pines. It took a long time to buy the land and build my cabin. As soon as it was inhabitable, I moved in and never looked back. Most of all, I never regretted it.

If my parents had lived, I'd probably be living a very different life. Instead of a t-shirt and jeans, I'd be in a suit. Instead of helping set up a stage in the middle of tourist central, as Gladys calls it, I'd be stuck in a boardroom. Instead of sleeping next to Kira every night, I'd go back to a penthouse alone. I'd be a regular human without a hint of the shifter world. My cat hisses in my head and I wince. Apparently, I'm not the only one who doesn't enjoy thinking about what could have been.

"Chase, can I have a word?" Slade says from behind me, and I glance over my shoulder.

The last thing I want to do right now is have a conversation with him. He clearly doesn't like me. Before, I thought it was just because I morphed into a sliver cat. Seems hypocritical since he's friends with Jake, who is clearly a cryptid being a bigfoot shifter. Now I wonder if it's because of how Kira acts around me. I'm sure to Slade, she seemed enamored with me while I was shifted.

"What can I do for you, Slade?" I ask as I tighten one of the screws on the stage.

"Probably should apologize," he mutters, stepping up next to me.

"Go on then."

He runs his hand through his dark hair and sighs. "I'm sorry I insulted you."

I dust off my hands and face him. "You didn't insult me. Your bias doesn't matter to me. I'm not the one who deserves your apologies, anyway."

He has the good grace to look ashamed. I press my lips together, trying to keep my judgements to myself. Butting into their sibling relationship would be the start of a shitshow. The need to protect my mate overrides my good sense.

"When are you leaving?" he asks, raising an eyebrow.

I cross my arms and dig my nails in to keep myself from punching him. "Haven't decided yet. Maybe I'll stick around."

"That would be unwise. You've got a whole life halfway across the country. Not much for you here." He narrows his eyes as if challenging me to deny it.

I don't bother responding. I can't tell if he's trying to goad me into reacting or confessing. He's not going to get either. Maybe he thinks if he's enough of a dick, my emotions will bubble over and force me to shift. I don't know why he'd want that since it'll wreck everything and piss off everyone. He wouldn't sabotage his parents just to get me out of here. At least I don't think he would.

His nostrils flare, and a flush spreads up his neck. "You need to stay away from my sister. She's already in too deep and if you drag her down more, she'll never recover. I'll drag your ass into the forest and bury you so fucking far into the ground even the goddess won't be able to find your goddamn body."

"You sure have a funny way of showing you care for your sister," I murmur.

He steps into my space, trying to force me back. "What the hell is that supposed to mean?"

"Slade Camden Livia," Kira shouts from behind me, and Slade jolts.

His brows pull low as he studies me. Maybe I should have reacted when she approached. Except I knew she was there. It's why I didn't punch him or yell back. I could feel her presence, and I wonder if it's a mate thing. I wish I could ask someone, but all the people who would know are connected to Kira. Even Jake is compromised. He'll spill the beans to Gemma, who will call one of her family members, and it'll be speculation at the next family dinner.

Kira pushes between us and stabs her finger into Slade's chest. Her claws come out and Slade winces. He has the good sense to not move. I'm sure she'd chase him if he ran away. Shit would be so much worse for him then.

"Why the hell are you harassing him? You're being a goddamn asshole to everyone around you, but especially to him, and I want to know why," she demands.

Slade's face turns stormy. "Everything was fucking fine until *he* showed up."

"You can't really be that naive, Slade. Chase is—"

"He's what?" Slade sneers.

Her shoulders tense. "He's a shifter. Just like you and me. And he's kind and accepting, unlike you."

"He's a problem and no one seems to care!"

"He's the problem? *He's* the problem?" she growls. "You're the problem, Slade. You blow into town and start bossing everyone around. You think you're the smartest person in the room when really you're just an insecure little boy who's still searching for a purpose in life. Worry about your own damn life before you start butting into mine."

"At least I'm not—" He bares his teeth as if biting back his words.

"Go ahead. Say it," she taunts.

I slip my arm around her waist and tug her back. "Put the claws away, sunshine. People are watching."

Her body melts into mine, and she lets me push her around him. Slade tilts his head as we leave, and I wonder if I've given myself away. He looks like he's trying to solve a mystery where the pieces hang just out of reach. Thankfully, Kira is too worked up to even notice.

"I don't know what the hell happened to him," she growls as I pull her around the corner of the general store. She shakes me off, then stomps toward the back door.

"Let's get inside and then you can rage at me," I say softly, guiding her inside.

"Why the fuck would I rage at you? I'd rather punch him in the balls. Maybe that'll take him down a peg or two," she snarls.

I shut the door to the large storeroom behind us and lean against it. "Which is exactly why you're going to take it out on me instead of him. I'm sure he'd like to keep both his balls in working order."

She lets out a sharp laugh. "I'm not going to take my anger out on you. I can't fucking believe him. He just accosted you in the middle of the damn street. What the hell was he thinking? You weren't even behind the boundary. Anyone could have heard him. Not only that, but he was *way* off base."

She paces back and forth, throwing her hands up and muttering. I watch her for a while, letting her get it all out of her system. Nothing I say will make it better, anyway. She needs to work through everything running through her mind before she can open up. Hopefully, she won't shut down again. I'm determined not to walk away like I did the other night.

I clear my throat when she seems to settle. "I'm not concerned with Slade's opinion of me, Kira."

"That's not the point," she snaps, riling herself up again. "For some reason, people listen to him. They care what he has to say. Usually, I don't give a shit because he's often spot on, but he's way off base here."

"You said that before," I murmur.

"Well, maybe I'll just scream it from the rooftops. He's *way* the fuck off base. He pops up, stirs shit up, and blows out of town again. I don't understand why he's so set against you. It's not like you're an asshole or trying to change shit. In fact, when Gemma asked if you could come, Slade said it was a great idea. What the hell changed?" She stops and faces me, eyes pleading for an answer I don't have.

I pull in a deep breath. "I morphed into a sliver cat. When I was a cougar, I wasn't a threat. Now I am. He's just trying to protect his family."

"But you're not a threat," she cries, throwing up her hands.

"Except we don't know that. I've only shifted around you and Alissa. Take you out of the equation and we have no idea how I'd react. And we were worried about it, too." Logic may not be the best way to talk her down, but I'd rather she not partially shift in the middle of the room. "How do you bring your claws out? And why are they longer than when you're a wolf?"

"What? That's what you want to focus on right now?" She huffs, running her hands through her hair. "Fine. I don't know why they're longer. They top out about four inches."

I grin and grab her waist to reel her into me. She settles between my legs, resting her hands on my chest. "So you're saying you're like bionic...like Wol—"

"Don't," she snaps, and her nails dig in. Thank the goddess she doesn't bring out the claws.

At least some of the tension is gone from her body. We probably shouldn't be this close even if we are sequestered away in a storeroom. The shelves lining the walls are stuffed with various products, waiting to go on the floor. I should grab one of the bigfoot stuffed animals. It's the perfect gift for Jake.

"And how do you do it?" I tuck a stray piece of hair behind her ear.

Her teeth worry her lower lip. "You know how when you're about to shift there's magic in the air and in you? At least, I'm pretty sure that's how it was…"

"How it was? Wait. Back up."

She smiles and warmth spreads through me. "I don't really think about it anymore. It's more reactionary, I suppose. Like a habit. It's hard to remember what it was like when I was first shifting. Anyways, when I want to shift only a little, it's like a sip of magic instead of a gulp. Does that make sense?"

I hum, wondering if it's something I'll be able to do. "Could you always partially shift?"

"Yeah. Actually, I partially shifted before I fully shifted. I didn't know what the hell was going on. Sloane almost went out the window when she woke up in the middle of the night and saw my eyes glowing. We shared a room at that point, and she moved in with Gemma for a while."

I close my eyes and scrunch up my face as I try to find some magic floating in the air. I concentrate on my tail, thinking it'll be the easiest thing to shift without hurting her. Letting go of her isn't an option right now. Even if I could, I wouldn't want to. My muscles tense and a headache forms behind my ears.

"What are you doing? Are you okay?" Kira's frantic voice floats over me.

I let out a harsh breath, and the back of my head hits the door. "I was trying to partially shift."

She laughs, resting her forehead against my chest. Her shoulders shake, pure joy radiating from her. I tug her closer, soaking up her happiness. The longer I'm here, the more hopeful I get. Then I have to remind myself to be realistic. It's why I was so disappointed when she opened up to me about her family. She was so adamant she couldn't leave. I don't want to bring her down by talking about it again, though.

"I doubt you'd be able to. You're already a cryptid. Do you really want to add more to your plate?" She grins up at me, then leans up and pecks my cheek. "Let's go back out. I'm sure Slade ran to Mom to complain by now."

She steps away and I drop my hold on her, though my palms itch to keep her near me. I shuffle to the side as she opens the door and slips into the hallway. I swallow hard, trying to pull myself together before I follow her. She'll probably notice soon, but I can't make my feet move. Sooner rather than later, I need to come up with a plan. And figure out how to ask her to come to Whispering Pines with me.

Chapter 30: Crying Wolf

Kira

"I'm not sitting next to him," I hiss to Mom, and she glares at me.

"He's your brother. Of course you're sitting next to him. We need to show a united front. These producers are more thorough than the others. I hate the internet." She huffs, fussing with the vegetables she spread on a platter.

I roll my eyes and glance over my shoulder. She always blames the internet for any problems shifters have. People moving into town? Internet's fault. Someone's electricity went out? Internet's fault. Dad had a little too much of Johnny's bootleg vodka? Internet's fault. Although that last one might be true. She doesn't care that the internet isn't sentient and can't actually affect what she's complaining about.

"Fine, but why can't Slade sit next to you or Dad?" As much as I don't want to be next to my brother, I also don't want him anywhere near Chase. Slade is less likely to lose his temper in front of the guests.

"Because we need to spread out, but I assumed you didn't want to be stuck between two assistants who didn't know their ass from their end."

"I'll have Chase." If I wasn't staring at her, I would have missed her wince. I narrow my eyes and grit my teeth. "Don't even tell me..."

"You know, for someone who was adamant he wouldn't step foot in your house, you certainly have taken to having him around a lot," Mom says flippantly.

I cross my arms, wishing she would stop messing with the plates. "Don't even try changing the subject, Mom. Tell me you didn't revoke his invitation."

"Of course I didn't, dear. Although Dad did talk to him when you two got here. Whatever Chase decided to do then is none of my business."

"What the fuck is that supposed to mean?" I snarl.

She spins, shaking a wooden spoon. "Language. We have company. Now you know we like Chase and we enjoy having him here, but this is very important. If he's volatile or loses his temper, it could very well cost us this program. It's nothing against him, sweetie."

"This is Slade's doing, isn't it? He voiced some bullshit concern, and you lapped it up."

Her mouth opens like she'll deny it, but snaps it shut again. "It wasn't like that."

"It was exactly like that. And it's pathetic on his part and disappointing on yours."

I stomp from the room, passing Dad on the way. He tries to stop me, but I slip by him without a word. Mom can explain why I'm pissed off. For people who were excited to welcome him into our community, into our home, you'd think they'd be more understanding. I can't imagine what Chase thinks. If he left without a word, I wouldn't be surprised. It would be out of character and I don't think he'd do that, but I wouldn't blame him.

I rush out the back door, almost taking out Slade when I step into the cool night. He tries to catch hold of me, concern mixed with laughter in his eyes. I snarl at him and he grabs my arm. I try to tug away from him, but his grip is too strong.

Suddenly, my hand flies through the air and slaps him across the face. I didn't even mean to, though I don't know if I can blame it on my wolf. I've been itching to smack him for a while now. It's enough to loosen his grip and I yank away, then stumble down the path.

"What the hell, Kira?" he shouts after me.

I push myself faster, wishing I could shift. With the producers and crew crossing the boundary, no one's allowed to shift. Kids are kept inside or out in the forest. After the incident with Gemma all those years ago, protocols were put in place. No one wanted a repeat incident. Guilt washes over me when I remember the aftermath. I may have played it up to Gemma, but it was a blessing in disguise. It forced the town to address the way we moved forward. Doesn't mean it probably wasn't terrible for her. Not only did she have to deal with everyone talking about it, but she also had to deal with shit at school. And then she came home, and I made her life harder. But Moon Cove changed the way we do things—all because of her.

My cabin comes into view, and I breathe a sigh of relief when light shines from the front window. A shadow flits around inside, and my muscles relax. My feet stutter to a stop when another shadow crosses the room. Chase isn't the type to...he's not the one. Obviously, there's an explanation.

Still, I sneak up the stairs and slowly ease the door open. Voices float from the back. There's only a half bath and a small office before the exit to the backyard. It's not like I use the room for anything, but I still don't want random people in there. I wouldn't care if it was just Chase. Whoever else is there puts me on edge.

"Maybe I should just leave..."

"Alissa?" I call, and her head pops into the hallway. "What the hell are you doing here?"

She shuffles into the room, grimacing. "I didn't realize the television crew was at Mom and Dad's or I would have waited."

"No, it's fine. I just—" My gaze meets Chase's as he comes out of the office. "They're over there now. You could take my place."

She rolls her eyes, glancing down at her outfit. "I'm not exactly dressed for the occasion."

"Perfect. Slade's been pissing me off. Now you can return the favor."

She smirks and rubs her hands together. "Well, in *that* case. If you'll both excuse me, I've got some ass to kick."

She slides past me, and I call over my shoulder, "Just a heads-up, I slapped him right before I left."

Her peals of laughter heal something inside me. The door shutting cuts off the sound, and I shake my head.

"What are you doing here, Kira?" Chase says, some emotion I can't pinpoint lining his voice.

I wander toward the island and lean against it. I'd rather collapse on the couch, all the adrenaline from earlier seeping out of me. Slapping Slade wasn't my finest moment. Especially since he's clearly going through something. This can't be entirely about Chase. Instead of yelling and hitting him, I should have asked him what the hell happened.

"I wasn't going to sit there after they kicked you out," I mutter. Now that I'm here, I'm wondering why I left since Chase is looking at me like I lost my mind.

"No one kicked me out. Ben asked if I'd be able to keep myself under control since shifting would be a little too real for the producers, so I left. I made the decision, Kira. Not them. You should go back." He grabs a book and sinks onto one of the beds. I scan his face when he opens it up, but his eyes don't move.

I tug at my shirt, trying to get it away from my throat. The neckline feels like it's strangling me. I didn't want to wear this thing, anyway. It's too tight and squeezes my arms. I'm constantly pulling down the hemline to cover my stomach. My mother gifted it to me and insisted I wear it. When I can't take it anymore, I rip it over my head and breathe out a sigh of relief. Until I realize my bra straps are digging into my shoulders.

Tugging at the fabric, I try to ease some of the tension. When it doesn't work, I reach around and attempt to unhook it. My mind scrambles when I can't find the right way to pinch it, and my shoulders ache. My cheeks heat and I swear I'm sweating. Telling myself it's not that big of a deal doesn't help. It never does, but I try it every time.

Chase appears in front of me, and I freeze. He reaches around me and unhooks my bra, then guides the straps down my arms until it falls to the ground. Before I can process what's happening, his own shirt envelops me and his scent washes over me. I don't know what to say. Doesn't matter since he retreats to the bed. Usually when I take my clothes off, he's all over me. Disappointment crashes into me and I swallow hard.

I wish I could run. It would take too long to make it to the forest, though, and I'm already exhausted. The need to shift and get away from this feeling welling up inside me is too much. I'm too scared to even name the emotion. Labeling it will only make it more real and I'm not ready. Is it ridiculous as a thirty-something-year-old woman? Yes. Should I have a better way of dealing with things? Also yes. Will I change things tonight? Nope.

"Was there something you needed?" Chase asks, and I jolt.

"Why are you mad at me?" The question slips out before I can stop it. "Never mind. I'm going to shower."

I already showered before I went to my parents', but there's literally nothing else to do. It's going to get too dark to garden since I can't shift my eyes. It's too early to go to bed. Chase clearly doesn't want to have a conversation. I could clean, but then I'd be around him and I'd constantly worry I was bothering him.

"I'm not mad at you," he murmurs, and I stop at the bottom of the stairs.

"It's fine."

"No, it's really not." He sighs and sets down his book. "I'm not mad at you, Kira. I'm not upset about being excluded from dinner. I'm not even pissed about Slade. And you shouldn't be, either. No one's done anything wrong other than Slade treating you like he has."

"Except he's treating you shitty for ridiculous reasons."

"And he's treating *you* shitty because of *me*. Which is unacceptable. However, I doubt my scolding him will hold any weight." He glances at me, then away. "It might be time for me to think about going back to Whispering Pines."

A chill washes over me and I shiver. My immediate thought is to reject him. Either tell him he can't leave yet or to just go. My mind fizzles out like a sparkler at the end of its life. My eyes blur as I imagine what it'll be like without him. Waking up alone. Having no one to talk to. No one to eat with. Shifting by myself. Alone. Utterly Alone.

I swallow down the emotions threatening to drown me. I could tell him I don't care either way. Dismissing his impending departure would be hard. I'd feel like I was lying to him. He'd probably see right through me.

You could ask him to take you with him, a small voice whispers.

As soon as it fades, my responsibilities here weigh me down. My shoulders slump as I recognize how incredibly ludicrous the idea is. My parents need me. The store needs me. The community needs me. Hell, even Alissa needs me. Chase doesn't need me. Whispering Pines is his home—where he belongs. He has Jake and Gemma and his house and his hobbies and he helps with the camp. He'll be fine without me, which hurts more than anything else. It shouldn't, even though I gave up thinking this was a fling a while ago.

"Whatever you think is best," I whisper.

I make my way up the stairs, keeping my steps even and quiet. I bite my tongue to keep the tears at bay. As long as I can get to the shower, it won't matter. Plenty of water to wash them away when I'm under the spray. I don't have the right to cry over him. He's been nothing but amazing, unlike me. I don't deserve him, anyway. I need to let him go.

Chapter 31: Sage Advice

Chase

I don't know what I expected from Kira, but it wasn't to give up so easily. If I wasn't watching her, I'd think she didn't care at all. It was as if she shut down completely—like her mind needed to reboot. I'll need to bring it up again. It was hard enough to say something in the first place. Thinking about doing it again makes my stomach turn.

As the shower starts up and I close my eyes, trying to keep the images of her naked from my mind. I jolt when my phone buzzes. Jake has been calling the last couple of weeks. I've been dodging him. It's not like I have anything to say to him. Everything I'd usually tell him will flow straight to Gemma. Since most of my news has to do with Kira, I'd rather not have to lie, even if it is a lie by omission.

Right now, I need the distraction and accept the call. "Hey, Jake."

"Finally," Jake growls. "Listen, I get you don't want to talk to Gemma, but I'm by myself and we need to discuss some shit."

I grit my teeth, wondering if this is how all my conversations will be from now on. Jake sounds like Slade, inserting himself where he's not needed. Then again, I can't blame Slade for his concern. I'd be worried too. I can't guarantee I won't black out again. Or lose my shit and my cat will take over. Kira's confidence in me isn't as warranted as she thinks.

"Go ahead," I sigh.

"First of all, what did you tell Gemma? Because she's been moping around for weeks now and won't tell me. Says it's not a big deal, but I know it is."

"We're dealing with sisters, Jake. Neither of us understands what it's like to have siblings. I may have inserted myself where I didn't belong, though. She was blaming Kira for my wanting to come home in the beginning. I set her straight. I apologized, though." I don't know why she'd take it so hard. It's not like my opinion matters.

"Yeah, I saw that. Not that I was supposed to. It's been a long time since they've seen each other."

"Maybe Gemma's realizing how much she's missed by staying away from Moon Cove. Might do her some good to visit. You should go with to run interference, though. You could come out for Samhain."

A plan forms in my mind. If I can get Jake and Gemma to come here, then it'll distract everyone from my own leaving. Kira and her parents will be wrapped up in Gemma returning and meeting Jake. Slade will probably be gone by then, though he might stick around if he knows Jake will be in Moon Cove. Alissa won't care either way whether I stay here.

"And where will you fit into this little reunion?" Jake grumbles, interrupting my thoughts.

"I'll go back to Whispering Pines and run the haunted house for you. You've got plenty of counselors coming back this year, so I'm sure I can handle it. And you can tell Gemma not to worry about people talking. No one's going to say shit about something that happened over twenty years ago. They've got other shit to worry about."

"What are you running from?"

I shouldn't be surprised he saw right through me. We've been friends long enough for him to know when I'm hiding shit. I hate doing it. My life was so much simpler before I became a shifter. Part of me longs to go back in time. I wouldn't have met Kira, though. Or maybe I would have if she and Gemma ever made up. I'm pretty sure I wouldn't feel the strong pull of her being my mate, then. I would have missed out on what life was truly meant to be.

Shoving to my feet, I strain to make sure she's still in the shower. I quietly make my way to the back door and out toward the lake. I probably shouldn't be wandering around at night. No one's allowed to shift, though, and the shore should be empty.

"Something may have happened. I'm not running away, but I may have overstayed my welcome."

"Well, any amount of time in my book is overstaying. So you're going to have to explain."

"You can't tell Gemma. I haven't told anyone some of this."

He sighs, and I imagine rubbing his hand across his beard. "Fine. But if you're going to tell me you met your fated mate or something..."

He lets the words trail off, and I don't know how to respond. If I deny it, he'll clock the lie again. If I confirm it, he'll figure out it's Kira. I don't know what the hell to do. I should have known he'd guess within the first ten seconds.

"Holy shit," he breathes. "Okay, I'm not asking any questions. I don't want to know. What else?"

I suck in a deep lungful of chilly air as I reach the lake. "You know what a sliver cat is?"

"Uh, a cat who's silver?"

"Sliver, asshat. That's clearly a no. Okay."

I take the next ten minutes to explain everything I've learned about what I am. He doesn't comment or ask questions, which isn't a surprise. He'll process the information slowly. I shouldn't be nervous, but with the way Slade reacted, I am. Hell, even the way Alissa treats me now has changed. When she stopped by earlier, she was standoffish. I chalked it up to her being back in Moon Cove after she left in the middle of the night. Now, I'm wondering if it was because she was nervous around me. I don't blame her.

I fall silent and wait for his judgement. He doesn't rush into things and has always given me good advice. Sometimes he's a dick about it since he thinks everyone should have common sense, but he'll have something that'll help me through this.

"Okay. What else?" he asks.

I pull the phone away and glance at the screen. "That's it?"

"You just told me, a cryptid, that you're also a cryptid. Am I supposed to be impressed?"

"I assumed you'd have some sage advice or bolstering support. Plus, everyone knows you exist. Hell, even humans know you exist. Apparently, no one knows what the hell a sliver cat is and they haven't been seen for like a century. So, yeah, I thought you'd be a little stunned or impressed or something." I run my hand through my hair and glance over my shoulder.

He sighs. "Well, being a cryptid sucks. Everyone says they believe you exist, but they're still awestruck when they find out it's true. Some people think you're going to go off the rails at the drop of a hat. Getting mad around anyone sets them on edge more. Which is ridiculous. You don't see honey badger shifters getting treated like that. And they *do* snap when they're threatened in their shifter form."

"Maybe they just use it as an excuse when people piss them off. Then they won't be held accountable for their behavior."

He chuckles, which with anyone else would be a boisterous laugh. "I suppose it has helped me keep people away. What else is eating you?"

"You ever wonder what life would have been like if your parents had stuck around? Or if they had more than one kid?" I murmur, staring at the stars overhead.

"Not really. I grew up knowing they would leave. It's in our nature. Though, if Gemma and I ever have kids, I doubt I'll do the same. Plus, Gemma wouldn't be able to, anyway. Hard to imagine something you never had. Being around their family hard?"

"It's different. Ben called me 'son' and I about lost it. Which isn't the look I was going for." I shouldn't be ashamed and normally I wouldn't be. I'm pretty sure my reaction caused everyone to see me differently. Then I turned into this cryptid no one's heard of, and it just added fuel to the fire.

"Don't know what look you were going for, but Ben seems like a good guy."

I drop to the ground as emotions overwhelm me. "He is. Gladys is great and Alissa is nice—wicked smart, too. And Kira...she's not like Gemma described. I know they've got all their shit from the past, but she's not..."

"Not how Gemma remembers? Yeah, I told her that. After you called her out, we talked about it. Which is why she's moping. The question is, what are you going to do about it?"

I clear my throat and push to my feet. "Nothing. It's not my place to fix their relationship."

"No. I mean with your mate. You said you were going to come home. Are they coming with you?"

That's the ultimate question. I've tried broaching the subject, but she shuts me down every time. She's made it pretty clear she doesn't want to leave. Or rather, feels like she can't. If I could get her parents on board, I might be able to convince her to come with me. They're not my biggest fans right now, especially if Slade keeps whispering in their ear. They won't want their last remaining child to run off halfway across the country with a volatile cryptid.

"I don't know if that's possible. She's pretty settled here. And staying here might not be an option either."

"Why not?" he asks, then curses under his breath. "Hold on."

He shouts to Gemma he'll be inside in a minute. I imagine he's pretending to chop wood instead of talking to me. Being snowed in every year means a lot of wood for fuel. Plus, he insists on keeping me stocked as well, even though I have someone to plow my road when it gets bad. I wouldn't mind being stuck if Kira was with me.

"I gotta go. She's getting suspicious. Listen, I'm not saying you should, but there's nothing tying you here. I get there might be some hurdles moving to Moon Cove, but you'd figure it out. Just talk to your mate and figure it out." He snorts. "How's that for sage advice?"

He hangs up before I can respond. Not that I know what to say. As I make my way back to Kira's, my mind whirls with options. If she'll let me, I'll stay here. Giving up my home and the life I've lived for years will be hard. It'll be worth it if I get to keep her. I won't even have to tell her we're mates. I can wait until she figures it out for herself. She'll be pissed I didn't confess, but she'll get over it. Maybe.

"Chase?" Alissa calls when I pass the garden.

"How was dinner?"

She rushes toward me and drags me behind a tree. "Sorry. Slade is just out front and I didn't want you two to get into it again."

"You heard about that?" I whisper.

She snorts as she peeks around the plants. "Slade hissed the whole thing under his breath the entire damn meal. And my parents pulled me aside when everyone else left."

"You don't have to tell me what they said. It doesn't matter."

She straightens and gives me a look. "Oh really? Because your face says otherwise."

"Obviously I'm not happy about it, but I can't change their mind. Slade thinks I'm going to be a problem. Your parents clearly have the same reservations. And I don't blame them."

Her mouth drops open. "He's just being preju—"

"No, he's not. He's being cautious. I don't like how he's treating me, but I can't fault him for it. Just a few weeks ago, I *was* volatile. I wasn't able to shift, constantly blacked out, woke up with blood. Hell, I almost attacked Gemma the first time I shifted in front of her. And that was before I was a sliver cat. You know the most about my species—is it species?"

Her head tilts and she purses her lips. "I actually have no idea. I never really thought about it. We call them shifter forms or something like that. Then again, most of us are typical animals."

"Which is why it's understandable they all are worried I might spiral. Do you think if I stuck around longer and proved myself, they'd realize I'm—" I snap my mouth shut. Apparently tonight is for opening up to fucking everyone except for my mate.

"Start with Dad. Mom won't snub you, but she's superstitious. Do not tell them about the dark watchers," she mutters.

Slade steps around the corner and crosses his arms. "Dark watchers? When the fuck did you see dark watchers?"

Chapter 32: Feels Like Goodbye

Kira

The last thing I wanted to do tonight was be crammed into my living room with my siblings and Chase. Especially after the night I've had. Slade hasn't looked me in the eye once. Alissa keeps glancing at Chase like he's going to jump out of his skin. To be fair, Chase doesn't seem like himself. I wonder what the hell they were talking about. Or maybe it was whoever he was speaking with. I came out of the shower and spotted him from the window with his phone pressed to his ear.

Then Slade showed up and Alissa appeared, and my hopes for a quiet rest of the night went down the drain. I'm not going to be the one who starts this conversation. I'm sure it's going to be more lectures and pleas for Chase to leave. No one else can see who Chase really is underneath his shifter form. He's not a danger to me and if everyone keeps insisting he is, I might lose it. I don't even know why it matters so much. Just tonight, he was talking about leaving. Why am I fighting with my family for someone who's going to abandon me?

I tense when the thought runs through my mind. He's not abandoning me. We haven't talked about being more than temporary lovers and friends on the side. Every time I think about broaching the subject, fear chokes off the words. I need to grow a fucking backbone.

"Slade?" Alissa prompts, widening her eyes at him.

"What?" he spits out.

Alissa huffs. "You're the one who insisted on coming over here. So, why don't you...say whatever you need to say."

"So I can get slapped again? No fucking way," he sneers.

"Maybe you should get the hell out, then," I mutter.

Chase pushes to his feet. "This seems like a family thing, so I'm going to bed."

"Sit down," I hiss, glaring at him.

He plops down next to me, careful to keep a few inches between us. I doubt we're fooling anyone. Then again, they probably assume we're just friends. We're living together. We're shifting together. We're practically inseparable. Shit. We're in a goddamn relationship. Which means we'll have to actually break up when he leaves.

You could ask him to stay.

I shake my head, recognizing this is not the time to think about it. When I'm lying in bed later, I'll figure it out. Or I'll just avoid it some more until he brings it up again. It might be cowardly, but I can't handle the inevitable rejection. Avoiding disappointment is the only thing that's kept me going the last ten years. He'll tell me this was temporary, we're not meant to be, we're too different.

"Okay, how about we just agree to disagree? And stop bringing Mom and Dad into this...shitshow," Alissa finally says.

I shove to my feet. "Slade, outside. Now."

I march to the porch, hoping he follows me. As the front door shuts, I spin around and cross my arms. Slade has the decency to look a little ashamed of himself.

"Okay, bucko—"

"We don't live in the south, Kira. Cut the shit," he snaps, mirroring my stance.

"Shut the hell up and listen. Chase isn't about to attack anyone. He hasn't blacked out since he started shifting on his own. He hasn't given any indication he'll go rogue and rip me to shreds. And, might I remind you, I am a damn wolf shifter. I'm pretty sure I can at the very least get away from him if need be." I glare at him, daring him to argue.

"Put aside the fact that I'm not the only one worried about it—"

"They're only worried because you planted seeds, you a-hole."

He throws up his hands and spins away before facing me again. "*He's* worried, Kira. Your own boyfriend is scared he's going to hurt you. Doesn't that say something?"

My brain short circuits when he calls Chase my boyfriend. Doesn't mean I need to acknowledge it. Until Chase and I talk, no one else needs to be involved.

I pull in a calming breath. "I get you're worried about Chase, but I'm a grown-ass woman. I can take care of myself, and *I* decide who to interact with. Not you. Being my big brother doesn't give you the right to waltz in here after months and pretend you know what's going on with my life."

"Fine. But what happens when you spiral again? What happens when he leaves and the rest of us are left to pick up the pieces?"

My spine snaps straight and my breath stalls in my lungs. "I don't know what you're talking about."

I thought I was hiding it better. I thought none of them noticed how hard life has been for me. I've been fine the last few years, living the life I was handed. It might not be everything I thought it would be, but I'm fine. Everyone wishes for things they'll never get. They hope their dreams will come true. And when they don't get what they want, they get sad.

"Of course you don't know what I'm talking about," he retorts, and I glance at the door over his shoulder, making sure no one is about to come out. "Except you disappear into yourself for weeks, barely noticing anything around you. I don't know what you think will happen when he breaks—"

"That's enough, Slade," Chase says from behind me, and I deflate. I wonder how he got into the yard.

Slade's mouth snaps shut, and he storms off the porch. I watch him walk away, my neck straining. Slade's shoulder hits Chase's, and my brother mutters something I can't hear. Chase doesn't respond, his eyes fixed on me. Alissa comes out of the house and brushes past me. I wonder how much Chase heard, but I'd rather not discuss it.

I hurry inside while Alissa mumbles to Chase. Maybe if I pretend I'm sleeping, he'll leave it be. If we ignore it long enough, it'll go away. I rush upstairs and into my bedroom. By the time the front door closes, I'm in my pajamas and slipping between the sheets. His footsteps echo through the space and I close my eyes, attempting to even out my breathing.

"You don't have to pretend to sleep, Kira. If you don't want to talk, that's fine. Just say it, though. Stop hiding," Chase says quietly as he moves about the room.

Huffing, I roll onto my back and stare at the ceiling. "Let's get it over with."

"Get what over with?"

"There's a plethora of things we could choose from. We can talk about Slade. Or what you talked about with Alissa. I'm not going to pry into who you were talking to on the phone earlier, but it clearly affected you, so we could talk about that. There's also what you overheard between Slade and me." I pull in a shaky breath as he sits on the bed and leans against the headboard. "Then there's when you're going to leave."

His fingers work their way through my hair as he stares out the window. "We could talk about my shifter form."

"Why? I'm not concerned about it."

"I am," he whispers. "I won't hurt you. I could never. My cat—" He shakes his head. "I've thought a lot about it, and I know I wouldn't hurt you. Except I don't know how I'll react around others. If someone startles me, I might black out. Being in Moon Cove...it's more stressful now."

"Is that why you want to leave?" I hold my breath, hoping he doesn't say it's because of me.

"Part of it."

"We don't have to talk about it," I mutter.

He sighs, his fingers stalling. "Slade's comments were bullshit, Kira. However, I get the feeling there's something else going on with him and he's projecting it on you."

"I thought so, too. Maybe Alissa can get him to open up. I doubt he'd talk to me right now."

"It's late. We should just go to bed." He pulls his hand away and swings his legs over the edge of the bed. "I'm going to take a shower."

Part of me wants to stay awake until he actually comes to bed. Exhaustion swamps me and my eyes flutter shut. My mind doesn't want to shut off, and I run through every scenario. If he stays, everyone will be on edge. He'll end up being sequestered in my cabin and ostracized by the townspeople. It's exactly like what Gemma went through. The town turned on her, and I knew she'd never live it down if she stayed. I can't put him through that.

If he goes, though, I'll be heartbroken. I'm finally able to admit it, even if it's only to myself.

I don't want to be separated from him.

I'm happier when I'm with him. A future I never knew was possible has unfurled before me. I may not be perfect for him, but I'd try. Striving to be better for him wouldn't be hard. He makes it easier to want to be *more*.

The door squeaks as Chase closes it behind him. Seconds later, he slides in next to me. Tears prick my eyes when he slips his arm around me. His chest presses against my back and my muscles relax. As his thumb traces circles on my stomach, heat builds between my legs. He probably has no idea what he's doing. He just likes being close to me.

His lips brush my neck. "I need you."

I roll in his grasp and his fingers skim up my side. When our mouths meet, I give myself over to the sensations flowing through me. Usually, we're crashing together, each seeking a release. This is softer and quieter, a melding of two people needing something more. I'm not ready to name what I'm searching for, though I know what it is.

He strips my shirt from me, groaning when he realizes I'm not wearing underwear. I didn't do it on purpose. Since we started sleeping together, I haven't been wearing anything other than his shirts.

"So fucking beautiful," he breathes before his lips wrap around my nipple.

I arch my back, sliding my fingers into his hair. A whimper leaves me when he switches to the other and slides his hand down my body. Desire explodes in me when he circles my clit. When he kisses his way across my skin, a rush of heat envelops me, and I fling off the covers. I hum as the cool breeze from the window washes over me.

When he covers my body with his, a shudder runs through me. He grinds his hips into mine and a groan leaves him.

"Do you know how goddamn sexy you are?" he murmurs, burying his face in my neck.

"I think you should tell me again. I might have forgotten."

He snorts, then sinks his teeth into my skin. I hook my thumbs in the waistband of his boxer briefs and try to shimmy them off. He chuckles when I get nowhere.

"Need some help there, sunshine?" He doesn't wait for a response and shoves them down his hips, then kicks them off.

Then he's on me again, gathering me in his arms as he surges into me. Desire builds in me gradually as he rolls his hips. My pussy spasms around him, and he grunts. His hand slides to the back of my neck, and his forehead rests on mine. It's intoxicating and disorienting—a connection I've never known before. I give myself over to the sensations rising within me.

Chase thrusts into me, coaxing whimpers from my lips. When my eyes flutter closed, he growls and I open them once more. I wind my legs around his waist, forcing him deeper. When he pushes to his knees, I expect him to take full control. I'll give in—I'll give him everything.

His fingers knead the flesh of my hips as he pulls out slowly and sinks into me. I glance down, watching his length disappear over and over. My back arches as his thumb circles my clit. He murmurs his praise when I cup my breasts and roll my nipples between my fingers.

Flames of desire lick at my skin as my orgasm dances just out of reach. I don't want this to end. Not so quickly and especially with him leaving soon. I need to commit to memory the way he makes me feel. I'll replay it for years to come while nursing my heartbreak in silence.

Chase's fingers grip my chin, forcing me to look at him. "Come back to me. Focus on me."

He punctuates his words with another thrust. My eyes blur as I hurtle into oblivion. Spasms wrack my body, and I grab his legs, digging my nails in. He groans out my name as he follows me. As his body covers mine, I cling to him, not ready to let him go.

Chapter 33: Whisker Away
Chase

I didn't think I'd be covertly meeting Slade, but here we are. I'm pretty sure he's been avoiding me the last week. Slade's been a ghost to the point where I asked Kira if he left town. I'm not surprised. I'd probably avoid me too if I were him.

Except it's not just him. No matter where I go, people seem to vanish. Gladys and Ben can't spend more than a few minutes in the same room with me. Alissa practically ran back to her cabin the morning after our little sit down when I came out on the porch. I don't know many others, yet everywhere I go they duck their heads and hurry past.

"Did you think leaking my secret was going to make me run for the hills?" I call as Slade pads into view. I glance back at the lake, soaking up the scene from the outcropping.

"I didn't say anything to anyone, actually." He settles next to me. There's less tension exuding from him than before.

"You weren't exactly subtle. Small town like this, news spreads like wildfire."

He sighs, resting his elbows on his knees while his feet hang over the rock. "True. I need to know about the dark watchers."

"Why didn't you ask Kira? Or Alissa?"

He glances away, hiding his face. "Neither of them are talking to me. Which I know is my fault, so you don't have to lecture me about it."

"Not my place. Your family is your business."

His head whips around, and he narrows his eyes. I gaze back steadily, wondering what he's searching for. Maybe he thinks I'm trying to infiltrate his family, poach them for my own. I doubt he knows anything about me beyond my shifter form. Jake isn't one to spill other people's business. I'm sure Slade will reveal his thoughts sooner or later. He's not one to hold back on his opinions.

"We'll see. Tell me about the dark watchers."

I explain every encounter we've had, including Kira's first contact with them. I still don't understand the issues surrounding them. They didn't seem unsettling to me like they did to Kira. They just stood there, doing nothing. Whether they're an omen of death or something else doesn't really matter to me. As long as they don't interfere with my life. I keep most of my opinions out of my recounting to Slade. He doesn't care what I think.

"And Alissa didn't have any insight into them?" he asks when I finish.

"Nothing more than I already said." I watch him as he rubs the back of his neck. "Just spit it out, Slade."

"I think they followed me."

His confession hangs between us. It wasn't what I was expecting. I thought he would blame me. If not me, then Kira. The dark watchers didn't show up until I came. Kira was the first one who saw them. Unless...

"Did you see them before you got back?" I ask, hoping he doesn't clam up on me.

"On the way here, actually. Several times. Then when I got to Moon Cove, they were just out of the corner of my eye. I swear they were following me." He scrubs his hands over his hair again and again.

"How close were you to Moon Cove when you first saw them? Wait, which way did you come?"

He ducks his head and mutters, "I was in Whispering Pines. Stopped at the same campground I met Jake at on the way back."

"Why are you acting like that's a secret? Who cares if you were in Whispering Pines?"

He sighs, his jaw jutting out. "My parents don't know I went to visit Gemma. And I was getting more info on you."

"Find anything interesting?" I doubt he did. Gemma may be more open than Jake, but there's nothing to tell.

"She said you smiled a lot."

I smirk, shaking my head. "I suppose I do, usually."

"Except you weren't smiling when I got here. Unless you were with Kira, that is. Which got me thinking maybe you were hiding something. Then to find out you were a cryptid...things were just not adding up. I may have jumped the gun."

It's probably the closest I'm going to get to an apology. Slade doesn't seem like the type to say he's sorry unless forced. I'm sure his parents made him when he was a kid. Then again, I don't know him very well.

"You realize you're not the only one who was blindsided by that shift. No pun intended."

He chuckles and some of the tension eases from my shoulder. We'll probably never be besties, but hopefully we can be civil for however long I have left. The thought has my stomach flipping. If Slade and I had a different relationship, I'd ask him for advice. Telling him Kira is my mate probably wouldn't go well. All the progress we've made tonight would crumble.

"Kira needs someone who will stick around. Not necessarily in Moon Cove, but by her side. She's not capable—"

"I'm going to stop you right there. I don't need you to tell me anything about Kira. Whatever's going on between us is our business. I may not know what it's like to be a part of a family like yours, but I doubt she'd appreciate your meddling."

I push to my feet, determined to leave the conversation there. If he keeps interfering, I might just push him off the cliff, and I'm not entirely sure he can swim. Besides, I'm not talking about Kira behind her back. I'm sure they all think they're doing it in her best interests. Doesn't change the fact they're still gossiping about her. And I don't like it. Anything they say to me, I'll funnel right back to her. They shouldn't trust me with their secrets. Her emotions are my number one priority.

"Fine. I get it," he says, scrambling after me. "All I'm going to say is, don't break her heart. Please."

Usually, I'd assume he was spouting big brother bullshit. With the concern in his eyes, I think this goes deeper than that. I wonder how many times he's left Moon Cove, worrying about Kira. It doesn't excuse him from going behind her back. However he's approaching things clearly isn't working.

"I don't know what you want me to say, Slade."

"You don't need to say anything. I just needed to say it before it was too late."

I don't have the nerve to tell him it's already too late. Unless I stay or she goes with me, I'll be leaving my heart behind. Maybe she won't care either way. I've been putting off the conversation about our future. Since I brought up leaving a week ago, we've been ignoring everything again. We can't wait any longer, though.

"If you see the dark watchers again, tell Alissa. She'll be able to figure out what's going on. At least she seems like the best option of finding answers," I say.

He doesn't stop me when I make my way down the worn path. Kira was having dinner with her parents, but she should be home now. She wanted me to go with. I didn't have the heart to tell her they didn't want me there. Neither of them invited me. She gave me a funny look when I told her I had something to do.

When I reach the cabin, she's already posted up on the porch. Her eyes flick to me before dancing away. With a heavy sigh, I collapse into the chair next to her. We sit in silence for a while. I'm not going to be the one who breaks it. If I wait long enough, she'll eventually bring up whatever's bothering her.

"You know, when I was a kid, I wanted to learn how to surf. Or waterski. Just something on the water. Our lake isn't big enough and even if it was, no one would have taken me. Growing up with a big family seems nice, but sometimes you just get lost in the shuffle. I don't blame my parents or my siblings. They all did what they could. Sometimes I just wish they would have chosen me. Which doesn't make any sense, really."

"Why doesn't it make sense?"

"Because it's not their job to choose me. My siblings have their own lives and my parents have each other. I missed my window."

"When? After high school? Or when Gemma left? Or a year ago, when your siblings started leaving?" I don't understand why she thinks she missed out. She didn't need an invitation to live her life.

She purses her lips, contemplating my questions. "I don't know. I suppose I just changed my dreams when I realized I wouldn't be waterskiing anytime soon. Gardening became my new dream. And helping my parents at the store. We need someone to take over when they retire."

Well, that answers that question. She won't leave Moon Cove anytime soon—if ever. I close my eyes and imagine what my life would be like if I stayed. Being with her would be amazing. It'd be everything I never knew I wanted. The rest of my time, though, would be like wading through mud. I'd end up getting her dirty just by being around her. Putting her through that wouldn't be fair. But if she asks, I'll stay.

"Where does that leave us?" I finally ask.

"I don't know," she breathes, then chuckles. "No strings, right?"

"If you still think there's no threads tying us together, Kira, I hate to burst your bubble..."

"Yeah. Yeah, I know."

My chest tightens and a headache forms behind my eyes. I could walk away right now—pretend we never had this conversation. We could continue on like we have been, enjoying each other's company. Except we've tried that and it didn't work.

She sucks in a deep. "When are you going home?"

A crack forms in my heart, widening the longer I sit here. She doesn't want me to stay. Telling her we're mates now would be manipulative. I won't keep her that way. I could move out of her house, try to woo her from afar. Staying at the hotel or the bed-and-breakfast in town would be fine. If she doesn't want me, though, fighting for her will only end in more heartbreak.

"I can leave tomorrow."

I push to my feet and make my way inside. I go through the motions of packing. My things are scattered around the house, and I realize how ingrained I've become. At least here. Not so much in the rest of the town. Which is just another reason I should leave. Anything I forget, I'll replace when I'm back.

I take one last glance around the living room before moving upstairs. The rest of my stuff is in both bedrooms and the bathroom. I keep expecting Kira to interrupt me. As the minutes tick by, my hope dwindles. She could come up here right now and tell me to stop. She could ask me to stay. She could beg me to take her with me. I'd give her anything she wanted. Yet she doesn't come. I'm pretty sure she's still on the porch, but I'm too chickenshit to check.

When I'm finished, I stand in the hallway at a loss of what to do. I could crawl into her bed, spend one last night with her in my arms. Or I could go into the spare room and make it easier on both of us. Sleeping away from her would hurt, especially knowing she's right across the hall.

I leave the curtains open in her room and slide between the sheets. It takes a long time for my body to settle down. There's a lot of things I wish would have happened differently. Right now, I just wish she would come to bed. I lie awake, watching the moon march across the sky.

Chapter 34: We Had a Fucking Deal

Kira

Wind shivers its way through the remaining plants in my garden. I sigh, picking at the dirt embedded under my nails. I've spent most of the last three days out here. It's the only thing keeping my mind off Chase leaving. I couldn't even bring myself to watch him drive away. Mom hounded me, saying I would regret it. Dad said I needed to do whatever was best. Neither of them understands.

"Kira?" Slade calls from by my cabin.

I tuck my body farther into the dying corn stalks. I can't handle him right now.

"I know you're here, Kira." His footsteps are soft but distinguishable as he approaches.

"What do you want, Slade?" I ask, keeping my head buried. Maybe he'll go away if he thinks I'm busy.

He rounds the corner and stares at me. "What the hell are you doing?"

"Hiding from you." I stab my small shovel into the dirt. Not that it's doing anything. "What do you want?"

He plops down next to me and sighs. "Is this what you've been doing the last three days? You realize most of these are dead, right?"

"Like you'll be if you don't leave me alone," I mutter.

Silence falls between us, and I wonder if he's here to keep me company. Every time I walk into a room, people avoid my eyes. It's been isolating, which is why I've been staying home. I feel like I'm abandoning Mom since she's had to cover at the store. They have enough going on with the show in town. It's been hectic and the worst time for me to hide out in my house.

"Talked to Mom. She said she hasn't seen you lately." He picks up one of the carrots I pulled earlier. He brushes away the dirt and takes a bite.

"I'm going into work later. I have to finish the inventory. And I'm taking over when they're at the production shoot at Samhain. It's coming up fast. You could help out if you want. We need to set up the decorations at the store and the haunted house. Not to mention the—"

"Stop," he growls. "Just stop. What the hell are you doing, Kira? Is this really what you want? To live in this town and follow in our parent's footsteps?"

"What's wrong with that? They're successful and raised a family. They're an integral part of the community. We're safe here and—"

"Safe," he murmurs, and I snap my mouth shut. I was just babbling anyway.

"Yes, safe. Moon Cove is one of the few safe shifter communities in the country," I snarl.

He nods, then sniffs, a smirk forming on his face. "Since I've seen more of the country than you have, I'm going to have to disagree. There's plenty of towns full of shifters. And they're all safe. But that's besides the point."

I huff, throwing my shovel on the ground and straighten. "Then what is the point, Slade?"

He pushes to his feet and brushes his hands off on his shorts. I'm surprised he's still wearing them this late in the season. Then again, he never did feel the cold.

"The point is, maybe safe isn't what you need."

He turns and saunters away. I wonder what the hell happened between Slade and Chase. Neither of them bothered to tell me they were sneaking off for a random rendezvous at the lake. Dad let it slip he saw them leaving—separately. Apparently, they weren't very sneaky. I wish I would have asked Chase when he returned from his secret meeting. I just couldn't bring myself to before he left town.

There were a lot of things I couldn't bring myself to question him. He would have stayed if I asked. I could see it in his eyes, though I tried to ignore it. I couldn't trap him here. The light would slowly fade from his eyes. Eventually, he'd resent me for having to stay in Moon Cove. Even if he wooed the other shifters, he still wouldn't be happy. Not in the long run. He'd definitely win them over, too. He's just that way.

Which is nothing like me. I've kept to myself since I graduated. I know the townsfolk don't like me particularly, and I don't blame them. I've burrowed further into myself since I realized how terrible I was as a teenager. Apologies didn't matter for some, and others couldn't let me grow into someone else. Most of it is my fault, though I spent a long time denying it. And then I didn't know how to fix it.

I make my way inside and shower, my mind bouncing between the past and my squandered future. I'm so lost in my thoughts I almost put body soap on my hair and end up conditioning my hair twice. An ache develops in my chest when I spot an errant bottle in the corner of the shower. Chase must have left it behind since he was in a hurry. Which is another thing that's my fault.

My mind wanders again and by the time I check back in, I'm walking through the back door of the general store. Shaking my head, I slip into one of the rooms and grab the inventory sheet hanging on the wall. Most of the numbers are already written down, but I need to count the keychains. It's the fucking worst. At least it's a mindless activity.

I pull out one box and start counting. When I finish one, I start on the next one. And then the next. I'm eight deep when the door opens behind me. Keeping my eyes fixed on the paper on my lap, I attempt to ignore my mom. Her scent gives her away. She's been wearing the same perfume my entire life, and it transports me back to my childhood.

She sighs as she lowers herself next to me. She tugs a box closer and paws through it. We work in silence until she finishes hers and grabs the clipboard. I bite my lip, then huff when I lose count. Tossing the ones I've already counted back, I grumble under my breath. I wanted a mindless task, but now it's just become tedious.

"Why are we counting keychains?" Mom asks.

"Because we need to finish inventory before the year is out. And I'm only halfway through. I lost a lot of time." I press my lips together and curl my hands into fists.

"You realize we have employees for this type of thing, right?"

"Don't trust anyone else to do it correctly. I've been doing it for a decade, so I know what to do," I mutter.

She sighs again and covers my hand with her own. "Why are you still here, Kira?"

My head snaps up. "Where else would I be?"

She gives me a look, and I glance away. I'm sure she saw more than what I wanted. But after everything that's happened, I didn't expect her to be questioning my decisions. She was the one who kicked Chase out of the dinner. She was the one worried at the party. She was the one who kept avoiding me.

"I'm surprised you let him leave. You defended him so eloquently. And vehemently."

I snort, smirking. "Did Dad get you a word-of-the-day calendar?"

She tugs a nonexistent strand of hair behind her ear. "He may have. That's besides the point. You want to explain to me what happened between you and Chase?"

"No, I'd rather not."

"You know, I'm a pretty good listener."

"Mom, I'm not talking to you about Chase. If you wanted to know something, you should have talked to him before he left."

She huffs, shaking her head. As she struggles to her feet, I leap up and grab her arm to help. She rests her hands on my shoulders, though I have to look down at her.

"I'm afraid we didn't do enough for you," she murmurs.

I stiffen, wondering how I made her feel that way. They did everything for us. They gave us what they could while dealing with the other responsibilities to the store and the community. Maybe I wasn't hiding things as well as I thought.

"Mom, you did everything for me. You and Dad. You're always there for me and you gave me a job and you—"

"Oh, dear. That's being a parent. We didn't do anything special. I'm not saying we didn't try, but it isn't your job to be grateful. It's your job to grow and live. And I'm afraid we made you feel like you couldn't." She cups my cheeks and pulls my head toward hers. "We want you to be happy. Nothing else. Do what makes you happy, Kira."

She presses a kiss to my forehead, and my eyes flutter closed. She lets go and makes her way out of the room before she can spot the tears. I knew they wanted me happy. I just didn't know what it looked like. It's not as simple as choosing happiness. Every step I've taken since I became an adult was maintaining the status quo. I strived to be better than I was and did whatever I could to achieve it. Which meant giving up.

I wander back to my house, my mind mush. It's probably the reason I almost run straight into Alissa. She skips to the side silently, then latches onto my upper arm. She drags me into the house, her nose wrinkling when she spots the beds stuffed in the living room.

"Why the hell do you have all these beds, yet nothing on the walls? It's like you moved into an abandoned frat house," she says, disgust lacing her voice.

"Mom needed a place to stick all the beds they couldn't break down. Couldn't leave them at the store, and she didn't want to get rid of them." I shrug and make my way to the kitchen to grab a bottle of water.

"This. This right here is the problem. You focus on fixing everyone else so you can ignore your own problems."

"I don't know what you're talking about," I mutter.

She scoffs, throwing up her hands. "What the hell are you going to do? Mope around here and live like this for the rest of your life?"

"What's wrong with my life? I *like* my life."

"Except it's one you could have anywhere," she cries. "I can't believe you let him leave. You didn't even ask him to go with, did you? I bet you didn't even ask him to stay. Did you even tell him you're in love with him?"

A hole opens in my heart, threatening to swallow me up. I've been avoiding this, walking around in a daze so I wouldn't have to feel the hurt. If she would have just left me the fuck alone, I wouldn't have to go through this. I could have shoved all the pain down next to all the other shit I haven't dealt with over the years.

I suck in a deep breath and face her. "I don't control Chase, therefore I didn't *let* him do anything. I wasn't going to invite myself with him."

"Why the hell not?" she yells, and the facade I've put up cracks.

"Because it would fucking hurt," I shout. "More than this, it would have broken me. Why can't you understand that?"

I spin and plant my fists on the counter as I try to get myself under control.

I slowly turn and try to keep my voice steady. "If he stayed here, he'd eventually hate it. Everyone thinks he's going to snap at any minute. Long distance wouldn't work, so we don't exactly have an alternative to be together."

"Did you tell him you love him?" she whispers.

"We had a fucking deal," I yell.

She stares at me with wide eyes and I hold my breath, desperate to keep my emotions in check. My chest aches with the effort. When she blinks, the dam breaks and I come undone, sliding to the floor as I bury my face in my hands.

She pushed and pushed and now there's nowhere to go. I can't get away from the pain eating away at me. Alissa's arms wrap around me and hold me while I sob. All the walls I built around me splinter, large chunks slamming into the wasteland of my mind. I didn't expect to be so distraught, and it takes me a long time to calm down.

Alissa sits back, concern hanging in her eyes. She keeps the rest of her arguments to herself. I don't think I'd be able to take much more, anyway. I'm already empty. There's no more fight in me.

"Go," she breathes. "Just go, Kira."

I scramble to my feet, a spark of hope flaring to life within me. Even if I get there and he rejects me, it'll be better than not knowing. Anything will be better than the pain.

Chapter 35: Get Your Shit Together

Chase

Jake pounds on my door again, and I roll my head around to stare at it. He's been coming the last four days. Not that I've answered. I texted him when I came into town since it was late. As soon as I got to my house, I sequestered myself inside and couldn't bring myself to go back out. I've been subsisting off whatever I had in the pantry before I left.

Leaving Moon Cove a week ago was harder than I expected. I almost turned around more than a couple times. The thread linking Kira and me seemed to stretch the more miles I put between us. I was so wrapped up in her rejection, I didn't think about how it would feel to leave my mate behind. No amount of telling myself she's better off without me made a difference.

Pain slices through me when I close my eyes, and her image appears.

"I know you're in there, Chase. Open the damn door or I'm breaking it down," Jake yells, and I sigh.

Lumbering to my feet, I spot the stains on my sweatpants. I'll need to do laundry. When I whip off my shirt, I stumble on the steps leading from the sunken living room. I grab a shirt from my bags I still haven't unpacked. This one came from a gas station on the way back home, but I threw it in with everything else. My feet stutter to a stop when Kira's scent washes over me.

Jake hammers on the wood again, and I shake my head. When I open the door, I'm met with my best friend's scowl, almost hidden behind his beard.

Glancing behind him, I spot Gemma in his truck. She waves, but I look away. I'm not upset with her anymore. I just can't handle dealing with more people.

"About time," Jake grumbles.

I drop my hand from the knob and turn to shuffle back to the living room. The couch is dented where I've been sitting. And sleeping. And eating. The huge picture window it faces highlights the lake. It's a peaceful view, calming the raging feelings within me. If I cared, I'd shift and make use of the water. I never did feel like I could do it in Moon Cove. There were too many people around to judge.

I've been putting off shifting, even though the new moon is less than a week away. I don't know what'll happen when I do. I'm terrified I'll slip right back into blacking out like I did before. Without Kira to center me, I might just slip too deep into my sliver cat. He'll take over, and I'll end up living in the woods for years, like Alissa told me.

"What the hell is wrong with you? I thought you'd figured everything out?" Jake growls as he drops into the chair across from me.

"If by everything you mean shifting, then yes. Everything's figured out," I mumble.

"Shit," he breathes, running his hands through his long hair. He props his elbows on his knees. "Have you shifted since you got here?"

"Nope."

"Have you talked to her?"

I want to pretend I have no idea who he's talking about. Actually, he doesn't know who my mate is, but he's probably guessed. I never confirmed either way. It would be easy to dismiss him or kick him out. He won't quit coming, though. At one point, it was me forcing him to interact. He'll think he's returning the favor, no matter how much I wish he wouldn't.

"Who?" I ask to buy time.

"Kira, asshole. We both know she's your mate. Don't worry, I didn't tell Gemma."

"Wouldn't care if you did."

My eyes blur as my mind wanders back to Moon Cove. I wonder what she's doing right now. It's midday there, so she's probably not in the garden. Maybe she's helping her parents at the store. Now that Samhain is closer, there'll be an influx of tourists. Then again, maybe she's helping with the production crew. She mentioned once she's in charge of setting up the ruse for them. Which is merely another reason she'd never come here.

"Well, maybe I will. Then she can call Kira and ask her why she'd let her mate leave," he snaps.

I explode from my seat, seething. "Don't you fucking dare. She doesn't deserve to get shit on. None of this is her fault, and I'm fucking sick of everyone blaming her."

He sits back and crosses his arms, a smirk playing on his face. "Thanks for confirming my suspicions. Why'd you leave?"

I deflate, collapsing onto the couch. "She asked me to."

"Did she ask? Or did you infer? Because those are two very different—"

"I'm not going into details. I couldn't stay, she wouldn't go, it's done." I doubt she cares either way.

I'd love to think even without knowing about the mating bond, she feels the strain like I do. Then again, it didn't seem to bother her all that much when I actually left. She didn't even bother to see me off or say anything. I waited for her, and it broke me when she didn't. Even Slade came. He tried to explain away her absence. We both knew he was lying. At first, I imagined she was hurting, too—she was so upset she couldn't say goodbye. I'd understand if that was the case. It was why I had to fight not to turn around.

By the time I got to the hotel that night with no call and no text from her, I realized the feelings were probably only deep for me. She made it perfectly clear we were temporary. It was a fling with a side of friendship. I was the one who pushed her, and I shouldn't have. I should have let her be. I never would have known she was my mate had I stopped pursuing her. Nothing will make me regret my time with her, but I doubt I'll recover. All I have now is my cabin.

"Did you need help with the haunted house?" I ask. Samhain is less than a week away. I'm surprised he's here at all. I don't really want to do anything other than rot on the couch, which only adds to the guilt. He won't leave me alone to waste away. Maybe helping will get him off my ass.

"Don't change the subject. What do you mean you couldn't stay?"

I sigh, tipping my head back and closing my eyes. "She didn't ask me to stay. Even if I wanted to, I wasn't welcomed by the community. Hell, even Slade was a dick to me until he figured out I was leaving. I'm not trustworthy while shifted."

"How the hell do you know that? You haven't even tried shifting since you got back."

"And I'm not going to," I mumble.

"Wait. You can't be fucking serious. Chase, if you refuse to shift, the moon will force you. Which might have you blacking out. You realize how terrible of a decision that is, right?"

"I'll be fine. I'm going to take off before the new moon so I'll be deep in the woods. No one else will have to deal with me." I let out a humorless laugh. "Just like it should be."

Jake grabs my shirt and twists the fabric before hauling me upright. He's larger than me, capable of throwing me around like a rag doll if he wanted. If he's trying to piss me off, he's succeeding. I try to brush him off, but he doesn't let go.

"What the hell is wrong with you?" I snarl.

"Get your shit together, Chase." He releases me, shoving me back onto the couch. "You didn't let me waste away when all I wanted was to be left alone. You knew I needed a friend. If it wasn't for you, I wouldn't have the summer camp. I wouldn't have Gemma. Now it's time for me to repay the favor. If you won't go to Kira, I won't interfere. That's your own mess to clean up. But I'm not going to let you lose who you are as a human because you're too stubborn to accept how you've changed."

He stomps toward the sliding door off the dining room and flings it open. "Get up and let's go."

"Where are we—"

"You're going to shift. I'll be there to keep your ass in line. One step at a time, we'll deal with this. Besides, I'm curious to see if you're actually silver or if you were lying about that."

I scoff, shaking my head as I push to my feet. "Sliver cat. I'm not fucking silver."

"Well, prove it, then." He flourishes his hand, presenting the way.

"This is ridiculous. And Gemma has to leave," I mumble as I pass him.

"She'll stay in the truck. She was the one who suggested this."

We take the stairs and start toward the lake. He walks a little behind me, as if I'm going to take off for the house or something. I could just run off into the woods. He might be able to catch me. Then again, I'm a lot faster than I used to be. He doesn't realize how much I've changed. Maybe if he saw what I've turned into, he'll leave me the hell alone.

We make it several hundred yards before I stop. My cat is already hissing in my head. He's been silent while I've wallowed. Another wave a grief washes over me, though slightly isolated from my own. I think I liked it better when he was hiding.

I spin to face Jake, and he stops, crossing his arms. Gathering the magic isn't as hard as I expected. It's almost become second nature. I wonder how easy it would have been had I stayed longer in Moon Cove. Maybe if I would have read more or talked to Ben about it or listened to Kira more or picked Alissa's brain...none of it actually would have helped. I have all I need to do what needs to be done. The idea of spending the next several months shifted sounds amazing right now.

In the blink of an eye, I shift and crouch, settling on my stomach. I don't want Jake to think I'm about to attack him. Jake's gaze widens, his mouth parting as he circles me. My cat rumbles inside my head, attempting to tug me toward the house. I struggle to keep us in place while Jake inspects me.

"Well, shit. You weren't lying. Except I can tell you're you. So, you can shift back, and we'll talk," he says.

I lose the fight with my cat, and he forces us toward the cabin. I expect him to hide inside or force me to shift back, but instead he takes the wraparound porch. My claws dig into the wood as he pushes us faster. Gemma's eyes widen as I leap from the deck and land close to the truck. I'm sure she thinks I'm about to attack her. Jake does too, based on the growl from behind me. He's already halfway to us, though he doesn't need to worry. I dash around his vehicle and take off down the driveway.

I could stop my cat. We're actually on speaking terms now. But I don't want to. I want him to take over. The less I know about what's happening, the easier it'll be. It's probably not the healthiest way to cope. I don't see any other way to deal with everything.

"Chase," Gemma calls, and my cat skids to a stop.

I wait for him to turn us, run again, collapse to the ground, something. He just retreats to the corner of my mind, letting me decide what to do.

"Chase, I'm sorry." She's whispering, yet I can hear her as clearly as if she was standing in front of me.

I glance over my shoulder and find her tear-streaked face. Slowly, I turn and pad back to her. She probably thinks I'm still upset with her. Doesn't help I dodged her calls for weeks. I could take the time to repair the relationship or let it lie. It might be safer for her. I'm not exactly great company, anyway. She's another tie to Kira and severing it might help. With the look of devastation on her face, I doubt I'd be able to hold myself to that.

I paw the ground in front of her, not ready to shift again. She nods as if she understands. It's not enough, but it's enough for now. Eventually, we'll get back to being friends. Jake comes up behind her and wraps an arm around her waist. His hand tenses on her hip as if he's seconds away from whisking her away.

"Stop it, Jake. He's fine. I'm fine. It's okay." A choked sob leaves her, and I duck my head.

Jake's reaction is the same as Slade's. I knew it was a possibility, but I hoped my best friend wouldn't think I was a danger to his mate. It's part of the reason I hid in my cabin instead of going to them. I knew Jake wouldn't want me around Gemma. His loyalty rests with her, which is how it's supposed to be. He should pick his mate over me. I'd do the same thing. Over and over, I'd pick Kira over everyone else.

"He's still a cat, Gemma. The last time you two were in this position, he was going to attack you. I'm protecting both of you. He'll feel terrible if something happens to you. He understands what I'm going through," Jake says, and her eyes flash in awareness. Leave it to Jake to give away my secret without even realizing.

A soft smile blooms on her face. "No, that wasn't him. That was his cougar or whatever he is now. He wasn't in control. But you can see he's in there. Aren't you, Chase?"

I shake my head, then swing around. I could shift and actually talk. Except I can't bring myself to face either of them. Since I'm not going to flip out and my cat isn't going to take over, I need to run. I take off for the woods, giving in to the feelings rolling through me. Maybe it'll help me forget Kira. Deep down inside, I know it won't.

Chapter 36: Spiral, Confusion, Exhaustion

Kira

I swear if Alissa calls me one more time, I might lose it on her. She's been blowing up my phone the entire journey. It doesn't help that I have no idea where the hell I'm going. She keeps interrupting the GPS. I've missed like three turns because of her.

My brother's car fills with her ringtone, and I let out a frustrated cry. Pulling over to the side of the road, I cuss her out under my breath. I could ignore her, but she'll just keep calling, thinking I'm lying in a ditch somewhere.

"What do you want, Alissa?" I snap.

"How close are you?" she asks, her excitement palpable.

"I'm five miles closer than I was when you last called."

She snorts, and I wonder if she's with Slade. "You should be farther than that."

"Well, I'm like twenty minutes away, and I had to stop to evacuate my bowels. I think I'm going to throw up. What if…never mind."

"Nope, let it out. Better now than when you're sitting outside his house and hyperventilating."

I bite my lip, wondering where to even start. I didn't really think this through. Alissa kept egging me on while I was packing. She practically shoved me into Slade's car since I don't have one of my own. Slade didn't even question it, which I should have asked about. I was too wrapped up in my own feelings.

"What if he isn't there? What if he didn't come home?" I breathe.

"Slade talked to Jake. Chase is definitely there."

I take a drink of water, then kick myself since I need to pee now. "Fine. What if he doesn't want to see me? What if he doesn't actually care, and him leaving didn't have anything to do with me? Maybe I was just an easy way to pass the time while he was in Moon Cove."

"You realize everyone could tell, right? He had stars in his eyes every time he looked at you. He's not going to turn you away."

I don't know if I can trust her judgement. She wasn't exactly around us while we were in town. I love my sister, but she doesn't understand everything that's happened. Chase morphing into a sliver cat was a twist no one saw coming. And Alissa doesn't think it's a big deal. Chase's situation is mesmerizing to her.

"It doesn't matter. He could still tell me to go away. We haven't seen each other in almost a week, and he could have changed his mind. And then I'll have come all this way for nothing. I'll have to drive back after being rejected. How the hell am I going to get home? It's not like I can just hop on a flight and leave Slade's car behind. He'll kill me." I gasp for breath and lean my forehead against the steering wheel.

"Okay, slow your roll, honey. It's okay to let out all the anxieties, but you're talking like it's a done deal. It's not. That man is in love with you. A week away won't change that. However, if he's not showered, give him a break, okay?" She laughs lightly, and I huff.

"Why the hell wouldn't he be showered? He takes care of himself, Alissa."

"Because he's probably wallowing because he misses you so effing much. Now get your shit together and drive the rest of the way. I promise everything will be okay."

"How do you know?" I whisper.

"Let's go with gut feeling. It'll be okay, Kira. Love you."

She hangs up, and I drop my phone into the center console. I was fine until I saw the sign for Whispering Pines. It was small and I almost missed it, but there it was. Whispering Pines—eleven miles. I have eleven miles to get my shit together. Gemma would take me in if I went to her place first. We might not be close and I'll definitely have to make amends with her—explain why I said the things I did. Having that conversation before I've settled things with Chase wouldn't help my nerves, though.

If he does reject me, I could always say I was there for Gemma. I wouldn't have to pour my heart out and beg him to give us a chance. I could wander around town and wait to run into him. That would be a bitch move. I can't do that. As I pull onto the empty road, I run through all the scenarios and what-ifs. Only one of them results in a happily ever after. It's the one shining hope I have left.

Going back to Moon Cove with my tail tucked between my legs would crush me. I'd become a shell of myself. I'd go back home and hide in my house. Maybe I'd go back to my routine of working and gardening and reading. And then...nothing. I'd have nothing because I wouldn't have him.

I spend the next twenty minutes wallowing in my imagined failing. I can't bring myself to admit how I feel about him. Alissa has all sorts of opinions about the many emotions I may have. Slade mentioned the L-word before I left. I'll have to face my feelings when I'm standing in front of him. As I pull onto a quaint little main street, I realize my plan isn't exactly a smart one. If I wait to acknowledge what I feel, I might not be able to get the words out.

I pull into a parking spot in front of a small general store. An older man walks past the large window, though he doesn't notice me. I rest my forehead on the steering wheel and mouth the words I've been avoiding. It takes a bit for me to buck up the courage to voice them.

"I love him," I whisper. It'll have to be good enough.

I jolt when someone knocks on my driver's window. A woman with short brown hair smiles and nods as if I need encouragement to speak with her. I press the button, but she doesn't wait until the glass no longer separates us before she starts speaking.

"Are you new to town? We don't usually get people in so early for the Halloween festival. Not that we're not happy to have you. We just don't get a lot of visitors around here. What's your name, honey? I'm Marcy." She smiles the entire time she's speaking, and it's kind of freaking me out.

"I'm just passing through. Needed some snacks for the road," I mumble.

I may not have spent any time outside of Moon Cove, but I was there when Slade gave Gemma a list of rules before she went off to college. One of them was don't talk to strangers. I'm not about to get scammed or kidnapped because I didn't listen to him. Then again, I'd probably be able to save myself if I was kidnapped. They probably wouldn't know what hit them when I shifted into a wolf right before their eyes.

"Oh, well, it is getting late." It's not. It's only like three in the afternoon. "You should probably stay the night," Marcy says.

"I think I'll be fine. Thank you, though."

Her face pinches while she struggles to keep up the pleasant demeanor. I glance around and spot a tall, bearded man sauntering toward us. He's probably going to the general store, but he keeps glancing at me. Or maybe he's looking at Marcy. She's pretty cute. Maybe it's her boyfriend. A zing of magic rushes through me, and I stiffen. The last thing I need is to give myself away where Gemma now lives. I've caused her enough problems. She'd probably refuse to acknowledge we're related if I effed up that badly.

The mountain man shuffles to a stop in front of my car and crosses his arms. Marcy's head whips around, and she straightens.

"Oh! Fancy seeing you here. Thought you'd be—" She stops when he holds up a hand while he stares at me.

Slowly, I reach for the keys dangling from the ignition. This place is starting to give me the creeps. There was a movie about this sort of thing, and I don't want to end up being chased through the woods by a guy with an axe. He *is* wearing flannel. It might be a stereotype, but he seems like the kind of guy to chop wood.

"Move along, Marcy. Paul's waiting for the jam," he says in a growly voice.

Marcy huffs, swinging around a basket I didn't even notice, and flounces into the general store. I should leave—abandon the wild plan to search for Chase and run back to Moon Cove. I wasn't meant to be out in the world. Everyone said they'd be fine without me. No one seemed to think my leaving would be disastrous for *me*.

It didn't occur to me I have no idea how to operate in a normal town. How the hell will I get a job? How will I find somewhere to live? I don't even think my driver's license is up to date. I probably just drove halfway across the country illegally. Slade planned my route so I'd avoid any major roadways since my experience with driving is minimal at best. Shit, I did not think this through.

"Kira?" the man calls, and my head snaps up. "Well, shit."

"Uh, no. Not Kira. Sorry." I fumble with the keys, and they slip out of the ignition. I curse as they fall to the floor, and I kick my foot around trying to locate them.

"Same brown eyes. Same flash of annoyance. Same clumsiness. Yeah, you're definitely related to Gemma. You looking for Chase?"

"Jake?" I ask cautiously.

I think he smiles under his unruly beard, but I'm not entirely sure. "That's me. I'll tell you where he lives, but don't mention to your sister I saw you first."

I nod, my mind in a daze. He points toward a street a couple blocks away and gives me directions. My brain doesn't check back in until the canopy of fall leaves close overhead. I follow the road deeper into the forest, keeping my gaze forward so I don't miss his house. Once the trees open up, I realize I didn't need to be so careful. A massive cabin comes into view, and I slam on the brakes.

"How the hell did he survive in my crappy little place? No wonder he didn't want to stay in Moon Cove," I mutter.

I swing my car around in case I need to make a quick getaway. If he tells me to get lost, I don't want to be doing a five-point turn while fighting back tears. I'd have to stare at him the entire time I tried not to hit a tree. It takes me a good five minutes to put the car into park, then another ten to turn off the engine. I keep glancing in the rearview mirror, expecting to see his face. When he doesn't appear, I finally push open my door and slide out.

A gust of air rushes past me, and the leaves shiver overhead. I pull in a deep breath and turn toward his cabin. The wraparound porch is massive, with several chairs and swings set up. I don't think he has any neighbors, which might be the best part of this place.

I wander, not to the front door, but to the lake. He said it was bigger than the one in Moon Cove. This one makes ours look like a pond. My eyes flutter closed as a calmness washes over me. Birds chirp and insects buzz, making the whole scene feel like it's straight out of a fairytale. No wonder he didn't want to stay in Moon Cove. I wouldn't want to leave this either.

As the tension bleeds from my body, I sigh before I make my way back to the front door. When I knock, I'm not expecting much. I'd imagine he'd already be out here if he was home. Doesn't stop my heart from pounding in my chest or my stomach from doing somersaults. I knock harder just in case he's sleeping, but he still doesn't answer.

And now I'm faced with the dilemma of sticking around for him to show up or drive away. I drop onto the rocking chair and close my eyes. Now that I've stopped moving, weariness hits me hard. I'll take a few minutes and then decide whether or not to stick around. Just a few minutes is all I need.

Chapter 37: I'll Never Let Go

Chase

I should name my cat. He sits there in my head—part of me, but not fully me. Calling him Chase seems wrong. He's not me, but he is. A pulse of pain hits me behind the ear, and I swipe my paw at the spot.

Maybe having an existential crisis while shifted isn't the smartest thing. Instead of shoving the thoughts aside, I start throwing out random names. He hisses at every single one. I table it for later, though I might just call him Bob for now.

I wish I could keep running, but I'm hungry and would rather not catch a rabbit or something. I'm always a little nauseous after I let Bob fill my stomach with woodland creatures. Plus, I don't think I could bring myself to do it while aware. It might be the circle of life and all that, but I don't like thinking about it. I don't have much at the house to eat. I don't have it in me to go into town, though. If Jake is still hanging around, he'll insist I come home with them. I'm sure I've got a can of beans or something.

The closer I get to the house, the more Bob perks up. He hasn't been very alert while we've been in the forest. Once he realized we weren't going to be sprinting for Moon Cove—for our mate—he's been listless in my head. As the trees thin, he lunges for control, and I stumble. He must sense something I don't. Glancing behind me, I search the muted area for a threat.

A familiar scent drifts past me, and I freeze. My cat throws himself at me, and I snarl at him. It's a strange sensation, fighting with myself. I don't know how to explain it might be a ruse. Actually speaking with him is a skill I haven't learned yet. I slowly pick my way through the brush to get him to back off.

As my cabin comes into view, my gaze instantly flicks to Kira sitting on my porch. It's been a week, yet it feels like years. With her eyes closed, she looks peaceful, as if she's always been here—as if she's home. I shake my head, my ears twitching with the move.

No reason to jump the gun. Maybe she just wanted to come visit Gemma and didn't want me to be surprised. Maybe she's a mirage and my broken heart conjured her to ease the pain. Relief floods my system when I spot only one car in my driveway. Jake and Gemma must have left before Kira showed up. I'd rather not have her see Jake tear into my ass again about wallowing.

Slowly, I approach her, padding across the lawn. She doesn't stir, though she sighs as I mount the stairs. I probably shouldn't be shifted when she wakes up. She might not know where she is or who I am. Plus, we clearly need to talk.

If she's only here for Gemma, I'll need to stay out of her way. With the way Jake and Gemma have been acting, I doubt they'll leave me in peace while I deal with everything. Gemma will want to fix things. Not that there's anything *to* fix.

Kira isn't broken. Just because I left doesn't mean she owes me anything. If she wants to visit her sister, so be it. She shouldn't feel like she has to get permission from me first. I don't own Whispering Pines.

My tail twitches, and I realize I'm spiraling. I don't know why she's here. Until she wakes up, I won't have answers. Curling up at her feet, I resign myself to waiting. I'm not about to rouse her. She clearly needs sleep based on the dark rings under her eyes. I take the time to scan the forest with her scent wrapping around me. It might be the last time I'll truly be at peace, and I'm going to soak up every minute I can.

As the sun marches toward the horizon, Kira stirs. I keep still, waiting for her to realize where she is. A soft *oh* leaves her, and I lift my head. Her eyes fill with tears, and I wonder if I should shift now. I wait for her to move or say something. When she doesn't, I fidget slightly, and she straightens.

"Hi," she whispers.

I back up and close my eyes before I shift. She lets out a shuddering sob, and I wrap my arms around her without a thought. It takes a few minutes for her tears to slow, and I ease back into the chair next to her. She wipes her face with her sleeves, sniffing.

When she glances up, her mouth drops open. "What the hell are you wearing?"

I glance down at my stained sweatpants. "What do you mean?"

"Is that...is that a wolf on your shirt?" She leans closer, tilting her head.

"Oh," I murmur. "It's actually three wolves howling at the moon. I, uh...yeah." I'm not about to tell her I found it at a gas station on my way home and bought it on impulse. It made me think of her. I hold my breath, hoping she doesn't take offense.

My fears were unfounded since she busts into giggles. A smile blooms across my face, and the ache in my chest eases. Maybe this won't be so hard after all. I'm still clinging to the idea she's here for Gemma. It's the only way I'll avoid a complete meltdown of my entire life. I was already teetering on the edge before she showed up.

"Well, that's certainly...it's good to see you," she mumbles, then tucks her chin to her chest.

"Are you okay?"

"I suppose I shouldn't be surprised since I lost it when you showed up. I'm good. Fine. Okay, I guess. I'm—" She sucks in a sharp breath.

"I'm not," I say softly.

Her head whips up and she stares at me. "What do you mean? What's wrong?"

My mouth goes dry, and my heartbeat thunders in my ears. "Jake showed up earlier. With your sister. He thought I'd be fine after I shifted, but once I did...things didn't exactly pan out."

Her nostrils flare, and grooves appear between her eyes. My palms itch to soothe her, but I don't know if she'd push me away. Her reaction might hurt more than if she never showed up in the first place.

"Did he act like Slade? Bastard. He should know what it's like to be—"

My hand covers hers, and she jolts as if she's been shocked. "It wasn't like that. Gemma got out of the truck and called out to me. I was aware of everything. He was afraid I would attack her. I don't blame him since I'm not exactly the same as when I left. It makes sense he would be worried about his mate around a cryptid like me."

"That's bullshit. I'm sure he'll come around, though. Slade did, right?"

I force a small smile. "Sure. I'll just have to wait and see. Is that why you came? To see them?"

I hold my breath, no longer sure what to feel. Bob stirs in my head, practically vibrating in anticipation. She bites her lip, and the urge to kiss her overwhelms me. We could abandon this conversation and connect like we're used to. Except I can't go another minute in this limbo.

"I actually saw Jake earlier. He told me where you live."

"Great. That's...that's just great." I push to my feet and put some distance between us. "Did you want something to drink?"

She springs to her feet, and I step back, giving her enough room to get by me if need be. Her lips part, and I avert my gaze so I don't end up grabbing her. I feel like I'm losing her all over again. It's why I didn't seek her out before I left. She never came to bed, and I wasn't about to go searching for her. I wasn't hiding and she could have found me whenever she wanted.

"Chase," she whispers, but I pretend I don't hear her. The desperation in her voice is too much.

"I'll get you a water. Do you need directions to Gemma's? She's probably at the cabin, but the camp is on the way if you need to check there. I'm sure you two will have a lot to talk about after so long." I shuffle back another step, angling for my front door. If I don't get away from her soon, I'll end up doing something I'll regret. Like shifting or crying or blurting out all sorts of things.

"Chase, please."

"You can tell Jake he can crash here if need be," I mumble as my hand wraps around the knob.

"I love you."

I freeze as her confession hangs in the air. A gust of wind laced with a shiver of magic swirls around me. I don't know if I heard her right. Maybe she never even spoke and it was just my imagination. It's the only thing I've wanted to hear from her, and I'm afraid I merely manifested her confession. I'm scared to move, worried about breaking the spell.

I glance over my shoulder. "What was that?"

"You heard me," she whispers harshly.

I turn and lean against the wood. "Do you know?"

Confusion hangs in her amber eyes. "I mean, I can't exactly define love, but yeah, I know."

It's not what I'm asking, but she answered my question, anyway. She has no idea she's my mate. I thought it would make me feel worse for some reason, like I was lying to her. Except if she loves me without knowing, it means it goes deeper than the bond. I didn't care much about the thread tying us together because I knew she was it for me. Weeks ago, before I could admit it to myself, I knew. I open my mouth, but she holds up her hand and I snap it shut.

"I love you because you make me feel alive. In a way I haven't been in years, if ever. You woke me up and made me laugh. And you did it with seemingly no effort. I know I won't be easy to be with. I'm hard to—"

"Stop," I growl, and she falls silent. "If you're about to say you're hard to love, you're wrong. Being with you is as easy as breathing."

"I didn't mean sleeping together."

"Neither did I."

I sigh, holding out my hand, and she takes it. I reel her in and fit her body to mine. Her head rests on my chest as I wind my arms around her. I don't know how long we sit like that, just soaking each other in. I pull in a deep breath, bracing myself for what's to come.

"Say it again," I whisper.

"You first," she whispers back, and her body tenses.

"I love you."

She grins up at me, joy radiating out of her. It's as if all the stress and anxiety have vanished in the wake of my words. My cat presses against the corner of my mind, urging me to tell her everything.

"I'm sorry I didn't ask you to stay," she murmurs.

"I'm sorry I didn't ask you to come with."

"Why didn't you?"

My head knocks into the door as I tip it back. "Because I knew you were entrenched in Moon Cove. Because you kept talking about how you needed to be there. Because I couldn't be the one who took you away from your family. I don't understand what that's like, Kira."

She snorts, and I glance at her. "Yeah, you do. You've been living it for weeks now. Plus, Jake and Gemma, they're your family. It's why you didn't want to move to Moon Cove. And I don't blame you. This place is amazing. I probably didn't help when I kept bringing up the fling thing."

"Not exactly, but I figured you were just scared. So, what do we do now?"

"Would it be weird if I said I want to stay in Whispering Pines? I can get my own place, and we can see where this thing goes."

"No. If you think you're staying anywhere other than here, you're out of your mind." I slide my hands up her body and cup her face. "Stay with me."

"I'd ask if you're sure, but I think you'd bite my head off if I did."

"You'd be right."

I kiss her gently and she sighs. Whatever else we need to figure out can wait. She's here and she loves me, and that's all that matters. Another piece of my heart slots into place as she melts into me. She's meant for me, and I'm never letting her go.

271

Chapter 38: Fated, not Forced

Kira

As I trail after Chase, I try to catch my breath. I didn't think he'd give in so easily. Actually, I didn't think we'd get to this point. Expecting the worst was the only way I could protect my heart. Now it's like I'm catching up.

Chase waves his hand around as he shows me the cabin. Calling it a cabin seems a little blasé. Four of my houses could fit in here. With each step, I realize how out of my depth I am. I've never had to worry about money, but Chase is in a different tax bracket. Part of me wonders if he kept this quiet. How many others have tried to use him because of his money? I don't blame him.

We step into the living room, and I gasp. A wall of windows looks out on a massive deck, but it's how it frames the lake that's truly breathtaking. I press my nose to the glass, not caring whether I get prints on it. He chuckles behind me, then presses his chest to my back.

"Whole reason I built this place," he murmurs, burying his face in my neck.

"It's beautiful." I can't seem to take my eyes off the scene.

"It's okay. I can think of other things I'd like to stare at, though."

I snort as the cold seeps into my palms. "Doubt it."

His nose brushes my jaw. "Would you like me to show you?"

His fingers dig into my hips, and I shudder. He hooks his thumbs in the waistband of my shorts and pushes them down. I close my eyes, letting the sensations he's eliciting from me take over. It hasn't been that long, yet it feels like a lifetime ago.

He drops to his knees as the fabric falls to my feet. Gently, he guides one foot out and then the other. He slides his palms up my calves, and my knees almost give out. He growls, the sound reverberating through my body. When he stands, I shiver, anticipating his touch.

"Don't move," he murmurs as he gathers my hair and pushes it over one shoulder. "And no peeking."

He presses a kiss to the back of my neck before he tugs off my shirt. His hands drop and I squeeze my eyes shut. He might think he's sneaky, but I can hear the rustling of his clothes. His scent washes over me, familiar yet not. I can't place how it's different, but it is. Maybe it's being here or our confessions of love. It has an extra layer now. I'm so focused on deciphering the individual notes of his scent, I jolt when his fingers tweak my nipples.

His hand slips between my legs as he pushes his chest into my back. He strokes me slowly, and I moan, my breath fogging up the glass.

"Ever since I got home, I've sat on my couch, staring at this window. I've fantasized about fucking you as the sun dies in the sky, your body awash with the colors of the sunset. I've imagined you panting and moaning, begging me for release. In my dreams, you're so fucking wet as you wonder who might catch us. Anyone could walk by and see your pussy greedily taking my cock. Is that what you want, sunshine?"

"Yes," I moan, tipping my head back until it rests against his shoulder.

His words conjure even more images and heat shoots through my body to settle between my legs where he's still playing with me. He pushes two fingers inside, then pulls them out slowly, only to circle my clit twice before repeating the move. He has how to work my body into a frenzy down to a science.

"Tell me how much you want it. Tell me exactly what you want me to do to you." His free hand cups my breast and kneads the flesh.

His words intoxicate me and warmth gathers in my gut. I could spin around and make demands. I could take control of the entire situation and force him to his knees. Something holds me back. He won't let me get away without answering, but I need him to be in charge.

"I want you inside of me," I groan. "Now."

He chuckles, then presses a kiss to my neck. "Your wish is my command, sunshine."

He pulls his hand from between my legs and steps away. I glance over my shoulder and he growls. I whip back around, focusing on the sun setting behind the trees. He kicks a pillow next to my feet, and I step onto it. He clearly thinks I'll be able to keep my balance. It's fluffy, though, giving me an extra inch or two of height.

When he grips my hip with one hand, a shudder rolls through me. A rush of pleasure races through my veins as his cock slips between my legs. He pushes the tip into my core and I wiggle, attempting to take him deeper. He freezes, his hand flexing on my skin.

"Patience, Kira. I plan on taking my time with you. It's been too long since I've been inside you, and I refuse to rut you like an animal." The strain in his voice is evident.

I turn my head, not quite looking at him, and huff. "Take your time later. I want it hard and fast."

He groans and plunges into me, stealing the breath from my lungs. Something deep within me pops into place. A thread shines behind my lids as I slam my eyes shut. When he rolls his hips, I whimper and tears spring to my eyes. A voice whispers in my mind, too low for me to decipher at first. I don't need it, though.

Mate.

My shoulders slump, and I tuck my chin to my chest. I don't bother wiping away the tears from my cheeks. I'm too overwhelmed by the emotions hammering my senses. Chase's low murmuring infiltrates my breakdown. They're words of love as he wraps his arms around me. He tucks his face into the curve of my neck. Does he know? Has he felt the pull between us? Did he realize long before I did? Maybe he has no idea what this feeling is. Maybe he thinks this is normal between two shifters.

"Chase," I gasp, and he hums. "We're...we're..."

"I know," he whispers. "My beautiful mate."

My knees buckle, and he grips me tighter. I expect him to bask in the realization, savoring the moment with slow thrusts. Instead, he surges into me. I moan as my orgasm builds much quicker than normal. Whether it's the awareness of the bond or our time apart doesn't matter. His teeth sink into my neck, and I explode without warning. As I shudder, he buries himself into me again and again. It doesn't take him long to follow me into oblivion, and we're left panting.

"Such a good little mate. Did you see stars while I fucked you?"

Anticipation stirs within me. We've done this dance enough, and I know he's not finished with me. He'll demand everything my body has—all the orgasms he can force from me. We'll end up christening every surface of this cabin, and I'll beg for more. I didn't question it before. I should have, but I was too wrapped up in my own head. Of course mates would be insatiable. Coupled with his shifter form being horny pretty much all the time, and I'm in for a long night.

"I don't remember stars. Maybe we should try again. For research," I say, smirking over my shoulder.

He slips out of me and spins me around. I almost slide on the pillow, but he seizes my waist and steadies me. His eyes darken as his gaze drags down my body as fire flashes through my veins. I lick my bottom lip when I glance between us. He's already hard again, even with the evidence of our time dripping down my thighs.

Chase slides his hands around my body and grips my ass before hauling me up. A thrill races down my spine. He slams my back against the glass, and it rattles. He doesn't give me a chance to recover before he thrusts into me. I moan and hook my ankles behind his back. Our eyes meet, and I get lost in the depths of his gaze.

"Harder," I whine, and the back of my head hits the window.

"Eyes on me, Kira," he grits out, and my gaze dips to his.

I quiver in his hold, the thread between us shining brightly. My wolf brushes up against the strand, and I shiver at the emotions overwhelming me. I never thought I'd find my mate. I have a feeling I'll be basking in the glow for quite a while. Chase plunges into me, and I grip his shoulders, digging my nails into his skin.

"Touch yourself," he grits out.

My hand drops between us, and I rub my clit. It doesn't take long for me to spasm around him, and he follows me into oblivion. Being with him has always been different than I was used to. It's stronger, deeper—more. Everything with him is just *more*. I didn't understand why and I never questioned it. Maybe I should have. Then I would have known he was my mate long before now. Except I wasn't ready.

He gathers me closer and carries me to the couch. He settles me onto his lap, still buried inside me. His hand grips the back of my neck and guides my face into his neck. A weightlessness takes over, and I close my eyes. I wonder if he plans on going for round three before letting me sleep. I won't complain either way. After a week apart and a shit ton of heartbreak, we need this.

"How long have you known?" I whisper into his skin.

He hums, pressing a kiss to my temple. "Are you sure you want to know while I'm buried in your pretty little pussy?"

I snort and clench my muscles, earning me a grunt. "It's probably the safest place for it right now."

"True," he sighs. "I've known for a while. Since I shifted in front of Alissa after the dark watchers showed up."

He groans as I sit back, his fingers digging into my hips. I stare at him while I search my brain, running over the last few weeks. I've seen Alissa a lot more than usual since Chase showed up. Trying to pick out one incident among a plethora of them isn't as easy as it should be.

"After you morphed into a sliver cat? When you shifted in front of her the first time?"

"That's the one," he murmurs as he brushes his hands up and down my sides. It's soothing, though not enough to stop the questions building in my head.

I swallow hard, staring at his chest, but not really seeing him. "Why didn't you tell me?"

He cups my cheeks, forcing me to look at him. "Because you wouldn't have believed me. No one would have. And I wasn't going to use it to make you stay with me. You needed to make the choice on your own. Not because of some invisible bond linking us together."

A heaviness sits in his eyes, and I try to keep it together. I really do. When I can't hold back anymore, I grin and roll my hips. His face tightens as his cock hardens even more. I need to do more research on why he's always half-mast around me. Maybe it's the mate thing or the sliver cat thing. Either way, I'm not complaining.

"You know the whole fated mate thing is only a means to find your soulmate, right? It doesn't force you to be together. Either one can walk away anytime they want. The goddess isn't into that. It's called fated mate, not forced mates for a reason."

He grits his teeth, gazing at me through hooded eyes. "I know you said really important things, but I can't think straight when you're teasing me, sunshine."

I rock back and forth, just to see him squirm. "Bond or not, I always had a choice."

His head tips back as if he'll never get through this conversation if he's looking at me. "Then why the hell did it hurt so much to leave?"

"I think that had more to do with you"—I suck in a deep breath—"loving me. The bond is stronger then."

He smiles, grabbing my waist. "So, you're stuck with me now. No getting away. All fucking mine."

"I wouldn't have it any other way."

As our bodies move together once more, I have a feeling I won't get any sleep tonight. We have to make up for all the time we missed being apart. Whatever the future brings, I know we'll be okay because we're together. It'll be new, and we won't always agree, but we'll get through it. Peace settles over me as I realize I've found exactly where I'm supposed to be.

Epilogue: Wolf Lingerie
Chase

Six Weeks Later

Wind whistles around the cabin, creating a backdrop to the holiday music ringing through the kitchen. Snow piles up against the windows while a fire blazes next to me. Kira's singing rises and falls, adding to the festive atmosphere. I close my eyes and soak it all in. If someone would have told me six months ago I'd be here, I never would have believed it. When Kira showed up on my porch, I didn't want to get my hopes up.

Now I can't imagine a life without her here. She's made this place a home. I've lived here for so long, I got used to being alone. Didn't get rid of the loneliness, though.

"Chase, where's your sifter?" Kira calls, and I set my book down before pushing from the couch.

I make my way into the kitchen, smirking when I spot her sweater. "If you wear that around Jake, he's going to get a big head."

"What? Oh, Gemma gave it to me for solstice. Mom sent a couple of them early, along with a bunch of towels with bigfoot printed on them. We figured we'd wear the sweaters to dinner just to see how red his face gets." She smiles and swipes at her cheek, leaving a dusting of flour behind.

I crowd her against the counter and kiss her nose. "I want one."

"I'm sure that can be arranged. Sifter?"

"Don't know what that is. From the sounds of it, though, I think it's in the bottom cupboard by the oven." I cage her in and press my hips to hers.

She gives me a look. "You realize I can't get to it if you don't move, right?"

"Is there anything in the oven?" I murmur as I dip my head and bury my face into her neck.

Pulling in her scent calms the beast inside me. He doesn't like being cooped up, but with the blizzard outside, we haven't been able to go out. The only thing that's helped is being buried in Kira's heat. The bond between us has only grown stronger.

"There's nothing in the oven, but I have to get these cakes in soon or we'll be late."

I hum, nipping my way up her skin. She melts under my touch, and I grin. It doesn't ever take long for her to give in to me. She likes to pretend she's busy, but her body knows who she belongs to. Her wolf submits long before she does. Unless I've pissed her off. Sometimes I goad her just to watch her take control. A shiver rolls through me at the thought.

"I think they'll survive if we're late. I have some plans first," I whisper in her ear.

She tilts her head and runs her hands under my shirt. "Plans?"

I pull back and grin. "Take it all off."

She scrambles to obey, the baking forgotten. I grab the box I stashed on top of the fridge, complete with a bow, and hand it to her.

"You want me to open a present while I'm naked?" She raises an eyebrow and purses her lips.

I kiss her swiftly, then retreat to lean against the island. "Yup. You'll be wearing it."

She pops off the lid and peels away the layers of tissue paper. The lingerie dangles from her finger, confusion flooding her face. We're not ones to gift each other things like this. Then again, we haven't really had the chance. I couldn't pass this up, though.

"What the hell," she breathes. "You bought me...lingerie. With a wolf on it? You've got to be kidding me."

I toss the box aside and pluck the scrap of fabric from her before I crowd her against the counter once more. She swallows hard when I grind my cock into her.

"I thought it would make you smile. Crotchless panties with a wolf howling at the moon? What could be more fitting than that?"

She rolls her eyes. "I expected a maid costume or something."

I kiss her softly. "I'd never disrespect you like that. Especially since I do most of the chores inside."

She narrows her gaze, searching for the insult. She won't find it. I like taking care of things the way I always have. We built a shed and stockpiled all the supplies she'll need to put in a garden once spring comes. She'll have her garden and I'll make sure everything is set in here.

"Fine. But if this thing digs into my hips, I'm cutting it up and burning it in the fireplace," she warns, and I drop to my knees and help her step into the panties. She huffs. "You're putting it on backwards."

"Nope. The wolf sits right above your pretty little pussy," I murmur and bury my nose between her legs.

Her hands grip my shoulders as a needy noise falls from her lips. I'll never tire of the sounds she makes. It fills a hole inside me bit by bit. I grab her leg and guide it over my shoulder, opening her for me. As I swirl my tongue around her clit, I breathe her in. Her pleas fill the air and I chuckle as I work her into a frenzy. We both know I'm teasing her, but she doesn't complain. She never does.

Her fingers tangle with my hair, and she wrenches my head back. "Stop playing, Chase."

I smirk and her eyes darken. "Not a chance, sunshine."

A delicious burn spreads along my scalp as I fight my way back to her pussy. I nip at her clit, and she yelps. When I suck the small bud between my lips, her grip eases. Her leg is already trembling with the effort to hold herself up while I play with her body.

"Please," she moans. "Please let me come."

My growl explodes from my chest, and I grip her ass to keep myself in check. Hearing her beg is usually my downfall. I give her anything she wants when she does. Tonight, I'm too enamored with burying my face in her pussy to give in. She keeps up a steady stream of appeals even as she rocks against my tongue. I lap at her core, her taste exploding within my mouth.

When I think she's had enough, I stand and whip my sweater over my head while she attacks my pants. Her hand wraps around my cock as soon as it's free, and I growl, gripping the counter to keep myself upright. My head tips back as she strokes me slowly. I'll gladly take whatever punishment awaits me—consequences for my teasing.

"Are you going to be a good boy and fuck me?" she asks as her hand squeezes at the base.

I nod, my panting filling the space between us. She hums, and I glance down as she sinks to her knees. Her eyes meet mine, and she smirks before her lips wrap around the tip. As she swallows, a groan spills from me. I don't know how long I'll be able to hold back. Not that I want to. When her gaze meets mine again, I almost lose it.

I cup her face and run my thumb along her cheek. "Do you know how beautiful you look right now?"

She smiles and a giggle bursts from her. She leans back and wipes her mouth. "You can't say shit like that." Her shoulders shake, and I tip her chin up.

"On your feet. I need to be inside you. Now."

I haul her upright and dig my fingers into her ass before I pick her up. I spin us around and set her on the island. It's the perfect height, and I thrust inside her. Dipping my head, I capture her nipple as I plunge into her over and over. I release it with a pop, and she whispers my name. She wraps her limbs around me, holding on while we move together. Nothing else comes close to how it feels to have her spasming around me. As she shudders in my arms, I follow her over the edge.

Gathering her closer, I wait for my heart to stop thundering in my ears. The oven beeps behind us, and she chuckles.

"It's pre-heated. Guess we won't be late after all," she mumbles, contentedness coating her voice.

I slip from her heat, and she whimpers. "If you keep making those noises, we won't just be late. We won't even make it, sunshine."

"Are you saying this is *my* fault?" she cries, gesturing down to her panties.

She rolls her eyes and hops down from the counter. When she turns away to find her clothes, I almost lose it. Stamped across her ass is another wolf. I didn't even notice the back when I bought them.

She glances over her shoulder, still bent over. "What?"

I press my lips together, unable to pull my eyes away from the image. There's a hole in a very strategic place, making it look like a moon with a wolf howling at it. She probably won't think it's as funny as I do.

"Happy solstice, Kira."

She straightens and marches toward the mirror in the hallway. I close my eyes, bracing myself for the shriek that's sure to come.

"Are you serious? Why is there another one on the back?" she bellows.

"Bend over, sunshine."

I close my eyes and count to ten. Her screech echoes through the space, and I burst out laughing. She marches back to me and plants her hands on her hips, a scowl firmly in place. It's hard to take her seriously when she's still wearing nothing but the lingerie, but I attempt to rearrange my face.

"You realize why they put it there, right?" she demands, and I nod slowly.

"I'm not howling at your dick," she snaps and swipes her clothes from the floor before marching toward the bedroom.

"You howl *for* my cock enough, sunshine. I'm sure I'll survive."

She slams the door behind her with a huff. I chuckle as I gather my own clothes and pull them on. I turn to put the cakes in the oven and am halfway through cleaning up the kitchen when Kira's phone rings. I glance at the screen and sigh before answering.

"Hey, Slade, what's up?"

"Chase," he mumbles. "Where's Kira?"

"Shower. You want me to have her call you?" I wait for his response, but stop cleaning when he doesn't. "Slade?"

"It was me," he breathes. "They're following me. It was never about you or Kira or even Alissa."

I lean against the counter and stare at the bedroom door. "Wait, who's following you?"

"The dark watchers," he whispers.

"Are they there right now? Is that why you're whispering?"

He groans, and I straighten. "No, they're not. I'm freaking the fuck out, though. Alissa told me to stop asking her about it since she doesn't know any-thing. Mom doesn't believe me. Dad told me to just get on with it—whatever the hell that means. I swear the goddess is laughing at me. I hear it in the wind. And the moon keeps trying to force me to shift. I don't know what to do."

I'm not the person to give him advice for a plethora of reasons. Being a made shifter, not born, I doubt I'll have some great insight. I know next to nothing about the lore compared to Alissa. I'm not equipped to deal with his issue.

"I can talk to Kira. Maybe she has some advice."

"What would you do?"

"I'm not exactly qualified—"

He scoffs and something clatters to the floor on his end. "Just tell me what you would do."

"Uh, first I'd shift. I know what happens if you ignore the moon's pull. Then I'd listen to your dad. If he's telling you to get on with it, then that's what you should do."

Ben may not always make sense, but he usually knows what he's talking about. His advice isn't given lightly. I don't have anything better to give Slade. Life doesn't just hand us answers. I had to go out and find them in Moon Cove. And that choice led me straight to my fated mate. I wouldn't put it past the goddess to send the dark watchers to Slade to force him to pay attention.

The bedroom door opens, revealing Kira with wet hair and a towel. It's probably the worst time for her to appear. Being horny while on the phone with her brother is awkward.

"Get on with what?" he cries, and Kira freezes.

I shake my head and clear my throat. "What were you going to do after winter solstice?"

"Got a friend down south who wanted me to check some things out. But I might need to stay in Moon Cove. I don't want them following me to other shifter communities. It'll be chaos."

"Except no one in Moon Cove other than you, me, and Kira has seen them. I'm pretty sure they're excellent at playing hide and seek. Maybe sticking with your plans is the best course of action."

He sighs, and I wait for him to process everything. We didn't part on bad terms, necessarily. If he takes my advice, it'll go a long way to repairing any animosity between us. My gaze meets Kira's, and she raises her eyebrows in question. I'll have to explain everything when I'm off the phone. Hopefully, since he was calling her in the first place, he won't mind.

"Fine. Might stop by Whispering Pines on the way, though. Pick your brain some more," he grumbles.

"Uh, okay?"

"Oh, and convince Kira to come back for the equinox. Without making her think everyone's pissed at her."

I have no idea when the equinox is. Jake only celebrates Samhain and winter solstice. I wasn't in my right mind over the last year to notice whether or not Gemma did.

"Things are different now," I murmur.

"Old habits are hard to break, Chase. She might not say it, but—"

"I'm pretty sure I know how to deal with my mate."

I hang up while he yells on the other end. Kira scowls as I set her phone down and advance on her. We had a plan on how to tell everyone. It wasn't much different from what happened. She still should have been the one to tell her brother. Wrapping my arms around her, I murmur my apologies. She shakes her head and runs her hands up my chest.

"I don't care. What's wrong with Slade?"

While I explain everything, her muscles ease until she's completely melted into me. When I get to the part about visiting Moon Cove, though, she tenses again. We haven't talked about going back. Maybe we should have, but we've been focused on building our relationship. Bringing in her family and the responsibilities she left behind wouldn't have helped.

"Are you okay?"

She rests her cheek on my chest, and I press a kiss to her hair. Her fingers dig into my back and my shirt bunches. I'll give her all the time she needs to deal with her emotions. She's gotten better at leaning on me and working through things without shutting down completely. It's not perfect, and I have no idea if I'm truly helping.

"I'm okay. I think we should go."

"Go...to Moon Cove? Or to Jake and Gemma's?" I ask hesitantly.

She laughs lightly. "Both. Equinox isn't until March, so we have time to get snowed in for the winter."

She smirks as she tips her chin up. I kiss her softly, and she relaxes. Whatever the future brings, at least we'll have each other. She's everything I didn't know I was missing. My life will never be the same. And I wouldn't have it any other way. The moon guided me exactly where I needed to be—straight to her.

Thank You

Thank you so much for reading Chase and Kira's story!
Ready for another adventure?
Check out the other works available by Emilia Abraham

If you'd like to hear about the other stories that have been living in my head, sign up for my
newsletter (including extra scenes & epilogues), visit my website, or follow me on social media
visit:

emiliaabraham.com

Special Thanks:
K.B. Barrett Designs-Cover Artist and Formatter
Emily Michel-Editor
Erenee-Beta Reader
Krysten-Omega Readers

Other Works

Also by Emilia Abraham:

Stuck at Sundown

Write on the Edge

The Cryptid Chronicles:

Bewitched by Bigfoot

Seduced by the Sliver Cat

Also by E. Abraham:

Shadows of Synd:

Under the Shadows-Book 1

Between the Shadows: Novella

Running From Shadows-Book 2

Becoming Shadows-Book 3

Shadows Within Us-Book 4

Beyond the Shadows-Book 5

Ruins of Rima:

Chasing Darkness-Book 1

Charmed by Darkness-Book 2

Available on Newsletter:

Bridging Epilogues, Extra Scenes

Author Bio

After many years of dreaming of becoming a full-time writer, Emilia Abraham took the leap, bringing her words to print. From sweet contemporary romance to spicy why choose and everything in between, she focuses on the happily ever after.

Emilia lives in the Upper Midwest with her husband (who's probably sick of listening to her expound on fictional men) and three kids (who try to steal her post-it notes). When she's not writing, she enjoys reading, playing video games, and consuming copious amounts of energy drinks.

www.ingramcontent.com/pod-product-compliance
Lightning Source LLC
Chambersburg PA
CBHW032351310726
48973CB00007B/1965